EYEING THE NORTH STAR

So AUG 00

D0618507

⤜ EYEING THE NORTH STAR ⤛

Directions in
African-Canadian Literature

George Elliott Clarke (signature)

Edited by

George Elliott Clarke

M&S

CANADIAN CATALOGUING IN PUBLICATION DATA

Main entry under title:

   Eyeing the north star : directions in African-Canadian literature

ISBN 0-7710-2125-9

1. Canadian literature (English) – Black authors.* 2. Canadian literature (English) – 20th century.* I. Clarke, George Elliott, 1960–   .

PS8235.B53E93 1997   c810.8'0896071   c96-932274-7
PR9194.5.B55E93 1997

The publishers acknowledge the support of the Canada Council and the Ontario Arts Council for their publishing program.

Typeset in 12 pt. Fournier by M&S, Toronto
Printed and bound in Canada

McClelland & Stewart Inc.
The Canadian Publishers
481 University Avenue
Toronto, Ontario
M5G 2E9

1 2 3 4 5   01 00 99 98 97

For my Mother,
      with adoration.

For Ayanna Black,
      with humility.

For the Writers,
      with respect.

CONTENTS

GEORGE ELLIOT CLARKE

Introduction

UNE RAISON D'ÊTRE

I am a voice crying in the wilderness, on the fringe of the diaspora.
— Carol Talbot

As a child, I became African American. My soul instinct. At four, lodged near Halifax with my parents and two brothers, I lived heart-pure. One April day, three young white boys, passing our home, pitched rocks and yelled "niggers" at I and I. Unstung by the word, I hurled it back — with choice stones — at their surprised eyes. Alerted by the commotion, my father shooed the white children away, ushered us sons indoors. Before a stunned mirror he sat us, uncupboarded two bowls of sugar — one white, the other brown — and preached, gently, that "some white-sugar folk don't like brown-sugar folk." I can still see that history-long mirror, still taste that bitter sugar. From that moment, I was, irredeemably, African American, sipping a testament of slavery, struggle, and flight that was "mine" — a bouquet for my mouth. I tippled tales of "General Moses" — Harriet Tubman — who shepherded hundreds of fugitive slaves to freedom in "Canaan" (Canada), by eyeing the North Star. I felt only semi-Canadian. I was not alone. In Coloured folks' antique homes — aged oilstoves and linoleum, images of pallid, unsatisfactory Christ and *Ebony* photos of chic Martin

Luther King flanked newspaper portraits of classy Elizabeth II. Bagpipes and fiddles were "official" 'Scotian music, but we crafted uppity drums from garbage cans and wooden crates. I consumed the National Film Board "shorts" about the mighty Québécois lumberjack Ti-Jean, but more nourishing were the books I devoured about the mythic John Henry, born with a hammer in his hand. Quasi-Canadian, I dreamed in the haven of a hyphen. Yet my bloodlines run deep in *Megumaage*, the Mi'kmaq name for Nova Scotia – to 1813 on my African-American/Mi'kmaq mother's side and to 1898 on my African-American/Caribbean father's side. My heart surges with the North Atlantic and leaps at the North Star.

As a youth, then, I was stirred not only by Robert Hayden, a Dee-troit poet, but by Alden Nowlan, a poet born where I was born. I wept over Malcolm X's *Autobiography* (1965) *and* over Margaret Laurence's *The Stone Angel* (1964). Slowly, I began to mix African-American and Euro-Canadian culture, to blend Little Milton's blues with Milton Acorn's poetry. Still, I did not discover African-Canadian literature until I was nineteen, when I took up Harold Head's anthology, *Canada In Us Now* (1976), and, especially, Gloria Wesley-Daye's chapbook, *To My Someday Child* (1975) – her occult, sweet poems that lyricized seaweed, fog, alleys, and pain – my Nouvelle-Écosse reality. Here was a voice that was black – *and* Canadian – like me; here was a writer who was ushering my world into words. I soon realized African-Canadian literature to be a species of hybridity. The King James scriptures melded with East Coast spirituals, New Orleans jazz, Bajan calypso, and Nigerian jit-jive. Steel drums and steel guitars harmonized. A discourse diced with Motown slang, Caribbean Creole, approximated Queen's English, gilt Haitian French, Canuck neologisms, and African patois.

Indeed, Canada is an assembly point for all African peoples, both Old World (Africa) and New (North and South America). Aware of this *mélange* of homelands, previous anthologists of African-Canadian literature have stressed its heterogeneous nature. Introducing *One Out of Many: A Collection of Writings by 21 Black*

Women in Ontario (1975), Liz Cromwell lists writers who either "migrated from the United States, Jamaica, Trinidad, Guyana, Africa, South America, and elsewhere" or are "native born Canadians."[1] In *Voices: Canadian Writers of African Descent* (1992), editor Ayanna Black counts writers who "come from Jamaica, Trinidad, Barbados, Ghana, Haiti, Guyana, Nigeria, Canada, the United States, and South Africa."[2] For Lorris Elliott, "the term 'Black writer' includes not only the descendants of Africa, but also the Afro-Asians and others of the diaspora."[3] To continue to validate this variety, I note that the writers in *Eyeing the North Star* hail from Alberta, Antigua, Barbados, Haiti, Jamaica, Kenya, Nova Scotia, Ontario, St. Vincent, South Africa, Trinidad, the United States, and Zimbabwe.

Arguably, African-Canadian literature was fated to manifest such multiculturalism, for it evolved from the historic traffic in cod, sugar, fur, lumber, rum, and slaves among West Africa, Western Europe, the Americas, and the Caribbean. Mapping this "Black Atlantic," Paul Gilroy sketches "the image of ships in motion across the spaces between Europe, America, Africa, and the Caribbean. . . ."[4] Though Gilroy omits Canada from his chartings, pan-Atlantic trade not only fostered Nouvelle France and British North America (Canada's inchoate imperial forms), it also cosmopolitanized the first black populations in these North Atlantic territories. To Louisbourg, for instance, on Île Royale (Cape Breton), slaves arrived from St. Domingue (Haiti), New England, Canada (Quebec), Martinique, Guadeloupe, Senegal, and France; others were born in the fortress.[5] J. L. Dillard reports that "slaves were transferred from one place to another, as from Nova Scotia to Surinam, . . . quite freely in the eighteenth century."[6] Consequently, African-Canadian literature is a patchwork quilt of voices. Its creators are, like their forebears, exiles, refugees, fugitives, pilgrims, migrants, and natives.

History clarifies this fact. The first anglophone authors were Black Loyalists: African Americans who, during the Revolutionary War, spurned the slaveholders' revolt to rally to the Crown's offer of land and liberty. Planted in the Maritimes in 1783,

a third of the original 3,000-strong contingent, fleeing local preju-
dice, left for Sierra Leone in 1792. Among this party, David
George, a Baptist minister, and Boston King, a Methodist, published memoirs in 1793 and 1798 respectively. Another Black
Loyalist, Susannah (Susana) Smith, became the first African-
Canadian woman writer by composing, on May 12, 1792, this letter
to John Clarkson, the superintendent of the Sierra Leone colony:

> Sir I your hum bel Servent begs the faver of your Excelence
> to See if you will Pleas to Let me hav Som Sope for I am in
> great want of Som I have not had aney Since I have bin to
> this plais I hav bin Sick and I want to git Some Sope verry
> much to wash my family Clos for we ar not fit to be Sean
> for dirt.[7]

The first African-Canadian author was, however, John Marrant, a
Calvinist missionary, who published, in 1785, his *Narrative of the
Lord's Wonderful Dealings with John Marrant, a Black (Now Going
to Preach the Gospel in Nova-Scotia)*, an account of his Joseph-like
captivity among the Cherokee. These early writings were supple-
mented by works authored by African-American fugitives who
settled in the Canadas and in British Columbia between the British
abolition of slavery in 1833 and the collapse of American slavery
in 1865. For instance, Josiah Henson's *Life of Josiah Henson, for-
merly a Slave, now an Inhabitant of Canada* (1849) prepared the way
for Harriet Beecher Stowe's incendiary abolitionist novel, *Uncle
Tom's Cabin* (1852). Mary Ann Shadd published the first major text
by an African-Canadian woman, *Condition of Colored People*, in
Wilmington, Delaware, in 1849. John William Robertson wrote
and issued his excoriating, yet coruscating, polemic, *The Book of
the Bible Against Slavery*, in Halifax in 1854. Martin Robinson
Delany, the first African-Canadian novelist, inked his famous abolitionist work, *Blake*, in Chatham, Ontario, where he dwelled from
1856 to 1859.[8] Toronto-born M. E. Lampert published two poems,
"Hymn to the New Year" and "My Dreams," "in the United States

around 1868,"[9] thus becoming the first African-Canadian woman poet. As the twentieth century dawned, new *émigres* contributed to the literature. Antiguan native Peter E. McKerrow's *History of the Coloured Baptists of Nova Scotia* became, in 1895, the first text published by a Caribbean-born writer in Canada. An African American, John Clay Coleman, published, in Toronto in 1898, a protest against Mississippi's segregation laws. Reversing directions, Ontario's Nathaniel Dett published a book of poems, the first collection by a native-born Canadian, in Tennessee in 1911. I testify: African-Canadian literature has always been international.

This decisively outward veering is inscribed in three ways: 1) a concern for African peoples everywhere, 2) the expression of solidarity with Third World peoples, and 3) the utilization of a diverse range of rhetorical styles. To check the first point, see the innumerable poems, essays, and fictions condemning apartheid South Africa and dictatored Haiti, or celebrating revolutionary Cuba and Grenada, or glorifying Harlem and Trench Town. For the second point, consult Claire Harris's "Where the Sky Is a Pitiful Tent" (1984), which articulates her sympathy for Guatemalan peasants, or Lawrence Hill's *Some Great Thing* (1992), whose black hero bears the unorthodox "Christian" name of Mahatma. To verify the third point, read aloud Pamela Mordecai's *de Man* (1995), a "Xamaican" Creole dramatization of the Crucifixion, or luxuriate in the Faulknerian richness of Frederick Ward's blackened English, or attempt the Joycean multiplicity of speech *chez* David Odhiambo, or the honed, incisive tone of Olive Senior's vernacular. As Cyril Dabydeen maintains, "There is a demotic, creolese and *dub* strain in [West Indian-originated] poetry, which is integral with the general cadence and lilt of West Indian speech rhythms and vernacular forms. . . ."[10] This observation applies, I think, to all African-Canadian writers who compose with an ear attuned to the frequencies of black popular speech. The literature is heteroglossic, a callaloo of languages (English, French, Spanish, Ge'ez, etc.), a medley of accents.

If the literature is distinguished by its pronounced catholicity, its critics are distinguished by their fixation on its politics. Hartmut Lutz theorizes that "the published writing of African Canadians comes out of a political struggle – and quite consciously so."[11] He proposes that "the 'coming out' of Black authors in Canada shows strong parallels with the struggle of African American writers in the U.S.A. in the Sixties and Seventies, and it also ties in with the ongoing process of decolonization in literatures of the former Commonwealth, written in various 'englishes.'"[12] But the truth cuts deeper. Though many writers chronicle social wounds, others bless religious faith or a blissful aestheticism. Dionne Brand champions a womanist, Marxian vision, but André Alexis indulges a *film noir* surrealism. Nor are there clear parallels between the U.S. Black Arts/Black Power movement of the 1960s and the *floraison* of African-Canadian writing in the 1990s. For one thing, the best-known African-Canadian writer, Austin Clarke, expounds a Red Toryism that vitiates any aesthetic influence. (Only Cecil Foster follows Clarke's style.) Bluntly, no African-Canadian intellectual has been able to shepherd his or her sistren and brethren along a single ideological path. Every attempt to achieve such hegemony has failed. For example, in *Canada in Us Now*, the so-called first anthology of black Canadian writing (it was, in fact, the third[13]), Harold Head exalts "revolutionary" black writing: "This anthology is representative of the collective consciousness of people in the act of liberating themselves (and us) from a legacy which denied their humanity and heaped scorn on the culture of colonial peoples. . . ."[14] Despite the attractive *recherché* messianism of phrases like "collective consciousness," however, writers have preferred to eschew party programmes to discuss, simply, their personal interests. See Paul Tiyambe Zeleza's Kafkaesque story, "The Rocking Chair" (1994), which defies description, and Althea Prince's story, "Ladies of the Night" (1993), which treats incest and prostitution, *sans* moralistic assertion. Writing in 1992, Ayanna Black maintains that "historically, African-Canadian writing has been overtly political, with little reference to the romantic or erotic."[15] But she also finds that "Black writers are now, it seems, struggling between the political and personal landscapes in their work. . . ."[16] Hence, M. Nourbese Philip's heavy-natured story, "Commitment to Hardness" (1992), straddling politics and erotica, seems to slide into a beautiful romanticism.

If no African-Canadian writer has been able to play the role of Black Arts Don that Amiri Baraka dramatized in the United States in the 1960s, the reason is anchored in the specificities of Canadian life, that is to say, the structural conditions that impinge upon all Canadian intellectuals and artists. The location of the nation's thirty million in self-contained cities and regions, often geographically distant and socio-politically distinct from each other, means that opinion-makers in Toronto, say, are not able to impose their aesthetics and agendas upon artists in Halifax, Montreal, Winnipeg, Vancouver, or even in cheek-by-jowl Kingston. Because provinces set educational priorities, battles for black history modules and other cultural initiatives are *entirely* localized. The absence of a guaranteed mass audience means that art must be created via a shifting combination of self-reliance, communal initiative, and public-sector support. (Hence, because African-Canadian writers were seldom published by major presses during the period of the literature's modern expansion – the 1960s to the 1980s, they self-published or banded together to produce their works through collectives.) Language dynamics drive some black francophone intellectuals to prioritize linguistic issues ahead of racial matters. (I reference the pandemonium that then-Parti Québecois MNA Jean Alfred, a Haitian Canadian, aroused at a National Black Coalition of Canada meeting in Toronto in May 1979, when he declared, before a hundred delegates at the King Edward Hotel, that Quebec's "liberation" was more important than black national unity.) The primacy assigned the Canada–Quebec schism marginalizes *all* other ethnic-racial-linguistic questions. Likewise, English Canada's desire to assert its moral superiority *vis-à-vis* the United States muffles discussions of racism, which is cast as an *American* problem. African-Canadian history and literature, feared as potential spoilers of white Canadian "innocence," are, then, necessarily repressed. ("Black poets . . . are treated," observes Ann Wallace, "like orphans and have been omitted entirely from . . . cultural, feminist and political history."[17]) Too, like Canada itself, the African-Canadian "community" fissures along regional, linguistic, gender, class, and ethnic lines, thus rendering the incarnation of race solidarity a difficult enterprise. Thus, *race*, per se, is not everything for African Canadians. No, it is the struggle against *erasure* that is everything.

A lucid difference between African Americans and African Canadians is that the former projects an identity, steeped in a visceral history, that is only fitfully available in Canada. That is to say, it is easier, in Canada, *à être français*, or Somalian, or Manitoban, than it is to be African Canadian. If the phrase "African American" denotes every person of African descent in the United States, no matter his or her origins, the phrase "African Canadian" denotes a fragile coalition of identities, consisting of Rastafarian "Dub" poets from Jane and Finch, African Baptist "gospelaires" straight outta Preston, and Haitian *péquistes* in Côte-des-Neiges. The variegated composition of the African-Canadian community frustrates trans-ethnic, trans-linguistic communication. (Hence, no truly "national school" of African-Canadian literature has been created, nor will we ever see one.) Happily though, the mosaic aspect of Canadian "blackness" produces a palette of discourses: Dany Laferrière's witty and knowing prose; Archibald Crail's catastrophic, blues-tinctured ironies; H. Nigel Thomas's meditative, spiritual fiction; Makeda Silvera's gynocentric comedies. Ayanna Black verifies this perception, affirming that "African Canadians incorporate diverse cultural, ideological, and geographic references in our works and further represent various literary influences ranging from western classics to the literature of developing countries."[18]

Commonalities do exist, nevertheless, among the varied African-Canadian constituencies. Hartmut Lutz cites three major themes in the literature: "the African *griot* tradition, a Black sense of community, solidarity with the Third World."[19] Liz Cromwell finds that black women writers in Ontario share "a bond of Blackness, a common history, a desire to communicate, and a Black tradition of sharing."[20] Ayanna Black posits that "we write out of a collective African consciousness – a consciousness embodied in the fabric of oral traditions, woven from one generation to the next, through myths, storytelling, fables, proverbs, rituals, work-songs and sermons meshed with Western literary forms."[21] These arguments are just but debatable. Essentialist nostalgia scores the *griotisme* that Lutz, Cromwell, and Black propound. Talk of a "collective consciousness" is perfumed dreaminess. Ancient Africa was a kaleidoscope of spiritual beliefs and political systems: Which one configures our posited "consciousness"? Our real commonality is rooted, as Cromwell suggests, in our history of forced relocation (the "Middle Passage"/immigration), coerced labour (slavery and domestic/agricultural worker schemes), the struggle against white-imposed economic discrimination (*de jure* and *de facto* segregation/colonialism), and the articulation of cultural links to Africa. Even so, Black's recognition of the centrality of orality to African diasporic literatures is correct, for New World African audiences demand an attendance to the *sound* and the *rhythm* of our texts. They crave signifying speech that moves body and soul. (Rhetorical analyses of New World African literatures should demonstrate, I dare say, our heightened usage of such techniques as anaphora, parimion, chleuasmos, litotes, etc., in contrast to European diasporic literatures.)

A commitment to pan-Africanism and black nationalism – that is to say, an adoration of the thought of Frantz Fanon, Malcolm X, Marcus Garvey, C. L. R. James, James Baldwin, Walter Rodney, Toni Morrison, and Audre Lorde – marks many African-Canadian texts. Surely, Fanon haunts Archibald Crail's "The New Order" (1992), while Garvey shadows M. Nourbese Philip's work. Such ideologies exert a *necessary* counter-influence to the mainstream dream of Canada as a "white" country ("The Great White North"), a fantasy which stigmatizes blackness. Illustratively then, when *Show Boat* (1927), the progressive American musical by Oscar Hammerstein and Jerome Kern, opened in Toronto in 1993, it provoked a fierce brouhaha. Praised in the United States for depicting blacks "as characterful individuals rather than racial stereotypes,"[22] it was bashed, picketed, and boycotted by activists and intellectuals from both the African-Canadian community and the larger concerned public. An acceptable commodity for African-American audiences, *Show Boat* was, for many African Canadians, grimly insulting *kitsch*. Similarly, Samuel Clemens's *Huckleberry Finn* (1884), a proven American classic, was trashed in 1993 by black New Brunswickers for its "racism" and by Lawrence Hill, in his *Some Great Thing*, for its illogical grammar. As these examples indicate, African-Canadian culture is no mere echo of its African-American counterpart.

Moreover, because African-Canadian history is ignored in Canada, African-Canadian writers are forced to act as historians. Hence, Diana Braithwaite's drama, *Martha and Elvira* (1992), recounts the fugitive slave experience in Canada; and Frederick Ward addresses this history in "Mary" (1983). Lorris Elliott admits that his anthology was assembled in reaction to complaints "about the scarcity of, and the need for, literary works which could inform [Black] children on the cultural background and also on the experience of Blacks who had been born in Canada or who had come to Canada before them."[23] If black children require such education, however, so do whites, for they often do not even know that slavery was practised in Canada. (For the record, Nova Scotia, New Brunswick, Prince Edward Island, Lower Canada [Quebec], and Upper Canada [Ontario] were all slave colonies.) Generally, African-Canadian writers are called to bear witness against Canadian racism: the shooting-downs, in cold blood, of unarmed black men by white cops; the pitiless exploitations and denials of black women; the persistent erasure of our presence; the channelling of black youth into dead-end classes and brain-dead jobs; the soft-spoken white supremacist assumptions that result in our impoverishment, our invisibility, our suffering, our deaths.

Given the specific socio-political, economic, and geographic context in which African-Canadian literature exists, a knowledge of its history is crucial for those who would not commit misreadings, a too-popular offence. For instance, the Trinidad-born playwright Lennox Brown, writing in January 1972, asserts, "There is no substantial Black culture in Canada"[24]; in fact, "Black culture in Canada was born in the cradle of Whiteness."[25] Lorris Elliott charges that "there is no real evidence of extensive literary writing by Blacks in Canada before the 1970s."[26] No, "the emergence of Black literature in Canada coincides with the peaking of immigration of Blacks into Canada, especially from the West Indies, from which the exodus of writers seeking better working conditions had begun in the 1950s."[27] Carroll Morrell, introducing *Grammar of Dissent: Poetry and Prose by Claire Harris, M. Nourbese Philip, Dionne Brand* (1994), insists that "when these authors take up the black, feminist, signifying subject-position, they create a new subject-position: they become teachers of the white Canadian literary and political communities."[28] Then there is Dionne Brand's dehistoricizing pronouncement that "We" – i.e., contemporary African-Canadian writers – "will write about [Canada's] internal contradictions."[29] M. Nourbese Philip cites, in Canada, "the absence of a tradition of Black writing as it exists in England or the U.S."[30] André Alexis theorizes that "black Canadians have yet to elaborate a culture strong enough to help evaluate the foreignness of foreign ideas."[31] All of these suppositions reveal inadequate primary research. Were Brown, Brand, and Nourbese Philip to scour histories of African-American literature, they would uncover many "lost" African-Canadian writers, including, to name only two, William Stowers, a novelist born in Canada West in 1861, and Theodore Henry Shackelford, a poet born in Ontario in 1888.[32] Elliott not only overlooks nineteenth-century records of sermonic, historical, and journalistic writing, he erases writers like the Montreal-born novelist John Hearne, who emigrated from Canada *to* Jamaica.[33] As for Morrell, her commentary values Harris, Nourbese Philip, and Brand as mere tutors of whites. Miserably, she eliminates nine generations of African-Canadian women and men who attacked racism in their petitions, sermons, speeches, and songs.[34] For his part, Alexis fails to note that the foreign (American) influences upon African-Canadian writers become *Canadianized*, a process which leaps into relief when one sets Austin Clarke's *Nine Men Who Laughed* (1986) beside Richard Wright's *Eight Men* (1961).

In the end, many critiques of African-Canadian literature are mere periphrases. They evade a felt cleavage in the canon, namely, that between "aboriginal (descendants of early settlers)" and "naturalized (immigrant)" African-Canadian writers, to employ the fine classifications of Anthony Joyette, the Vincentian-Canadian artist and editor.[35] If the latter are noted for "the 'immigrant novel' in which the protagonist and the setting are usually foreign,"[36] the former have emphasized Canada-centred, documentary, spiritual, and historical writing. Intriguingly, old-line African-Canadian communities are mainly rural and African-American in derivation, while the post-1955 new black communities are urban and diverse. Significantly, too, relations between "aboriginal" and "naturalized" writers replicate those between First Nations and mainstream Canadian writers, with tensions developing *vis-à-vis* resource allocations (arts and research grants) and appropriation of discourse. Yet, the pointed commonalities among African-Canadian authors do foster a degree of solidarity. In addition, if "naturalized" writers' first works are aimed at the audience "back home," or at their fellow and sister *dépaysés*, their subsequent works often begin to chart their surroundings. (The *oeuvres* of Dionne Brand and Cecil Foster exemplify this arc.) Joyette posits that African-Canadian literature is evolving from "plantation culture into a space of its own."[37] Surely, as second-generation writers like Calgary's Suzette Mayr and Montreal's Robert Edison Sandiford emerge, the distinction between "naturalized" and "aboriginal" will blur, leaving only the usual, insurmountable divisions between metropolis and hinterland, French and English, to continue to quarter the literature. If there is justice in André Alexis's complaint that he misses "black Canadian writing that is conscious of Canada, writing that speaks not just about situation, or about the earth, but *from* the earth,"[38] such attentiveness appears in his own writing – as well as that of Diana Braithwaite, Lawrence Hill, Suzette Mayr, and Frederick Ward.

Traditionally, anthology introductions offer the editor an

opportunity to explain his or her selection criteria and to justify the project. Let me say, then, that the time's ripe for the issuance of *Eyeing the North Star: Directions in African-Canadian Literature*. I'd wanted, originally, to title this book *New Provinces II* in provocative allusion to the famous 1936 anthology that proclaimed the triumph of High Modernism in Anglo-Canadian poetry. Sixty years later, the "New Provinces" that I have in mind are those being created by *les écrivains de couleur*, those insisting upon new, more inclusive definitions of Canadianness. To affirm this effort, I've sought to assemble a cast of significant suspects and to reprint their representative work. For instance, with the exception of André Alexis and David Odhiambo, each of these writers has published at least two books. Only three submissions are new works: Cecil Foster's "The Rum," David Odhiambo's poem-fiction, and one poem by Pamela Mordecai. Admittedly, however, it would be impossible in any one book to depict the full range and multiplicity of voices that is the wealth of African-Canadian literature. Ideally, a *compleat* anthology would range from the pioneer writings of John Marrant and Susannah Smith to the punk proems of Lawrence Braithwaite and the Dub drama of Ahdri Zhina Mandiela. Because I've covered some of the historical writing in *Fire on the Water: An Anthology of Black Nova Scotian Writing* (1991–1992), I've striven, here, to construct a democratic canon of diverse, contemporary voices, one which respects the regional, linguistic, cultural, and aesthetic differences that give African-Canadian literature its essential variety. Hence, Alberta's Suzette Mayr joins forces with Ontario's Makeda Silvera; New Brunswick francophone Gérard Étienne meets Québécois anglophone Frederick Ward; the native-born Lawrence Hill greets Jamaica native Pamela Mordecai; and Dany Laferrière's satirical impulse complements the social anger of Claire Harris. Because I've chosen to accent page-oriented, rather than stage-oriented, writing, performance artists have been omitted. Though I've not been persuaded to include a writer because he or she has garnered awards, or because he or she has appeared on university syllabi, it should be noted, duly, that many of the writers in this anthology can boast of one or both of these achievements. I have wanted, though, to revise previous anthologies that have praised, for instance, Austin Clarke's social realist fiction at the expense of his more imaginative work. Ultimately, then, I've favoured an eclectic selection of interests – or, rather, directions. No single approach to the literature can suffice, for the realities of any literature are complex. (I confess, though, that I prefer the eccentric, the perverse, the Gothic attitude that Canada inspires in many artists.) For me, then, *African-Canadianité* is Gérard Étienne's Négritudinous passion as well as Claire Harris's projectivist classicism; Dionne Brand's confrontational confessionalism and Althea Prince's *femme noire* voice; H. Nigel Thomas's elegant simplicity and Austin Clarke's undermilkwoodian exoticism; Suzette Mayr's magic realist rendition of Ovid and M. Nourbese Philip's demotic, domestic version; Olive Senior's poetic prose that sings like Virgil and André Alexis's cinematic prose that "screens" like Cronenberg; Dany Laferrière's adoration of indiscretions and Paul Tiyambe Zeleza's pleasure in *bizarreries*; Frederick Ward's astonishing musicality and Archibald Crail's arresting plainsong.

These writers avoid nothing. They speak the raw blues of truth, no matter how raucous, hideous, odious, bitter, or sore. They talk about everything that is loud, ugly, irrepressible. They talk about incest, self-hatred, alienation, and the wintry coldness of modernity and its vituperative capitalism. They remember original homes of love and warmth, even as they build new homes amid a cool hostility. They remember the seductive winters, the abbreviated summers. They have cursed the slate-grey, murderous Atlantic and wept out love in paradisal Grenada. They have stumbled across plains and across veldts. They have cut sugarcane, they have cut down dictators. They have made a *fête* of fate. Their poems on roses descend from their poems on corrosion.

Naturally, I wanted to enlist more writers. My attempts to include Lillian Allen were unsuccessful; Maxine Tynes was, unfortunately, incommunicado; Anthony Phelps *et les autres écrivains afro-canadiens* await translation into English; Yvonne Vera came too late to my attention; Ayanna Black, Hazelle Palmer, David

Woods, Jan Carew, John Hearne, Arthur Nortje, Kwame Dawes, Louise Bennett, and Robert Sandiford would have been included had there been space enough and cash. Despite these regrettable omissions, to quote James Brown, "I feel good."

Fugitive slaves were once directed to "follow the North Star to Canaan-land"; later, black migrants odysseyed north to "monarchical America" in search of a wider vista for grander dreams. And we are here. Where we have always been. Since 1605. *Eyeing the North Star* marks the further blessing of African-Canadian writers, eyes on our history, because we deserve no less.

George Elliott Clarke
Duke University
Durham, North Carolina
January 1997

Notes

1 Liz Cromwell, ed., Foreword, *One Out of Many: A Collection of Writings by 21 Black Women in Ontario* (Toronto: WACACRO, 1975), p. 5.

2 Ayanna Black, ed., Introduction, *Voices: Canadian Writers of African Descent* (Toronto: HarperCollins, 1992), p. xi.

3 Lorris Elliott, Introduction, *Literary Writings by Blacks in Canada: A Preliminary Survey* (Ottawa: Department of the Secretary of State of Canada/Secrétariat d'État du Canada, 1988), p. 4

4 Paul Gilroy, *The Black Atlantic: Modernity and Double Consciousness* (Cambridge, MA: Harvard University Press, 1993), p. 4.

5 Kenneth Donovan, "A Nominal List of Slaves and their Owners in Île Royale, 1713-1760," *Nova Scotia Historical Review*, 16.1 (1996), pp. 151-162.

6 J. L. Dillard, "The History of Black English in Nova Scotia – A First Step," *Revista Interamericana Review*, 2.4 (Winter 1973), p. 513.

7 Qtd. in Christopher Fyfe, ed., *"Our Children Free and Happy": Letters from Black Settlers in the 1790s* (Edinburgh: Edinburgh University Press, 1991), p. 24.

8 Gilroy, p. 27.

9 Ann Wallace, ed., Introduction, *Daughters of the Sun, Women of the Moon: Poetry by Black Canadian Women* (Stratford, ON: Williams-Wallace Publishers Inc., 1991), p. 8.

10 Cyril Dabydeen, ed., Introduction, *A Shapely Fire: Changing the Literary Landscape* (Oakville, ON: Mosaic Press, 1987), p.11.

11 Hartmut Lutz, "'Is the Canon Colorblind?': On the Status of Authors of Color in Canadian Literature in English," *ZAA: A Quarterly of Language, Literature and Culture*, XLIV (January 1996), p. 61.

12 Ibid, p. 63.

13 Head's anthology followed Camille Haynes's *Black Chat: An Anthology of Black Poets* (Montreal: Black and Third World Students' Association, 1973) and Liz Cromwell's *One Out of Many: A Collection of Writings by 21 Black Women in Ontario* (Toronto: WACRACRO Productions, 1975).

14 Harold Head, ed., Introduction, *Canada in Us Now: The First Anthology of Black Poetry and Prose in Canada* (Toronto: NC Press, 1976), p. 7.

15 Black, p. xii.

16 Ibid.

17 Wallace, *Daughters*, p. 9

18 Ayanna Black, ed., Introduction, *Fiery Spirits: Canadian Writers of African Descent* (Toronto: HarperCollins, 1994), p. xvi.

19 Lutz, p. 63.

20 Cromwell, p. 5.

21 Black, *Voices*, p. xi.

22 Bruce Kellner, ed., *The Harlem Renaissance: A Historical Dictionary for the Era* (New York: Methuen; London: Routledge & Kegan Paul, 1987), p. 322.

23 Lorris Elliott, ed., Introduction, *Other Voices: Writings by Blacks in Canada* (Toronto: Williams-Wallace Publishers Inc., 1985), p. 2.

24 Lennox Brown, "A Crisis: Black Culture in Canada," *Black Images* (January 1972), p. 8.

25 Ibid, p. 6.

26 Elliott, Introduction, p. 4.

27 Ibid.

28 Carroll Morrell, ed., Introduction, *Grammar of Dissent: Poetry and Prose by Claire Harris, M. Nourbese Philip, Dionne Brand* (Fredericton: Goose Lane Editions, 1994), p. 12.

29 Qtd. in Morrell, p. 13.

30 M. Nourbese Philip, "Who's Listening?: Artists, Audiences & Language," *Frontiers: Essays and Writings on Racism and Culture* (Stratford, ON: The Mercury Press, 1992), p. 45.

31 André Alexis, "Borrowed Blackness," *This Magazine* (May 1995), p. 20.

32 See my article, "A Primer of African-Canadian Literature," in *Books in Canada*, 25.2 (March 1996), pp. 7-9, for an extended survey of nineteenth- and twentieth-century African-Canadian writers.

33 Ibid.

34 My *Fire on the Water: An Anthology of Black Nova Scotian Writing*,

Volume 1 (Lawrencetown Beach, NS: Pottersfield Press, 1991), canvasses some early anti-racist writings.

35 Anthony Joyette, Editorial, *KOLA*, 8.1 (1996), p. 5.

36 Ibid.

37 Anthony Joyette, Review of *Voices: Canadian Writers of African Descent*, ed. by Ayanna Black, *KOLA*, 8.1 (1996), p. 68.

38 Alexis, p. 20.

→ ← ←

AUSTIN CLARKE

When He Was Free and Young and He Used to Wear Silks

In the lavishness of the soft lights, indications of detouring life that took out of his mind the concentration of things left to do still, as a man, before he could be an artist, lights that put into his mind instead a certain crawling intention which the fingers of his brain stretched towards one always single table embraced by a man and a wife who looked like his woman, her loyalty bending over the number of beers he poured against the side of her bottle he had forgotten to count, in those struggling days when the atmosphere was soft and silk and just as treacherous, in those days in the Pilot Tavern the spring and the summer and the fall were mixed into one chattering ambition of wanting to have meaning, a better object of meaning and of craving, better meaning than a beer bought on the credit of friendships and love by the tense young oppressed men and women who said they were oppressed and tense because they were artists and not because they were incapable, or burdened by the harsh sociology of no talent, segregated around smooth black square tables from the rest of the walking men and walking women outside the light of our Pilot of the Snows; and had not opened nor shut their minds to the meaning of their other lives; legs of artless girls touching this man's in a hide-and-seek under the colourblind tables burdened by conversation and aspirations and promises of cheques and hopes and bedding and beer and bottles; in those days when he first saw her, and the only conversation she could invent was "haii!" because she was put on a pedestal by husbandry, and would beg his pardon without disclosing her eyes of red and shots and blots and blood-shot liquor; the success of his mind and the woman's mind in his legs burnt like the parts of the chicken he ate, he was free and young and he was wearing the silks of indecision and near-failure. But he mustn't forget the curry: for the curry was invented by people and Blessings, Indians; or perhaps they were the intractable Chinese, the curry was the saviour of his mind and indigestion just as the woman guarded for no reason in the safe soft velvet of her unbelieving husband's love, guarding her in her turns as they sat opposite each other in the different callings of paint and metals and skin and negatives and thirst during all those dark days in the Pilot, the curry was the saviour of a madness which erupted in his mouth with the after-taste of the bought beer and the swirling bowels after the beer and after the curry; she was like the lavishness in the light except that the colour surrounding her in the darkened room hid everything, every thought in his mind just as the wholesome curry in the parts of chicken hid the unwholesome social class which it could not always distinguish from the bones any suitable dog in shaggy-haired and shaggy-sexed Rosedale would eat, and if the dog in Rosedale and the dog in him did eat them, the dog might make them, like this woman sitting with her drinking man, into an exotic meal packaged through some sense of beer and the sense of time and place, and looking at it in one imaginative sense, turn it into something called *soul food*: now, there are many commercial and irrelevant soul food kitchens these days in night-time Toronto, and any man could, if he had no soul and silks on the body of his thoughts, if his soul were occupied and imprisoned only with thoughts of *her* sitting there badly in the wrong light of skin, he could make a fortune of thoughts and sell them like dog meat and badly licensed food to all the becauseful people who wore jeans and heavy-weave expensive sweaters walking time into eternity in dirty clothes and rags because they were the "beautiful people" as someone called their ugliness, like *her* of soon-time piloted to a tavern, married to a man who did not deserve the understanding of her; these the becauseful people, people who didn't have to do this because they didn't want to think about that, because they were people living in the brighter light of the soft darkness which they all liked because they were artists and people; the becauseful people like her, liked her and likened her to a white horse not because of the length of her legs nor the grey in her mind, but because in the lavishness of the wholesome light of the Pilot she looked as secure and was silent as the fingers of the tumbling *avoirdupois* of the man who made mud-pies in the piles of quarters and dollars mixmasterminding them in the cash register. It is so dark sometimes in the Pilot that if you wear dark glasses, which all the artists wore on their minds, you may stumble up the single step beside the fat man sitting on a humptydumpling stool and where she always sat on her pedestal of distance and protection chastised in pickled beer, and you may not know whether it is afternoon on Yonge Street outside, for time now has no boundaries, only the dimensions of her breasts which her husband keeps in the palm of his flickering eyeballs; it is so dark in the early afternoon that with your dark glasses on, you might be in Boston walking the climb in the street climbing like a hill to where the black and coloured people live; or you might be here in Toronto walking where the coloured people and the kneegrows say they "live" but where they squat, here where E. P. Taylor says he does not live but where his influence strangles some resident life and breeds racehorses of the people, where Garfield Weston lives in a mad biscuit box crumbling in broken crackers; in the lavishness of the night thrown from your dark glasses, you might stumble upon a pair of legs and not know the colour of time, or what shape it is, or where you are, or who you are: he thinks he should haul his arse out of this bar of madness and mad dreams, drinking himself into an erection stiff to the touch of ghosts in her legs and the legs of the tables. He had seen her, "this young tall thing," walking to the bar through winter in boots and rain in blue jeans and sandals, insisting without words in the fierce determination of her poverty and dedication to nothing she could prove or do that this was her personal calvary to the cross of being Canada's best poetic-photographer, unknown in the meaning of her life beyond the tavern, unknown like the word she would use, "budgerigar," having years ago thrown out Layton, Cohen, Birney and Purdy in the dishwater of her weatherbeaten browbeaten body and heavy sweaters; he could see her mostly among women stuck to their chairs by the chewing-gum beer, free women freed by their men for an afternoon while art imprisoned the men with beer, wallpaper along the talking walls like flowers, their own flower long faded into the dust of the artificial potato chips they all ate in the nitty of their gloom because it was like grit for their reality, their "dinner" an unknown reality like her word, "budgerigar," in the despised bourgeois vocabulary and apartment-lairs of their lives; and in this garden of grass growing in their beds he had hand-picked her out five years ago, this one wallflowering woman who wore large hats in the summerstreet, and cream sweaters in winter. She always sat beside the man who sat as if he was her husband; tall in her thighs with the walk of a man, this white horse woman with the body of a bull; and the eye of her disposition through the bottom of the beer bottle warned him that "the gentlest touch of his desire might be fatal to the harmony" of the two ordered beers which they drank like Siamese twins in the double-bed of their marriage. He, the watchman-man, was harnessed by island upbringing and fear in the lavishness of the dim light, ravishing her ravishing beauty with his eyes they could not see, eyes they saw only once and spoke to once when they saw him entering or leaving; for five years. For five years of not knowing whether the sun would sink in the space between her breasts, or whether butter ever dried in the warmth of that melting space, he watched her like a timekeeper. Once he saw her leaving her husband's side and he followed her spinster's canter all the way in his mind down the railing guard of parallel eyes hon-ouring her backside sitting on the spinning stools where the working class reigned and into the bathroom, past two wash basins and the machine that saved pregnancies and populations with a quarter, on to the toilet bowl, under the dress she had plucked her hand and had pulled up her dress and did not soil her seat or sit on it because it was in the Pilot, and he smiled when she reappeared with fresh garlic on her lipstick mouth; and he looked at the edges of her powder, and he looked into the lascivious dimness and saw her and smiled and she smiled but the smile belonged to the mud-piling man at the cash register or to another table where they were talking about the Isaacs Gallery and the Artists Jazz Bann where Dennis Burton's garter belts were exhibited in stiff canvas and wore houndstooth suits and the thick heavy honey of colours and materials thicker than words. He had walked around her life in circles and bottle rings of desire and of lust and she was always there, the centre of dreams frizzled on a pillow soaked with the tears of drinking; he followed her like a detective in the wishes of his dreams, and from his inspection of a future together got a headache over them and over her, and over the meanings of these dreams. *Mickey* and *Cosmospilitane* and other dream books did not ease the riders of the head in his pain, and nothing could unhinge his desperation from the wishful slumber of those unconscious nights of double broken vision. And then, like a cherry falling under the tree because the sun had failed it, after long thoughts and wishes of waiting she fell into his path, and he almost crushed her. He remembered the long afternoons waiting for the indelible rings of the melting bottles to ripen, waiting for the departure of shoppers who lived above the Rosedale subway station to stop shopping in the Pickering Farms market so he could shop and not have to listen to the loud-talking friendly butcher in the fluorescent meat depart-ment, and whisper loud under the sun-tanned arms of the meaty housewives and commonlawwives, "One pound of pigs feet, chicken necks and bones – for soup," and hear the unfeeling bitch, "Er-er! Who's next?" behind the counter dressed like a surgeon with blood on his chest, saying, "You're really taking care of that dog, ain't you, sir?" Godblindyou, dog! godblindyou, butcher! this meat is for the dog in front of you; and he remembered her now, single, on this summerstreet under the large hat as she was five years ago under the drinking mural under the picture of hotdogs and fried eggs that some heartless hungry painter drew on the wall where she sat beneath when she was in the Pilot. He fell into the arms of her greeting like an apple to the core and he looked down into her dress and saw nothing not even one small justification for the long unbitten imprisonment of his mouth and his ambition, thinking of the nutseller selling his nuts next door. She was away now from the Pilot. And he did not even know her name: not for five years, he never was introduced to her name: "Hurley or Weeks . . . Weeks or Hurley . . ." either one would do? "they are both mine, and I use either one any time," but Weeks is her maiden time; although she was no longer a maiden, though single and with no husband for weeks and months now. There was no large gold ring on the finger of her personal self-regard, which she said ended mutual on a visit of her once-accompanying husband warming radically, like forgotten beer, into her haphazard lover; there was no bitterness in the eyes of her separation because she missed only the cooking which he would do every evening, when she said she was too tired, or couldn't be bothered to cook, which was every evening, when he would do the cooking in her kitchen and leave her afterwards like the dishes, panting from thirst and a thorough cleaning, so her eyes said on this summer afternoon, hungry in the frying pan of their double-bed bedroom, where he kept the materials of his stockings, feet and trade, his love of meddling with medals and metals and sculpture, and where she kept a large overgrown blow-up of her brother's success in the cowboys and movies in the West, shooting the horses over the head of the never-setting bedpost, her brother with a gun in his hand, a gun loaded at the ready to be fired at the nearest rivalry of badmen and bad women, a gun which he gave her, a gun which remained nevertheless loaded, hung-up, cocked and frustrated and constipated from no practice or trigger-happiness; and this she talked about; she did not stay in one place, she said she was rambling, not along the streets because she did not like to walk, but that she was rambling and that she had to be alone in the constitutional of her thoughts, from one bar to the next bar; she admitted she might have a problem, but it was not this problem which changed her husband's heart into a dying lover drifting apart at the semen in the widening sea of her jammed ambition: "I do not know what I want to do, I know what

I don't want to do, and that is stay married, but I don't really know
what I really want to do"; she bore her wandering in her hair, loose
and landing on her broad shoulders like the rumps of two cowboy
horses; and her dress was short, short enough for the eyes to roam
about in and follow her over all her landscape at a canter – that's
how she was put away; she was put away as if she could be put to
pasture for work and for love and for bearing responsibility: "I
know I don't want to have a child. What am I going to *do* with a
child? I know I can have children and I know I can have a child. I
want a child, but not now, because a child *needs* love . . . and and
and I I I haven't any left right now for . . ." He looked at her and
wandered and wondered why she couldn't give a child a chance, a
chance of love, with all the pasture in her body, all her body, with
all her breasts, with all her milk bottled in brassieres that had no
bones stitched in them, with all her thighs that spilled over her
dress-hem, "A-hem!", but perhaps she was really talking about
another kind of love and another need for love, which was not the
same as the need for love her lover-husband needed from her when
she was a child in his arms late at night, and was crying with him
in the doubleminded cradle of his sculptures. *Haii! Austin!* He
looked into her eyes and made a wish that her body under his eye
would not be completely bloodless as her hands sometimes seemed
five years ago when she was fresh from the basement washroom,
and the Snow on the women walking out of the cold corner of
Yonge and Bloor in the arctic months; that her body would not
reveal the theft he had in mind to put it through, the theft her
husband had put it through; that she would not be like Desdemona
and wax, but that she would be a queen from the entrails of Africa
and Nefertiti, plucked out in olive blackness luscious to the core of
her imagined seed, like the Marian from the alligator troughs of
Georgia. He dreamed a long dream standing there on the street
with summer before her, and he killed the colour of her body
because it needed too much *Eno* before it could go down; and he
wrapped her in a coffin stained in wood in blood, and made her
again to look like Marian from way across the bad lands of enroped
and ruptured Georgia. *Haii, Austin!*: he was back in those good

old days, good because they had no responsibility for paying the good deeds artists incurred in debts and made them bad, bad debts and artists on the segregation of walls and memories, he was here and he was there in Georgia in the double ghost of a second, for artists were bad for debts and for business in those young days when he was free and the only silk was his ambition; he remembered her in those days, and on this summer afternoon already obliterated in the history of the past, nights in the crowded Pilot Tavern, searching the faces of the girls and women for one face that would have had a meaning like Marian's, and he could not find one head with truth written in its clenched curled black-peppers of hair, one mask with the intelligent face of Nefertiti the history of Africa from Africa, not from the store on Yonge Street, "Africa Modern" selling blackness cheap to whites, written brazenly upon its ivory; a mask, a mask from that land not unlike Georgia, he had watched for one face like a timekeeper keeping a watch that had no end of time in it, and he had to paint the faces black, blacken them as he had blackened the red clay sculpture a woman did of him once, like an Indian in his blood, and had made it something approaching the man he wanted to be, something like the man Amiri Baraka talked about becoming in the later years of his new Muslim wisdom; he remembered the sweet-smelling Georgia woman in those soft nights when the bulbs were silk as moths among the books overhead like a heavy chastisement to be intelligent, like a too-self-conscious intention; with the sherry which she drank in proper southern quantities, like bourbon warm to the blood, and her fingers were long and pointed and expressive, impressing upon his back, once, her once beautiful intent, as they writhed in pain with glory and some victory, after she lay like a submarine in a watery pyre of soft soapy suds, white flowers of *Calgon* upon her black vegetation, going and coming, he remembered her in the shiny cheap stockings proclaiming her true colour of mind and pocket and spirit and background and intention: *a black student*; a black woman, black and shining in that velvet of time and black skin, a black woman, black and powerful down to her black marrow; there was something in the ring of her laughter, perhaps in the gurgle of her bourbon, in the *ding-ing* of her voice when she laughed in two accents, northern and southern, something that said she was true-and-through beautiful, and because she was black, and because she was beautiful, she was beautiful; she could withstand any ravages of history, of storms, of stories that wailed in the rope-knotted night of Georgia; she could stand on a pedestal under any tree which no village smithy in white Georgia would dare to stand up to: a man who had no burning conviction could not put his arms as high as her waist, for she had seen certain sheets of a whiteness which were wrapped around a black man's testicles in a bestial passion-play, and she had seen, in her mother's memories, this play as it showed the germ of someone's bed linen made into sheets that were worn as masks of superiority testing a presumption that some men would always walk on all-fours like a southern lizard; *Haii, Austin!* this woman standing on the summerstreet in the silk of time stopped without desire; and that woman lying in the rich water with her smell whom he remembered best holding down her head in love, in some shame, looking into a book of tears because his words were spoken harder than the text of any African philosophy. He remembered that woman and not this woman, well: Marian, his; ploughing the fields of poverty and a commitment in her barefoot days, dress tangled amongst the tango of weeds, sticking in the crease of her strength silken from perspiration, and her dreams cloggy as the soil, and in her after-days in the northern rich-poor city, her long-fingered hands again dipping into the soil of soiled sociology Jewished out of some context, maintained backyards, maintained yardbird poverty, backward in instruction the smell of soil the soiled smell of the land in which she was born, the smell of poverty, a new kind of perfume to freshen her northern ideas, a new kind of perfume truer than the fragrance of an underarm of ploughing, more telling than the tale in the perspiration of her body, in the fields, in the sociology, in the kitchen, in the bed, in the summer subway sweaty and safe with policemen and black slum dwellers from Dorchester, in the heat, in the bus stations, in the bathtub in Boston; a perfume of sweet sweat that clothed her body with a blessing of pearls, like a birthwrap of wet velvet skin: "Honnn-neee!" the word she always used; honey was the only taste to use; honey was the only word she used always; for it was a turbulence of love and time from the lowered eyelids from the vomiting guts up to the tip of the touch of her skin. She was a woman; she was a woman without woe; she was to be his woman, she should be here in the summerstreet; now in the summerstreet, he watches this alter-native of that woman, he understands that the transparency of this dress, tucked above her knees by the hand of fashion, is really nothing but the vagueness of this doll; he sees now that this transparency is the woman, like the negatives she meddled in, for five years' time, like the film on a pond's surface, like white powder, like a glass of water with *Eno* in it, like a glass of water in the sun, the water clear and unpolluted, the water the topsoil of the sediments at the sentimental bottom; he wanted to mix this water with that water in the bathtub in Boston, the water and the mud into some heart, into that thick between-the-toes soul of the Georgia woman; he wanted to break the glass that contained that water for the *Calgon* bath and the sherry and the bathwater; break the vessel, spill and despoil, spill and expel this watering-down of the drink of his long thirst; stir it up and mix the sentiments in the foundation with the upper crust of the water, shake it to the foundation of its scream and yell and turn it to the thickness of chocolate rich in the cup, thick and rich and hot and swimming with pools of fat, so he could drink, so he would have to put his hand into the black avalanche of feeling and emotion and sediment, deep and gurgling as the tenor in her laughter, down the tuningfork of her throat resounding with love and make her say a word, speak a thought, be some witness to the blood in her love. This was his Marian in the vision in the summerstreet. This was Marian. And the five-year stranger, estranged from her husband's love in a transparency, in the costume of a lover, this woman who used to sit upon the pin of his desires, now on this summerstreet where he thought he saw her, she is nothing more vivacious than a feather worn in her broad-grinned hat: not like the scarf *she* wore with conch-shells and liberty-scars and paisley marked into it with water; this negative of Marian passed like the cloud above the roof of the Park Plaza where one afternoon she sat drinking water, when he was playing he was playing golf in the new democratic diminutive green of the eighteenth floor bar; and a cloud passed overhead like the loss of lust of a now dead moment, with the woman; and when the sun was bright again, when the sun was like the sun in Georgia, fierce and full, when the sun was a purpose and passion, when the sun was as bright as the sweat it wrung from the barrels of a black woman's breasts, the laughing beautiful Marian was there, not in his mind only but larger, dispossessing the summerstreet in the buxom jeans of her hips, red accusing blouse belafonted down the ladylike tip of the gorge of sustenance between her breasts, and around her neck around her throat, a yellow handkerchief and a chain of a star and a moon in some quarter of her sensual religion. He saw her with passion and with greed, he saw her clearer than the truth-serum syrup of a dream, than the germ of love, true as the *Guinness* in the egg and the Marian was his stout, this woman. He remembered all this standing in the summerstreet: when before she climbed the steps to her hospital, she held his hands like a wife going in to die upon a cot, and drew him just a suggestion of new life closer to the relationship and her breasts, and with the sweet saliva of her lips she said in the touch of that kiss, "Take care of yourself." He was young and free again, to live or to travel imprisoned in a memory of freed love, chained to her body and her laughter by the spinal cord of anxious long distance, reminders said before and after, by the long engineering of a drive from Yale to Brandeis to Seaver Street to Brandeis dull in the winter Zion of brains, dull in the autumn three hours in miles hoping that the travel won't end like an underground railroad at the door of this nega-tive woman, but continue even through letters and quarrels and long miles down the short street up the long stairs in the marble of her memory, clenched in her absent embrace but rejoicing with his fingers in the velvet feeling of her silken black natural hair . . .

1971

+>- -<+

GÉRARD ÉTIENNE

Ah My Love Flutters . . .

(translated by Jo-Anne Elder and Fred Cogswell)

Ah my love flutters lighter than a bird-poem
and places sparkling feet on my hope grown tall with

                                                    darkness

This great weakness love tells of
Immense bogs painted with sun-rays
That long rope wrapping up human matter
the might of minerals and the heat of seasons
that flame of fire in the flesh of space like a beak or

                                                        a kiss

ripe fruit fleeing in the maiden dew
Oh it assumes the headaches of my piled-up loves
it assumes the reason for writing down all my loves
it warms beneath my palms this winter of

                                                  tenderness

this piece of my heart broken like a crystal
But if for a little of you in my reveries

                                                  metamorphoses

I sing you, a half-moon in myself and my torments
they will say that I sin against the strength that is
   your strength

they will say that my whole self is soft velvet in its folly
they will say that the sky is too light for my head
they will say who knows what
that your image dissolves in fog
and evaporates in sobbing vapours

There are oceans between our dreams and me
the world runs at my feet fresher than desire for

                                                            women

and in the evening's turbulence
as in the swift flight of crickets
I hold time in my hand
I squeeze time like a ripe fruit in the breeze

                                                        make love

time my poem that I love and that nurses me
my gluttony my driving force and my knowledge
reality
time that good fellow in my friend's eye
that mechanical thrust that makes my heart wander
through the too-frail waves of my desire

My love you are everything to me
you are the cry of Marie-Jude, my tenth sun
you are the sweet confession of Gladys
dewdrops of dawn in the indentation of leaves
my nourishment my eucharist my arteries my black nights
My love you are everything to me
slumber with its ample setting
a gaze silvered with sobs and inhuman farewells
the morning star which twinkles in my breath
life in its new suit
My love you are everything
the lynched dream of my fallen comrade in prison
manhood's kingdom coming open in the morning like a

                                                        petal

THE PEOPLE and their little hills of hope

My love you are everything
You are like Port-au-Prince in its frenzy
inside my room you take the form of Cuba
seeking Marti's voice
you are the heart of Africa, tom-toming the world in

its deep forests

You are Spain in my burning fever
those suns of Chile beyond my awaking

but why my love this dance so frail
in verse so poor from a poet
why all these gleanings in the field of my

inspirations

when their hands bring weeping
from the whip
from defiling
from lynching
from tearing to pieces

when they put a stop to children dancing in the moonlight
and break down doors and eat at reason

Of what use is love if it is not for loving

Of what use is love
if it is not for watering sorrow and grief

Of what use is love
if it is not for making heart-stalks bloom

Of what use is love
if it is not to join a great *coumbite*
of reunited days and nights

Listen my love
the season of love comes quickly
it runs away quickly and hurries up the time for loving
it clangs loud, the bell of love

Listen
evening enters your hair my love
hears the fierce shout from the *springfields* over there
that uproots your love my love
listen my love
the earth trembles at the approach of love
the hurrahs and applauses of the harvesters of love
O my love dialectic of the hymns of love
everything that is of you is me and us
they want to break you down as one breaks down a stare
they want to uproot you as one uproots from the sky a

                                                            star

you power and strength
God and demon
mountains and oceans
words and truths
illuminations and their opposites

My love leave my love
straighten your spine to heights loftier than reason
and pursue your course
in our flower beds of innocence and peace
for the great weeding-out of invented agonies

Be the wrath of a river
become my folly my form
my courage my light
For the happiness of nations I want to pile up suns
and want you my love to flutter like a dream

to lay yourself soundlessly on the layers of the world
where you will open with your hands of steel and flesh
The sluice gates of peace.

1961/1990

It Is Snowing Outside . . .

(translated by Jo-Anne Elder and Fred Cogswell)

It is snowing outside. Haitian slaves chained up in the Dominican Republic are coming into my room again. In their loose-fitting jackets they comprise dozens of skeletons. Haitian refugees are re-entering my grief as well. They have broken teeth, arms cut up; they wear their guts in their hair. Their laments reach the ceiling and their stinking sweat falls back on the growing helplessness of my face.

Out of that group of dead flesh invading my room, an old Negress stands out. Daylight narrows slowly in her eyes as the Chief's dragoons plunge their daggers into the breast of Jacques Stephen Alexis, the revolutionary. She refuses to hand over her system, that starveling stomach out of which pour caterpillars thirsting for blood.

I bear witness to an old dewdrop shaker. He dances around a coffin; his tones are snapped out as if his voice, beaten by ants and wasps, were going to make the timbers of the house collapse. Then once more I vomit my lack of power. Slaves and refugees bring me back to my negro intellectual shabbiness, to all the principles which make me a verbal magician caught in a trap of words.
but I scream
but I suffer

and poverty
and crime
both make your brains pop
love, too,
the illusion of believing
that you are useful for something in this corner of the globe
for they make you walk in shame
all those words
for the king's daughter's rose garden
all those words
for the voodoo spirits of the President
So it is snowing outside
they are in my room
monsters created by men
And monsters
have devoured my people my face
They have uprooted my soul
which walked beside a beggar-woman
They have swallowed up the mornings
no upside-down stories
and they have knocked on my bedroom door
until the curtain was lowered
on the monster comedy

It is snowing outside
You know very well, Dominique,
that the dream of the great evening has sprouted
that our lantern in the streets
the vermin of verminous quarters
the antennae-wearing centipedes
have cut off the current that feeds the power

You know very well that this boat will not leave
The ones who should go are waiting
grill in hand
to greet the poet's prophecy

It is snowing
A new stomach cramp
makes me clench my teeth
my cage is revolting
that niece who has just landed in Moncton
skin and bones
with nothing to restore the reality
watered down by contradictions of the spirit
and in those wells of the dead
where the General's Saints go to be born again

It is snowing outside
my cage closes again
heavy and without regret

1988/1990

La Pacotille [1]

(translated by Keith Louis Walker)

CHAPTER ELEVEN

The cell agonizes through the throes of death. The growling of the beasts, the execution of a rebel at every twenty-four hours, the absence of student demonstrations, the silence of the people, all of that lessens the little bit of hope of escaping the flames of the monster. More macabre the images I cling to. More bloodstained the robe of the prophet.

Something just pulled me from my delirium. The noises of the footsteps of a big Chief. On the watch out for the beast. As well as for his lackeys. They laugh. They applaud. A human body on the floor like a box of jumble. A mass of flesh in decomposition by my side. Impossibility of identifying the person. I have a swollen face. Blood-filled eyes. I make the supreme effort to identify the prisoner by the pitch of his voice which manifested itself in prolonged moans. No doubt in my mind. The monster is trying one last manoeuvre. Confront among them the revolutionaries. At least those who are still breathing since the Organization has lost its strategic heads. Justin Léon eviscerated by bayonet blows in the office of the monster. The rebel spat in his face. Pierrot Biamby is no longer moving in the cell next door. He was transported on a stretcher after a fourth session of torture to the National Palace. It is the same as far as concerns Gérard Michel. No sign of life either in his cell. The monster, it appears, did not obtain the confession of the prisoners. My guardian angel was readying itself to return to limbo when a strong voice brought me back to life.

"Fucking Pighead," it shouted. "We are making you a gift of

---

[1] Idiomatic: *The Wretched One.*

him. Your dirty nigger. Your dog of a nigger. I shall return in an hour. The truth, you understand, the whole truth."

Oh no, good God. I have prayed for a death in honour, not in the inability to be able to defend Guilène with arms. I have prayed, my God, for a death in glory. The glory of having been to the end of myself, of not having played games with myself, of having remained faithful to the honesty of my mother. I have prayed, prayed, in this shit to be spared the pardon of the monster, a freedom that would be my Calvary, a perpetual crisis of guilt because of the death of my friends. So there is the response to my prayers. Guilène at my side. Whom I cannot even see, smell, touch. To whom I can confess nothing. Guilène whose body has been sullied by the beasts of black men. Spare me this shame one last time. The shame of impotence in the face of this army of barbarians who are going to tear her to shreds.

We had no illusions. The way in which Guilène was arrested left no doubt about her immediate execution. A young woman who had invested so much money in the Organization, who had negotiated with the American bandits, the CIA included, the purchase of arms, had no chance of coming out alive from the jails of the monster. A whole battalion of militia in front of Guilène's residence. Slaughters. Guilène's grandmother Cecilia beaten to death. The residence first sacked and pillaged. Then set afire. The neighbouring houses vandalized. Two old men arrested. A horror film the arrest of Guilène.

Just barely arrived at the main door of the villa, a beast pounces upon Guilène. Blows from the butt of a rifle. Guilène falls. Swipes from the claws of the beast into the flesh of the young woman. A second beast attacks its prey. It strikes the temples this time. Guilène seems to be losing consciousness as blood gushes from her mouth. From her nose. Lifted from the floor, she is thrown into a paddy wagon.

The savagery reaches its climax. Taken off, torn, Guilène's dress is attached to the tip of a rifle fluttering like a flag while the beasts riddle the walls of the neighbouring homes with bullets. I realized that I had come to the most harrowing point of a youth of protest. The revolutionary undertaking of two living beings in perfect symbiosis. I was going straight for the goal through Guilène, for Guilène. The reason for my struggle, the unifying link between characters caught in a tragedy that has endured now for more than a century. . . .

I am waiting for the *coup de grâce*. I even provoke it by succeeding painfully in turning towards the beast, by raising my head in order to show him that I am deciding to confront him one last time. Less for myself for the minutes are slipping away than for Guilène. I shall not go to Hell before proving to him my courage. Even crushed. Even smashed. She had said to me that we would die together, that nothing could separate us. Through a recharging of the battery of the human body the mystery of which no one truly comprehends, my left eye painfully recovers its functioning. I am not dreaming. At my side the beautiful Guilène. The courageous Guilène. Her hair spread on the floor. The body covered with a cloth. The way she moves leaves me with the impression that she recognizes me.

A beast taking advantage of the absence of the Chief plays with Guilène's hair. The filthy beast. With a fierce expression, he caresses her legs. Surprise. A strength fills Guilène's face. A strength held in reserve deep within from the moment she realized she could not escape in the face of the battalions from the Dessalines army barracks surrounding her house. Trembling of the legs. Accelerated breathing so as not to fall into a coma. Yes. She is going to put up a fight. Until her dying breath. For the power so vaunted by the uncle of Ti-Blanc, a militant who was responsible for the indoctrination of a group of voodoo practitioners in the Bel-Air neighbourhood. For the uncle of Ti-Blanc who refused to join the ranks of the Organization, the power contains something which escapes non-believers, a kind of power that comes from heaven.

The death rattle, the sweat, the tears as well as the noisy breathing of prisoners form whitish masses in which one seems to see evolving the spirits of the monster. In spite of the blackness of the room, the setting sun succeeds in filtering through this stinking haze. Silence. Flag ceremonies. Funeral marches of an army battalion in front of the house of an officer who just executed a torturer of the President. . . .

"The names of your followers in Miami. The President promises you a pardon. You can see well for yourself, your poet is in robust health. In two more days he could be free."

Guilène does not move. One can see her biting her lips in rage. In a sign of impotence. . . .

Guilène's prolonged silence. One can barely hear her breathing. The end is approaching, one would say. In this filthy room where horrors take place that people will never know, that no one will be able to describe, that no one will be able to recount. Even with a new memory that the gods would procure for the prisoners who, through a miracle, will save their hides. Even with the accuracy of a movie camera cast upon the torture victims all along the way of the cross. Yes. So many horrors in the room which will evaporate into soap bubbles when the curtain falls on one of the bloodiest pages in the history of the pigsty, when the beasts will retreat to their lairs, satisfied at having sufficiently destroyed, bitten, debased the human species.

Too bad. No one will want to hear of a chest there, on the floor, torn out with a machete blow, from a little two-year-old girl arrested at the same time as her mother, deprived of food for quite some time, of old Léontine forced to eat her excrement. Oh no. One will not want to speak of those things, because those things are the product of morbid imaginations, invented in order to write books of poetry, to make horror movies, to give a bad conscience to the Whites who distribute food. . . .

At the hour when the locks of the heavenly vault are about to close, when peasants are returning to their huts of mud, at the hour when the awaited Messiah throws drops of dew on the burning embers at my feet, at the hour when one goes into mourning before even the departure of my soul towards other volcanoes, I hurl a last shout over and above the rooftops of the world. All the way to the end of my sigh, I shall sing of the eternal springtime of mankind so that no one will see the sun die before the last hour. . . .

Guilène is still not moving. On the cement floor that is torturing her. Her breathing is weakening more and more. A morgue the
room. Bells will soon announce the prayer for the dead. First
attempt to get my body closer to Guilène's. To take the hand
hidden under a cloth that covers her pelvis. In order to embrace
her. To bathe her in tenderness. We have already been through
hellfire. There remains for us at this point the supreme moment.
Among all others. To sign, in our comatose state, the fulfilment of
a dream of freedom. To sleep, carrying into our last delirious states
a people made to crawl on its knees. From Cerca-la-Source to the
capital, from the capital to Santo Domingo. To depart eternally.
With wounds all over the body, with voices made hoarse by
hunger, the faces of women, of men of children filled with pain
with always the expression of a little girl who trades her virtue for
a doll made of shells. Yes. To finish the dance in the light of the
moon so that we not make a last frown at life. We had gambled.
Not yet at the point of losing our hand. There still remains for us
a large portion of this illusion of having avoided the circle where
in broad daylight human sacrifices are held. . . .

The beast reflects while licking his paws, running his tongue
along his legs stained with blood. A pity words are not capable of
piercing the mysteries of life, that they are not voluminous enough
to contain all the ranges of reality. A pity. The earth would be a
book lacking in words to name the monster. His uglinesses. His
spasms. His regurgitations. To present a character whose smell
alone rots an entire country. There would be so much to say if
words had the swiftness of thought. The bedrocks of thought. The
beasts, it appears, have almost all deserted the room. Black hole.
Thick shadows. Another valley of tears to be crossed, there where
I am going soon to receive it, like a mass of air that makes hurri-
canes. Death. I had, during the torturing, imagined it as a liberating angel, that I would have coiffed with ribbons of satin, that I
would have received with arms full of flowers. No longer now.
I would have wished for a miracle in place of the death that appears
hideous to me. To the image of the beast, of all the foul things you
are forced to swallow in this low life. I look at it from a distance.

Black, quite black, the eyes of death. Volatile matter from within. The same burning. The same wrenching experience as humanity after the metamorphosis of the unknown serpent. . . .

Guilène still does not move. The hand under the cloth. I try a second time to get closer to her. For a bit more purity in the heart. To receive death in the calm of the just soul. She is going to awaken. She is going to rise. One does not die two times. I had indeed seen her in the truck. Her head under the boots of the policemen. I had indeed seen her decomposing in the sun. Her arms practically torn off. I had not dreamed. It seemed to me that there had been a flash in the sky. So, she is dead. No. She is waiting for my war cry. The passwords of the Organization. The voices of comrades. The signals of the full moon. Before taking the great leap into the space where the wild clamourings eclipse the song of nightingales. She has not yet said her last word. I am sure that the miracle is going to occur. It happens when her blood has been poured for nothing, when we have been trapped by the beasts with no arrows to defend ourselves. It happens when one carries a God in one's heart, when one denies him because of his absence in the enslavement of a people, when one consents to sign a pact even with the devil for the remission of the sins of beggars. Yes. The miracle occurs each time one wants to overturn the world, that one has in front of oneself a raging sea that the forces of evil refuse to part in two for easier crossing. Guilène has not yet let out a last scream. The beast wants me to cry, to rage, to condemn my God. The beast wants my repentance, my suicide for not having spared Guilène. The beast wants to kill me little by little tearing the flesh off my right side.

Twenty-two years old. Dead. Transported into a room of the Palace where, in the fashion of Clément Jumelle, the monster will take out her brain in order to pick out the secret codes of the Organization. If death wanted to do its work well, to tear Guilène away from the earth like a force one cannot control, quell, she would find in her sleep the lines of our melodies. The traces of our combat. We had learned, you recall, that there is no absolute death, that each death carries in it the elements of a new life. We had learned that one must not stop on the way even when invisible forces spike it with shards of glass, even when their Messiah hesitates to send us the promised guides.

The woman you had taken back to your house, you remember. In the sweetness of a summer's evening. She was bleeding. Her lips were burning. She was crying in your arms. She was telling you that you were created to bring light into the slums. The neighbourhoods on the cross. . . .

Guilène still does not move. A jagged image through my swollen eye. What a horror, my God. Indescribable, Guilène's body. Crushed, it looks like, under the wheels of the truck. Hacked, it looks like, with a machete. So, the end. No. Just a tiny little bit of breathing. Just enough for us to say one more time these unforgettable verses:

We shall not go to the goal one by one, but by two
Knowing each other two by two, we shall all come to know each
other.

Just long enough to go in search of the butterfly that followed us on the road to Kenskoff, that landed on her shoulder, taking on the colour of a time of royalty. . . .

We have won, Guilène. We have made him go mad. The monster of the Caribbean. The complexed Negro of the Caribbean. The Negro that no one dared approach. Too much a Negro in stone to be loved. Too ugly to please the creatures of this world, even to please house dogs. I had told you, Guilène. Remember. The monster is afraid of us. We who were fighting him only with ideas. Poems. Heartbeats. Here we are in front of the void. Here we are in the void. The ray of light on Guilène's body disappeared. I take a deeper breath. I gather my strengths.

Yes, Guilène. I give you my hand. You give me yours. Let's hold tight. That's it, my noble one. Go. Go. Push, push. It's coming. A little more, more. Breathe a little. Oh my God, thank you, thank you, thank you. Guilène's hand in my hand. The voyage will be less difficult.

1991/1997

→→ ←←

CLAIRE HARRIS

Where the Sky Is a Pitiful Tent

Once I heard a Ladino * *say "I am poor but listen I am not an Indian";
but then again I know Ladinos who fight with us and who understand
we're human beings just like them.*

Rigoberta Manchu (Guatemala)

All night the hibiscus tapped at our jalousies
dark bluster of its flower trying to ride in
on wind laciniated with the smell of yard fowl
Such sly knocking sprayed the quiet
your name in whispers
dry shuffle of thieving feet on verandah floors
My mouth filled with midnight and fog
like someone in hiding
to someone in hiding
I said *do not go*

* Ladino: a descendant of Spanish Jews who came to Guatemala during the
Inquisition. Quotations in italics are taken from the testimony of Rigoberta
Manchu, collected by Elizabeth Burgos, translated into Spanish by Sylvia
Roubaud and into English by Patricia Goedicke, and published in the Mexican
publication *Unomasuno* and in *American Poetry Review* (January/February 1983).

you didn't answer
though you became beautiful and ferocious
There leached from you three hundred years of compliance
Now I sleep with my eyes propped open
lids nailed to the brow

After their marriage my parents went into the mountains to establish a small settlement . . . they waited years for the first harvest. Then a patron *arrived and claimed the land. My father devoted himself to travelling and looking for help in getting the rich landowners to leave us alone. But his complaints were not heard . . . they accused him of provoking disorder, of going against the sovereign order of Guatemala . . . they arrested him.*

In the dream I labour toward something
glimpsed through fog   something of us exposed
on rock and mewling   as against the tug of water
I struggle under sharp slant eyes
death snap and rattle of hungry wings

                                        Awake I whisper

You have no right to act
you cannot return land from the grave
Braiding my hair the mirror propped on my knees
I gaze at your sleeping vulnerable head
Before the village we nod smile or don't smile
we must be as always
while the whole space of day aches with our nightmares
I trail in your footsteps through cracks you chisel
in this thin uncertain world
where as if it were meant for this mist hides
sad mountain villages   reluctant fields
still your son skips on the path laughing
he is a bird   he is a hare
under the skeletal trees

My mother had to leave us alone while she went to look for a lawyer
who would take my father's case. And because of that she had to work
as a servant. All her salary went to the lawyer. My father was tortured
and condemned to eighteen years in prison. (Later he was released.)
But they threatened to imprison him for life if he made any more
trouble.

I watch in the market square
those who stop and those who do not
while my hands draw the wool over up down
knitting the bright caps on their own
my eyes look only at sandals
at feet chipped like stones at the quarry
There are noons when the square shimmers
we hold our breath while those others
tramp in the market place
Today the square ripples like a pond
three thrown   what is left of them
corded like wood   alive and brought to flame
How long the death smoke signals
on this clear day
We are less than the pebbles under their heels
the boy hides in my shawl

The army circulated an announcement ordering everyone to present themselves in one of the villages to witness the punishment the gueril-las would receive . . . There we could observe the terrible things our com-rades had suffered, and see for ourselves that those they called guerillas were people from the neighboring villages . . . among them the Catequistas and my little brother . . . who was secretary to one of the village co-operatives. That was his only crime. He was fourteen years old . . . They burnt them.

As if I have suffered resurrection I see
the way the grass is starred with thick fleshed
flowers at whose core a swirl of fine yellow
lines disappear into hollow stems
so we now into our vanished lives
Dust thickening trees we turn
to the knotted fist of mountains
clenched against mauve distance
Because I must   I look back
heartheld to where the mudbrick huts
their weathered windows daubed with useless crosses
their shattered doors   begin the slow descent
to earth   my earlier self turns in
darkening air   softly goes down with them
The boy only worms alive in his eyes
his face turned to the caves

When we returned to the house we were a little crazy, as if it had been a nightmare. My father marched ahead swiftly saying that he had much to do for his people; that he must go from village to village to tell them what had happened . . . A little later so did my mother in her turn . . . My brother left too . . . and my little sisters.

If in this poem you scream who will hear you
though you say *no one should cry out in vain*
your face dark and thin with rage
Now in this strange mountain place
stripped by knowledge
I wait for you
Someone drunk stumbles the night path
snatching at a song or someone not drunk
I am so porous with fear
even the rustle of ants in the grass flows through me
but you are set apart
The catechists say *in heaven there is no male
no female*   that is a far foolishness
why else seeing you smelling of danger
and death do I want you so
your mouth   your clear opening in me

---

*We began to build camps in the mountains where we would spend the
night to prevent the troops from killing us while we slept. In the daytime
we had taught the children to keep watch over the road . . . We knew
that the guerillas were up there in the distant mountains. At times they
would come down in order to look for food, in the beginning we didn't
trust them, but then we understood that they, at least, had weapons to
fight the army with.*

You will not stop what you have begun
though I asked in the way a woman can
Since you have broken thus into life
soon someone will make a pattern
of your bones   of your skull
as they have with others
and what will fly out
what will escape from you torn apart
the boy and I must carry
In your sleep I went to the cenote[*]
in the moonlight I filled my shawl with flowers
threw them to the dark water
the ancient words fluting in my head
your son pinched awake to know what must come

My mother was captured (some) months later . . . when all she could wish for was to die . . . they revived her, and when she had recovered her strength they began torturing her again . . . they placed her in an open field . . . filled her body with worms . . . she struggled a long time then died under the sun . . . The soldiers stayed until the buzzards and dogs had eaten her. Thus they hoped to terrorize us. She doesn't have a grave. We, her children, had to find another way of fighting.

---

[*] cenote: a well occasionally used in ritual sacrifice (precolumbian).

Oh love this is silence   this is the full
silence of completion   we have swum through
terror that scared us to bone
rage lifted a cold hand to save us
so we became this surreal country
We have been bullet-laden air   fields that sprout
skulls   night that screeches and hammers
we have been hunger   whip   wind that sobs
feast days and drunken laughter
a rare kindness and pleasure
We have come through to the other side
here everything is silence   our quiet breathing
in this empty hut   our clay jugs full of light
and water   we are our corn our salt
this quiet is the strength we didn't know we had
our humanity no longer alarms us
we have found who we are
my husband our silence is the silence of blue steel thrumming
and of love
Our deaths shall be clear

---

*Our only way of commemorating the spilled blood of our parents was
to go on fighting and following the path they had followed. I joined the
organization of the Revolutionary Christians. I know perfectly well that
in this fight one runs the greatest risk . . . We have been suffering such
a long time and waiting.*

Your death is drenched in such light
that small things   the sky   branches
brushing against the cave mouth   the boy
stirring   make my skin crackle against damp blankets
As one gathers bullets carelessly spilled I gather your screams
all night I remember you   utterly lovely
the way you danced the wedding dance
rising dust clouding your sandals
your slow dark smile
You return to the predawn   leaving us
what remains when the flames die out of words
(small hard assertions
our beginnings
shards of the world you shattered
and ourselves)

Their death gave us hope, because it is not just that the blood of all those people be erased forever. It is our duty on this earth to revive it . . . I fight so they will recognise me . . . If I have taken advantage of this chance to tell the story of my life it is because I know that my people cannot tell their own stories. But they are no different from mine.

1984

Policeman Cleared in Jaywalking Case

> *The city policeman who arrested a juvenile girl for jay-walking March 11 has been cleared of any wrongdoing by the Alberta law enforcement appeal board.*
>
> *The case was taken to the law enforcement appeal board after the girl was arrested, strip-searched and jailed in the adult detention centre.*
>
> *The police officer contended the girl had not co-operated during the first five minutes after she was stopped, had failed to produce identification with a photo of herself on it, and had failed to give the policeman her date of birth.*
> *Edmonton Journal*

In the black community to signify indicates an act of acknowledgement of sharing, of identifying with.

The girl was fifteen. An eyewitness to the street incident described her as "terrified."

The girl handed the officer her bus pass containing her name, address, phone number, her school, school address and phone number.

Look you, child, I signify   three hundred years in swarm around me this thing I must this uneasy thing   myself the other   stripped down to skin and sex   to stand   to stand and say   to stand and say before you all   the child was black and female and therefore mine   listen   you walk the edge of this cliff with me at your peril do not hope to set off safely to brush stray words off your face to flick an idea off with thumb and forefinger   to have a coffee and go home comfortably   Recognize this edge   and this air carved with her silent invisible cries   Observe now this harsh world   full of white works   or so you see us   and it is white   white washed male and dangerous even to you full of white fire white heavens white words   and it swings in small circles around you   so you see it   and here I stand black and female   bright black on the edge of this white world   and I will not blend in nor will I fade into the midget shades   peopling your dream

Once long ago   the loud tropic air   the morning rushing by in a whirl of wheels   I am fifteen drifting through hot streets shifting direction by instinct   tar heel soft under my shoes I see shade on the other side of the road   secure in my special dream I step off the curb   sudden cars   crash and jangle of steel   the bump the heart stopping fall into silence then the distant driver crying "Oh Gawd! somebody's girl child she step off right in front of me, Gawd!" Black faces anxious in a fainting world a policeman bends into my blank gaze   "where it hurting yuh?   tell me!"   his rough hand under my neck   then seeing me whole "stand up, let me help yuh!" shaking his head   the crowd straining on the sidewalk the grin of the small boy carrying my books   then the policeman   suddenly stern "what you name, girl?"   the noisy separation of cars   "eh, what you name?"   I   struck dumb   dumb   "look child, you ever see a car in plaster of paris?"   dumb   "tell me what's your name? You ever see a car in a coffin!"   the small boy calling out my name into such shame   But I was released with a smile   with sympathy sent on in the warm green morning   Twenty years later to lift a newspaper and see my fifteen year old self   still dumb   now in a police car   still shivering as the morning roars past but here   sick in the face of such vicious intent

Now female I stand in this silence   where somebody's black girl child jaywalking to school is stripped   spread   searched   by a woman who finds that black names are not tattooed on the anus pale hands soiling the black flesh   through the open door the voices of

men in corridors   and in spite of this   yea   in spite of this black
and female to stand here and say   I am   she is   I say to stand
here   knowing this is a poem black in its most secret self

Because I fear   I fear myself and I fear your skeletal skin the spider
tracery of your veins   I fear your heavy fall of hair like sheets of
rain and the clear cold water of your eyes   and I fear myself the
rage alive in me consider the things you make even in the mystery
of earth and the things you can   an acid rain that shrivels
trees   your clinging fires that shrivel skin   This law that shrivels
children and I fear your naked fear of all that's different   your
dreams of power your foolish innocence but I fear myself and the
smooth curve of guns   I fear   Look   your terrible Gods do not
dance nor laugh nor punish men   do not eat or drink but stay a far
distance   watch the antic play of creation and cannot blink or
cheer   Even I fear the ease you make of living this stolen land   all
its graceful seductions   but I fear most myself   how easy to drown
in your world   dead believe myself living   who stands "other"
and vulnerable to your soul's disease
Look you child, I signify

1984

⤙ ⤚

FREDERICK WARD

Riverlisp

PURELLA MUNIFICANCE

When Grandma Snooks spoken'd you see'd

a sleeping bee
cuddled in a tear drop
hidden hind a elephant's ear

. . . cause she talked in them parable kind of visions to show her meanings: "Fuss is round all beautifull-ness. When you's in trouble, boy, you just seeks that inner place you got it! we all's got it!"

But Micah Koch's *inner place* was all fuss too. He'd seen Miss Purella Munificance.

Dear sweet Purella Munificance   the huckster man on his produce wagon, put light to your meaning so we can understand   huckster man be thinking on your continence   he sing the painter's brush strokes of your mouth; a low soft soothing: ahhhh   sound of the sea bird, leaning on the air! and shout:

"Oooo, tomatoes's red ripe!
Cabbage tender peas from the vine
Sweet . . ."

and draws them who wish to buy in a voice that forgits what he be selling. The womens is moved, tho. Huckster man be so taken he neglec'd and one woman is put to ask for her change: "Owe up, what you owe me, man!"

Mr. Makin It, say: "Yes, you bet. Sit down here with me . . . I tell you. Purella, could put a thot in your mind like, that what so you'd believe in her werent never gonna be lost or gone! And patient? I members she be waiting three days for a person to show up who promised to come'd over in fifteen mins. No, I dont lies. I be that friend and when I come'd acting out my lies to tell, Purella just sees me and a great sun come'd over her face and she says: 'Yeah, at last!'"

He look up at the sky to see if God were looking and take him a good drink lowered the bottle and his head   eyes closed squint bove a nose in s'pantion breathing on lips shaped after the raw persimmon touch: "Oooowhee! I'm gonna git caught one day . . ." as if the Lord didn't already know'd.

"When Miss Munificance be passing old mens on th street corner falls into th 'unpire slouch' position   bent over   shaking they head under a hand shading they eyes so to see th *strike coming in*, Purella Munificance gonna be home free – if she *just would!*

"O the boys were at her door   but usually got shush'd way. Her mama make her wear long skirts and dresses all th time she were growing up and Purella be obedient   aint never give her mama a moments bother. The pimps were always after her and th preacher's known for talking pass you in her direction, when she be round. Yet, she treated everyone with respec. She once were heard to say: 'Inevitably we is one.' She tol, she been dreaming of a great inte-coloured parade! and when she dreamt that, she clasp'd her hands and shouted: 'WHAT A LOVELY BOWL OF FRUIT . . .'

"But that aint had no meaning for most and some'd swear the girl were unhappy . . .

touch me
touch me
O let me see

". . . so when Micah Koch come'd to her home to sell his Bibles, I tells so you could understand why, for her, that parade dream come'd real and they says that Micah Koch's heart were taken! and that later, he cried as he were trying to sell a Bible when reading from Solomon and Sheba – Kings 10:1-13.

"No one knowed th moment what it were in which that Micah Koch and Purella Munificance see'd the Lord in each other's face and being. You may think it questioning that I says they see'd th Lord in each other's selfs   but the Lord, here means sacrifice – that's Love – and that's what they were ready and looking for to do. SACRIFICE! That, as far as I can says, were it. Sacrifice. No one knowed how they met, but they done. Aint none ever see'd them together, but people talked. Some out of fear   some were jealous   and others just vicious.

Fuss is round
all beautifull-
ness

"Seems like all th troublin things you could say were cut loose on sweet Miss Purella   the childrens would run to her on th streets – laughins – put they fist on they little hips – being in th ways of they mama's – switch dance and sang:

"you got a white man
you got a white man"

". . . and run way, they tongues jabbin at her. I sure Miss Purella's tears drained backwards directly thru to her heart, cause we who be sitting on th curbs and standing in th doorways never see'd a drop.

O hound
of the crucible!

"Put me in mind of Miss Jessups's boy's affair . . .

"Yes, you bet! many is the swift tongue of elegance to put words so to touch your inness and makes you to thinking on vision pictures of lovers that fill-heat the heart   huh, huh!   even lovers in hell trying to 'scapes. Micah and Purella werent th difference. What they had was private and maybe that's why people talked   made up and put words in they mouths and movements to they bodies over near the Japanese bridge one night. Poor Miss Purella.

"I guess the sweet child come'd to think in th way that the world was gainst her and in th middle one night, she just let a screamed. It took so long for th scream to reach nowheres that they werent no echo. She stop'd somewheres and aint been with us since!"

Makin It took a long drink look off after in the way of some noise: "You knows, I just worries bout God ketching me with my bottle. I worries lots cause I sleeps with it . . .

"Th worst thing in th world is to be goin thru something by your-selfs afore a audience, like people on the street. So Purella let to walking in th streets is always telling what she be going thru and why even to burst into tears in the middle of th street and then stopping a random person and telling them what was happening to her: 'I just been membering how daddy died of . . .' and she'd cry and embarrass the poor person way.

"Caint say what happened inside Micah Koch. He looked the same everyday cept he lost a might bit weight, tho. He didnt not sell many more Bibles, after just hung round.

"Mama Fuchsia – she truely loved that man – went to shushen and put shame in they hearts. She and the church women delicate in they care surrounded and gave assurance to Mr. Koch that everything would be put right if he'd only just come to th Lord come to th church! Took some time but one old Sunday night baptismal night it were up come Mama Fuchsia head high, but humble with Micah Koch. Come'd right in th church and sit if you please, afore th amazement! Rev. More were opening th doors of th church and asked: 'Is there a sinner among us? Th Lord ask me to ask.' All heads turned to Micah Koch. Mama Fuchsia leaned his way whispered: 'Raise your hand, Honey.' DONE.

"Rev. Mores come out of th pulpit walked up th ile and stood afore Micah: 'Th Lord welcomes every soul in th Kingdom. And th Kingdom here on earth is th church. Let's hear you say amens.'

(answered) 'You, young man been a servant of His for our people with your Bible selling and all. Th Community loves you as their own and what better than you show *your people* what th Lord done tol and we here believes – that all th Messengers is one spirit and loves us cause we is one.'

"Micah drop'd his head like to pray. Rev. Mores started to sweat, one stream catching th corner of his lip – left side – in a come-on-sinner-give-in smile. Th water in the baptismal pit stood cold and waiting waves rocking like th moaners who now filled th church with low chant . . .

"I likes to thinks on Mama Fuchsia's face brown and beaming bright.

"'Just like the Lord would say it; bless you, Honey
I buys one of them with the pictures.'"

1974

Who

Who gonna bargain for my soul
Who gonna bargain last

Her mouth stretched
withered and flush:
the crimson what come'd
round a bruise

though the voice
be a high sparrow-chirping:
the sudden flutter-ups-of-a-
startled thing

When she gripped a lone note
a breeze neath silk
be of report
and carried the thought of a

modest young girl
stooped to press her apron
gainst her dress
ironing it from the heat of her thighs

then standing erect
– surrounded by ancient

yet courageous tremblings.
shouts:

Who gonna bargain for my soul
Who gonna bargain last

1983

Who All Was There

MARY

Most I have were my fears and a hatchet when I
crossed over into Canada . . . I took my first night
in liberty high on a tree branch next of . . . all
as I could tell, a bird in shivers with its head
hid mongst a wing . . . I hummed to it to calm our
fears . . . give me confidence that the bird ain't
fly away during the night . . . be a sign to me,
owning up to my being human, that even not something shivering next to me I could consider with
a friendliness. Am I human. They never give me a
good characteristic to go on. Even my songs be
filled with the guilt grafted onto my soul. I
wanted to touch the bird but to do that I haves
to let go the branch and I'd lose my hold to it
cause my other hand grasped my hatchet.

The Lord do send us some tests, don't He? Breakfast be one of them. In the middle of my pity for
the bird . . . sunrise on my soul! I got hungry.

Since the bird's head were still neath its wing,
it had no head . . . I considered it cooked like the
fowl I served in bondage . . . and since it continued
to shiver. I thought what a mercy I'd bring to it.

But had not this been the lie what got me here:
were I not dead cause I possessed no tongue understood . . . were it even not a mercy, a right to beat
me cause I shivered with fear . . . have I not used it
gainst my own for proof? Am I mad? I am split
from my most confident self-assumption . . . yet the
Lord send a grace in some stranger's hand: a prayer
and a epistle . . . set my mind in "*the possibility*"
what changed the quality of my thought . . . kept it
safe whilst I seen them go crazy with their makings;
realized a spirit in me not noticeable as they checked
my teeth . . . snatched what be theirs from tween
my legs to beat on and chew on it . . .

The bird flown away . . . left its shiverings on the
branch and I climbed down into snow.

1983

Blind Man's Blues

The best thing in my life
was a woman named Tjose.

We never had to sneak for nothing
strong woman.

Put you in mind of a lone bird at dawn
standing without panic in the dew.

She kissed me so hard
she'd suck a hum from me

The best thing happen to her
were my own papa.

I found her
he had more experience

I think the hound in me sniffed out something —
something about her

And I caught her sucking that same hum from him.
I went dumb staring . . . and she seen it.

My to God, she tried to wave me off —
Papa say:
          — O son
          O son

And I don't think she wanted me
to look on my naked papa like that

She throw'd lye
in my face.

                                                            1983

Dialogue #1: Mama

Sure enough Lord, sometimes I just went and stood in the
corner . . . and had me corner. You know the day they come'd-
from room to room I moaned some tween me teeth til moaning
and quiet yelpings be all I had left. Then come'd the
knock. Me fears swelled up in me jaws . . . stretched the soul
of me to makes fer an explosion tween me lips, yet . . .

The bulldozer be next door to me friend Miss Chisholm's
place. Tweren't no crash such that would slide into a
child's crying, makes fer you to come running to the
window to see what fer. No! This sound'd keep me pressed
to me corner, covered over on meselfs and come'd to trembling.

I prayed: Please give me me tiny crimes. Fergive me me tiny
crimes. Fill the little emptinesses in me – and Lord bless.
I swear I heard something . . . a choir singing softly:
"*Have faith, Adeline!*" The knock come'd again. I lurched . . .
then folded me arms about meself. Most proudly I beckoned:
it's open.

Then shadows come'd right round me. Come'd in here without
asking pardon fer themselfs and took things from they place
whilst I mumbled and pointed. I touched me breath and tried
to slow them to take care. Some one of them apologized fer
moving me. But they made off with me evidence. I ACCEPTS!
But I expects they'd lease done the least, ceptin they ain't.
THEY MOVED ME IN GARBAGE TRUCKS![1]

1983

---

[1] The belongings of the people of Africville were moved by City of Halifax
garbage trucks because moving companies refused to do so. Africville, a community which had existed on the south shore of Bedford Basin since 1815, was
bulldozed by the City of Halifax in the 1960s and its residents relocated.

Dialogue #3: Old Man (to the Squatter)

– Listen here, son. Did you think this were gonna work?
Were you fool enough to think this were gonna work?
They ain't gonna let us put nothing up like that and
leave it. They don't intend to let us git it back. You
ain't a place. Africville is us. When we go to git a
job, what they ask us? Where we from . . . and if we say
we from Africville, *we are Africville!* And we don't git
no job. It ain't no place, son. It were their purpose to
git rid of us and you believed they done it – could do it!
You think they destroyed something. They ain't. They
took away the place. But it come'd round, though. Now that
culture come'd round. They don't just go out there and
find anybody to talk about Africville, they run find us,
show us off – them that'll still talk, cause we Africville.
NOT-NO-SHACK-ON-NO-KNOLL. That ain't the purpose . . . fer
whilst your edifice is foregone destroyed, its splinters
will cry out: *We still here!* Think on it, son. You effort
will infix hope in the heart of every peoples. Yet,
let's see this thing clearer. If our folk see you in the
suit, we may git the idea we can wear it. The suit might
fall apart, but, son, it be of no notice. We need the
example. Now go back . . . and put you dwelling up again.

1983

The Death of Lady Susuma

LIGHTNING were into the river. The weather turned to steel but Lady Susuma set herself gainst it to greet something in it. Her 'voices' were at her, say:

Not to worry bout the "Robes moving on the leaves"
We brought him come'd for to git you:
Kept Sweet Under the Pressure

When she heard it, she put her palm gainst her mouth then doubled it into a fist . . . crushed her lips . . . her hand flowered open afore her face, and she caught-smeared a tear . . . inside a shiver she done it:

"Yesssss, O Be Jesus, yes."
It were a quick and trembling-tickled "yes" hushed as through a hollowness neath ovals filled with finger pressings waved off by hen's down, tied at the hollowness's end in streamers . . . sing a softness.

She squinted out on shadows . . . choked the sobs in her, says of a memory:

"Sometimes when he be sleeping long . . . late, and I be feeling a bit alone, I walk to a tipping within myself to his room . . . pass my shadow across his eyelids . . . he always stirs his brow, and I imagine I be in his dream. And if he wakes, I be 'home' in his mighty stare: standing with no blouse on, in two pools of pale blue set in soft scottish pink surrounded by an autumn wheat field."

She peered out to see closely . . . sought him on the path. He started talking to her from down the road, shouting love:

"It's like a four letter word strung across a barn wall, trying to say it happened. DAMN!" He says this in his highland talk, waving,

Ar bidh
Is sinn
Cridhe

Mor
An daimheach

Uidhe agus eadar
A

Ar cridhe bidh mor daimheach
Agus a is an uidhe eadarainn[2]

Lady Susuma gathered herself together as he approached the porch-stoop. He stepped it. He bowed off his hat and she lowered her gaze but he weren't in it. Like a picture she sit, sit in her rocker in the doorway . . . barefoot, a fistful of hairpins resting on her lap, mostly covered by her other hand: its thumb drying tear-wet and favouring the veins in the fist . . . tracing them. She always have a little sweater over her draped around her shoulders . . . says, to keep the chill way from her.

She reach-caught the door frame and pulled herself up . . . took in a breath, balled it under her cheeks and stepped onto a twisting . . . she fuss of it in her smile but the hurt set trembling through her lips and neath her talk:

"Morning."

---

[2] Gaelic: Our are / Is us / Hearts // Great / The friends // Space and between / That // Our hearts / Are great friends / and that / Is the space between / Us.

Her mouth pruned it in dignity . . . says it like a bird do with the "goodgood!" and a "mymymy!" in it, the purpose subtle but bent as she sniffed:

"There's more truth in a dead baby's countenance than on your tongue. When you coming back? You always coming back."

She placed the hairpins in a neat pile on the banister, stepped and twisted to a window box and snatched a brown leaf from a bluish red fuchsia plant . . . hid it in her fist. She turned with his voice in her ear:

"You been carrying all that round with you?"

She paused:

"Yes, I done."

"I been carrying mine about with me, too."

"What do it all mean to you?"

"What?"

"Everything I just says to you."

"As much as it means to you. I love you, too, you know."

The rest be private. But it seems Lady Susuma drifted awhile . . . spent it gazing on "someone" and hugging the banister post about it . . . rubbing her cheek gainst it there in the rain. She dropped the leaf . . . waved a "go on way from here" but then stretched forth her hand into "somebody's" grip . . . gripped, and come'd off the porch dancing. Yes. Dancing. Once you can put your hand on the bush the curing berry be there for you.

1983

All Clear, 1928

I was beating chaklata when someone
came shouting: A stranger man come!

I dropped everything. Same way
in my sampata, my house dress,

my everyday head-tie, I rushed to
the square wondering: could it be?

How many gathered there so long
after our men disappeared into

the black water dividing us from
Puerto Limón, Havana, Colón

knew it was he? Not his sons lost
to a father fifteen years gone.

There he was. Leather-booted and
spurred, sitting high on a fine horse.

Never spoke a word. This Spanish
grandee sat on his horse and

looked at us. Looked through us.
Never could lump poverty. Used

to say: Esmie, when I strike it rich
in foreign what a fine gentleman

I'll be. And you with your clear
complexion will sit beside me,

your hands stilled from work
like silk again (silk of my skin

my only dowry!) Ashamed now of my
darkened complexion, my work-blackened

hands, my greying hair, a loosening
of my pride (three sons with Mr. Hall

the carpenter who took me in) I
lowered my eyes and tried to hide.

I needn't have bothered. He looked
so troubled, as if he'd lost his way.

And suddenly, with nothing said,
he wheeled his horse and fled.

And ever after we talked of the
wonder of it. The stranger never

spoke to anyone. Forgotten the young
man who left home with a good white

shirt (stitched by these hands) and
a borrowed black serge suit (which

the owner never recovered), a heng-pon-me
with four days' ration of roasted salt fish,

johnny cakes, dokunu and cerasee for tea
to tide him over to the SS *Atrato*

lying in wait in Kingston Harbour.
All, all the men went with our dreams,

our hopes, our prayers. And he
with a guinea from Mass Dolphy

the schoolteacher who said that boy
had so much ambition he was bound

to go far. And he had. Gathering
to himself worlds of experience

which allowed him to ride over us
with clear conscience. I never

told anyone. For I would have had
to tell his children why he hadn't

sent money for bread, why his fine
leather boots, why his saddle,

his grey mare, his three-piece suit,
his bowler hat, his diamond tie-pin,

his fine manicured hands, his barbered
hair, his supercilious air. Never

was a more finely cut gentleman
seen in our square. And I trembled

in anger and shame for the black limbo
into which my life had fallen

all these years till my hands touched
the coarse heads of my young sons

recalling me to a snug house clad
with love. And I cried then, because

till he came back I had not known
my life was rooted. Years later,

I learned that his fine gentlemanly air,
his polished boots, manners, and Ecuador

gold bought him a very young girl of very
good family in Kingston. And they wed.

He, with a clear conscience.
She, with a clear complexion.

1994

Swimming in the Ba'ma Grass

. . . Swimming? In the Ba'ma grass? Who ever heard of such a thing and a big man at that? Dress in him work clothes same way, him khaki shirt and him old stain-up jeans pants and him brand new Ironman water boots that I did tell him was too big for him, this old man playing the fool in the middle of the pasture, lying there pretending he swimming with his two hands out there like he doing the crawl and his feet kicking. Look how he playing the fool till one of his boots fall off and is what that red thing like blood stain up the back of him brand new khaki shirt, is only one time it wash and look how him gone stain it up now. And is why that police boy there, the one Shannon, why he standing there with his gun in him hand and that other one there from the station, Browning, standing beside him, and the two of them watching my husband there making a fool of himself pretending he swimming? Why all the people running and shouting and Shannon waving his gun at them telling them to back-back, Shannon waving his gun at me while I run to Arnold who not swimming at all – I know he jokify but this is going too far.

You don't think the one Shannon could mad enough shoot Arnold? That is what Dorcas big boy was calling out to me when I was hanging out the clothes? Him did really say "Shannon shoot Marse Arnold"? Me not even sure now me did hear what him did say good. He was making so much noise I get confuse. He was calling my name, calling my name, "Miss Lyn, Miss Lyn. Come quick," and something about my husband and Shannon, but if he really did say Shannon shoot Arnold why me poor woman standing here thinking seh Arnold playing the fool?

See here now. Is only because I know Arnold is a man come from the sea and like to play the fool sometime; he love the sea more than anything in the whole world and when he wanted was to go to Treasure Beach and I wouldn't let him, him would lie on the floor and pretend he swimming and laugh, doing it just to

annoy me, but not in a malicious way. Arnold don't have a mean
bone in him body which is why everybody so vex with the way that
that police boy Shannon been treating him since that time he went
up to the station to complain. Trying every which way to get
Arnold into trouble but he never succeed yet because everybody
in this town know Arnold is a decent law-abiding man. Telling
everybody, the boasy boy, say he going to get Arnold. And not a
soul, not even Sarge that say him is Arnold friend, do one thing
about it, because that Shannon is bull-buck-and-duppy-conqueror
and everybody fraid of him. Forever boasting that he going to get
Arnold. For what? Everybody know Arnold not a complaining
man. He not a quarrelling man. Look how long we live here in
peace with all our neighbours. Ask any one of them. Of all the
people living here, Arnold must be the only one never quarrel with
nobody yet. Me really can't say the same for myself because everybody know my temper well hot. But this time it wasn't me quarrelling with anybody why Dorcas boy was making so much noise.
Mark you, him was always a noisy little fellow. But what he was
calling out again ee? Lawd Jesus! A can't keep a thing in me brain.

Oh. I remember now. I was talking how my temper hot and that
is why when that Shannon show impertinence to me at the police
station I did fire him a box hot-hot. Me big married woman him a
go put question to! A tek him big dutty nayga hand a touch me.
Just because he see me there a clean up the place he must be think
I one of him dutty Kingston gal. I fire him a box, you see, and him
so shock, him just reel back so, and then I see some evil come into
him eye, you see, and a swear to Massa God he going to kill me.
But another policeman come into this room same time and Shannon
turn him tail and leave. This was one of the decent fellows there –
one of the Wright boys from out Christiana way – and when he
ask me what happen, I tell him. And me did expect him to laugh
but he look serious bout the whole thing and he say, "Miss Lyn,
you have every right to box him. Facety wretch. But Shannon not
a man to cross, you know. Them say is six man him kill aready in
town. Is 'Enforcer' them call him there, you know. And them only

send him here because town get a little too hot for him right now."
Then him look round good before him whisper to me, "Is Big Man
behind him, you know."

Cho! What the Wright think he playing? Everybody know bout
Enforcer and which politician him kill for. But that is Kingston
business. Me did hear say him was getting too big for him boots so
the Big Man glad to get rid of him, send him down here to cool him
off for a while. And like how no politics a go on down here,
Enforcer don't have nothing to enforce.

But see here, that Shannon is a rat though, you know, a stinking
dirty rat. After that, I couldn't do nothing right at the station.
Shannon cross me up every time. Is like him set in wait for me. The
minute I clean the floor, him would walk outside in the mud and
come tramping right across it, innocent like, and I couldn't say a
word. I would wash the sheets and towels and hang them on the
line, and when I come back to pick them up, I find that somebody
rub green bush and dutty into them. Me say, those things were so
childish. If him was big and bad like they say, why him was going
on like pickney so? I take the Sarge him coffee in the morning, and
Sarge take one sip and swear blue light at me for somebody put salt
in the sugar. Jus things like that Shannon do, like pickney. But still
and all he was a snake. Used to make my skin crawl. Any time I at
the station and he come in, my skin just crawl. Him never trouble
me again though, and I make sure to keep out of his way. But I get
the feeling the whole time he looking at me and laughing inside,
laughing and biding him time.

Then is what that Shannon doing standing there in the middle
of the pasture in this sun-hot, wearing him good Kingston shoes?
Why he not at the station, eh? I never even bother to tell Arnold
about him putting question to me, for you know how man stay.
Even though they there quiet, them like a raging bull when they
think another man even look at their woman. And then again
sometimes man you would never ever consider put question to
you, and your own man vex because they say is you encouragement them. So me don't say nothing. But all the little petty things

Shannon doing getting on my nerves. So I start complain about the job and I tell Arnold I want to leave.

Arnold don't want me to leave for he say is the best job I ever have, cleaning up at the station and doing a little washing on the side. Arnold say is good government work and I get my pay regular, I don't have to put up with some facety woman in her kitchen and if anything should happen to him, if I stay there long enough, I will come in for a little pension.

But I fuss and fuss every day till Arnold can't stand it no longer and he ask me exactly what is happening and I still don't tell him bout Shannon. I tell him bout all the trickify things somebody doing to me and how it making my work twice as hard. I don't tell him how it burn me up day after day to go to work and see that snakey smile on Shannon face.

Well unbeknownest to me, Arnold nuh decide to go and see the Sarge, who he know well — the two of them drinking all the time together down at One Love. But Arnold is a serious man when he ready so he don't tackle Sarge at the bar — he put on his good clothes one day and, after I leave work, he go to the station to complain to Sarge that one of the policeman have it in for me. So Sarge say he will look into it. Now, I don't know if Sarge did know what was happening — maybe Wright did tell him. Anyway, next day I go to work and he call me in and ask me how come something happening at the station and I don't tell him, look how long I work there and is my husband have to come in and lodge complaint. So then I explain to him what happen with Shannon and me and why I don't want to discuss it with Arnold. So he say "A-oh." And that is the last I hear of it.

Is the same fellow Wright did tell me how Sarge call in the Shannon there and chastise him for his treatment of me. But you see how life stay? Shannon get it into him head that is my husband that did lodge complaint to Sarge about him. And that is how the bad blood between my husband and Shannon start.

And is me cause it O God is me responsible for everything that happen in my husband life from he meet me. Is me cause him to be living here, working on the land, something he never want to do for he really wanted was to live by the sea. Is there him come from, down Treasure Beach way, is a hard set of people living down there, you know. If them not fighting with the sea them fighting the land, for it hardly ever rain and it hardly have any proper tree or no little green grass. Is Mandeville I come from, up in the hill where it green and cool all the time and me not lying at all, me just never like the part of the world that Arnold come from. It never look natural to me, the way place suppose to look, and the people them don't look natural neither. And I never never could stand the sea.

Is how me did get on to meeting Arnold? Me can't even remember, I tell you, mi brain gone.

Arnold used to deal with my Daddy, that time when I was a young girl and my Daddy did have a dray. He used to go down to Treasure Beach way and buy fish, and melon and tomatis and skellion, all those things what them Saint Bess people did grow, what nobody else was growing those time. And Arnold is one of the people he used to deal with.

When Arnold start put question, me never interested, because Arnold was a hard-back man and me was just a little bit of a girl. Used to ride with my Daddy sometimes for I was the youngest and he love me dearly. And I used to like travelling perch up on my Daddy dray, that time I boasy can't done, but I never like that part of the world he used to go to and me never like those St. Elizabeth red people. But after a while me just get used to Arnold, he know how to make me laugh, and my Daddy think highly of him. "That is a young fellow with nuff intelligence," my Daddy used to say. "Plenty ambition, girl. You can't do better." So my Daddy was happy when I marry Arnold.

When we married first, I did go to live at Arnold house, but me not lying, me could never get used to those people, no matter them was fambly now. Never could like them at all. And them never like me, that's a fact, for they just don't like black people.

So I pull Arnold and I pull him and I never stop till he agree to leave that place and come with me to my Daddy land in the hills.

So he come and I will say he make the best of it. He never say anything, but every chance him get he would go down to Treasure Beach and he would come back with fish and smelling of the sea. He never once blame me for nothing though, wasn't that kind of man, not even when I never have no children. I used to tell him I don't need more pickney than him the way he go on foolish sometimes. I tell you, that man can make me bus some big laugh. When I bother him, he say, "A gone leave you, a swimming to Treasure Beach," and then he carry on as if he swimming. Moving his hands and feet any which way. He mek me laugh till water come a mi eye. What a foolish man though ee.

Arnold go on too bad sometime. Now you can tell me why he lying there in the sun-hot in the middle of the Ba'ma grass?

You see him water boots? One of them fall off already and the other soon come off. Is stubborn he stubborn why they fall off, you know. Because he alway buying things larger than him size. Though him is such a little man, I think in him head he see himself as big as a king. If I didn't buy his clothes for him, nothing would ever fit him right. He swear even his foot bigger than it is and when he did go to buy a new pair of boots Saturday, I warn him to get the right size for I know how he stay. And lo and behold, he come back with a pair of water boots there that you could see was too big. He so stubborn, he argue with me say, no, water boots supposed to be big. Put them on this morning to leave for his ground and see here now, it look like these big boots mek him stumble and fall, why else he lying there on the ground? Him hat and all fall off. Lying there making me think is joke he joking.

Is what Miss Dorcas big son did call out to me just now when I was hanging out the clothes and he frighten me, he there bawling so loud? Why I can't remember? Lawd, my memory was always bad, from I was a young girl I forgetful. Is something Arnold tease me about all the time.

The boy say something about Arnold and I remember now I drop the clothes and run. My Father! I drop the good white clothes straight into the dutty ground. Is what happening to me poor soul, eh? And now I have more washing to do for Arnold new shirt soaking in blood and he lying here not saying a word and Shannon standing there like a snake and the people back off and standing over there fraid of Shannon and it can't be true what the boy run come tell me. It can't be true say Shannon shoot Arnold dead?

Arnold always say he want to die by the sea and is I take him away from where he wanted was to be. Jesus only know I have to take him back there. He can't just die here so.

Arnold, come mi love. Let me help you sit up. Look. Look over there and see a great wave rising. It coming from the sea. It bringing the whole of Treasure Beach rising up to meet you. See the boat them there. And your fisherman friend them. Festus and Marse George and Tata Barclay and Lloydie. See yu mother Miss Adina and see Grandy Maud, your sister Merteen, little Shelly your niece and baby Jonathan. Just sit up and look nuh, and stop play dead. You too jokify man, and everybody watching. Open yu eye and look, Arnold, if you think a lie. See the great wave there. Coming over the mountain. Coming to carry us home.

1995

✢ ✢

PAMELA MORDECAI

de Man

III: JESUS FALLS THE FIRST TIME

NAOMI   Well Samuel every rascal
            have him use. Tanks to yuh
            Sister renegade bwoy chile
            We cyan see everyting.

SAMUEL   Naomi dis long time . . .

NAOMI   (*Interrupts him*) Oh Jah!
            What me did tell yuh Samuel?
            De man nuh must fall down.
            Jesus? A what dat pon
            Yuh shoulder? One nasty
            Bloody meke-meke
            Mess wid splinter stick up
            Into it. Dem man deh
            Wicked bad Samuel.
            Yuh see all me? Me not
            Smadi believe in too
            Much mix-up mix-up. True
            Yuh and me, we cyaan do
            Much about de Roman dem.

Dem big and bad and everywhere.
Yuh look – a next centurion.
But dat don't mean yuh must
Associate yuhself
Wid dem. My granny seh
"Lie down wid dawg – arise
Wid flea." Left to all me
Dem wouldn't get a howdy-
Do. Dis blood-lust business
Is a Roman rub-off. A dem
Come round yah teach Israelite
Pikni fi gwaan so bad . . .

SAMUEL   Naomi dat not true.
Don't is a Jewish ritual
To stone a criminal
To death? Yuh never take a
Good good look pon man face
In a stoning crowd? Is
Not a pretty sight.

NAOMI   (*Interrupts him again.*) But me nuh
Understand dis man, Samuel.
(*Addresses Jesus who is below them.*)
Jesus . . . Like how yuh fall
Down – yuh nuh should tek a
Likl rest? What yuh a try
Fi get up for? Is like
Yuh dying fit put dat big
Old heavy ting back in de
Bloody hole it gouge out
Pon yuh shoulder . . .

SAMUEL   Naomi one ting me haffe
Seh fi yuh. Yuh don't change
Not one beeny bit from de

First day me set me eye
Pon yuh. Still love fi chat
No mind de circumstance.

NAOMI   *(Appears not to hear him.)*
Samuel dis man is very
Strange. Yuh know dat every
Crucifixion is a
Cussing match. So dem
Walk up dis hill, so dem
Mout get more nasty.
Prisoner cuss and soldier
Cuss dem back. Dis one don't
Have one so-so word fi seh.
And ku him face. Dat
Countenance grieving and
Puzzling me one time
One minute him resemble
Royalty. Like him face
Shining. Like de prickle-dem
Is crown fi true and him
Is a real king. Like all
De bad bwoy soldier dem
Is royal retinue.
Like none a dis nah gwann
And dem brute deh cyaan touch
Him if him don't decree.
Next minute him come
Like just anadda bruck-
Down beat-up smadi.

SAMUEL   Me tink me a go move
Up likl closer.

NAOMI   *(Hurries after him.)*
Samuel tek time.

Mi mout don't open good
Before him take off like
Mongoose. Old smadi mind
Yuh heart give out pon yuh.

SAMUEL   *(He continues on ahead of her . . .)*
Naomi who better
Dan yuh fi know just how
Strong my heart is? And now
Me come to tink bout it –
Don't dis same month
Is fifty-six yuh be?
So who yuh coming to
Call 'old smadi'?

X: JESUS IS STRIPPED OF HIS GARMENTS

NAOMI   Him get up, Samuel. Is now
Me know him not no
Everyday smadi. No blood
Nuh lef inside him body,
No strength in him bones,
And still Jesus de Nazarene
Get up and lift dat brutal
Cross and move wid it and
Reach top of dat hill.
(Covers her face with her hands.)
Oh Jahweh God have
Mercy on your sinful
Children who have brought
De sons of Israel to dis.

SAMUEL   Nuh badda look Naomi.
Yuh nuh want see dis.
Dem tearing off him clothes,

And scab and blood and skin
And flesh hold onto dem.
Him is a open wound,
A walking sore. Oh Jah
Mek dis thing finish soon.
Me tough but Lawd me cyann
Take nothing more.

NAOMI   (*Softly)* Yuh know Samuel yuh always
Was a man wid a big heart.
De Nazarene him always seh
"Forgive those that do wrong
To yuh." So is dat very ting
Me aksing yuh just now . . .

SAMUEL   *(Tender and a little sad.)*
Cho. Dat nuh big ting Naomi.
Yuh and me is old time story.

NAOMI   Ay Samuel. Book hard fi close,
And story hard fi done.

XI: JESUS IS NAILED TO THE CROSS

NAOMI   Well in a way it had
To come to dis. Is so
Life stay. If him was just
Anadda likl madman
Passing through, dem wouldn'
Haffe kill him. Him mussi
Really God fi true, else
Him would dead t'ree time
A'ready. And now dem
Going to lick some royal
Nail into him wrist

And kill him one more time
Before him dead. Look
Samuel. De man whole
Body jump each time dem
Bring de hammer down. Blood
Running from him two hand
Like two river. Is lift
Dem lifting up de cross
Now – Samuel, dem nail
So big him weight going tear
Him off it when dem drop
De cross inna de hole.

SAMUEL   Naomi yuh know is
Now I see de ting. Dis
Crucifixion is a
Sacrifice. Dis Golgotha,
Hill of de Skull, come like
De altar for de sacrifice.
And de man Jesus is de
Offering. And if him
Is God son fi true den
Any how dem kill him, some
Dread dread things going come
Upon dis land. So me
Nah heave yah till him dead,
No matter how it bruk
Up mi old body and
Tear mi soul apart. Mi
Time well short. Today me
Must find out which priest is
Really priest. Me haffe know
Who have de truth, who have
De power, who me must
Follow – de Pharisee dem
Or de Nazarene.

XIII: JESUS IS TAKEN DOWN FROM THE CROSS

NAOMI   Samuel is why yuh keep
Look-looking back up to
Dat hill? Listen mi bredda.
Come yuh and me mek
Haste put plenty space
Between de two of we
And dat renk wickedness
What Pilate and dem ugly
Priestman perpetrate
Top o' dat hill today.

SAMUEL   Well tell de trut' Naomi
One big piece o' me
Lef up dere wid de man
What dem just crucify.
As for de lady Mary –
Well me woulda easy give
Mi ears-dem eye-dem foot-dem
Hand-dem – all mi very life
Me woulda give fi bring
Him back. Compare to me,
Yuh know, de man is just
A likl youngster. Me
Cyaan stop memba how him
Use to chase dat likl ball.
Him and de dawg, de tiefing
Puss, him and de neighbour
Pikni dem.
           Den wait Naomi.
Look like yuh going back too . . . ?

NAOMI   After me cyaan lef yuh
One in de midst of dark-
Ness and of politricks.

     Oh Samuel, look – dem tek
     Him down. Dem putting him
     Into her hand.
          Listen sister
     Me grieve for yuh same like
     Him was mi very own.
     Me feel de dead weight in
     Mi arms. Me feel de limpness
     In mi lap. Me feel mi heart
     Leave from mi bosom drop
     Down to mi belly bottom.
     Sister Mary tell no lie
     Me know it hard fi carry
     Him and rear him up and
     Cherish him fi dis.
     Me know yuh want to tear
     Yuh hair out root by root
     And rend yuh clothes and bawl
     Until yuh eye dem don't have
     No more tears to drop.
     No mind. No mind. Yuh pikni
     Wasn't no criminal.
     Don't worry. Everybody
     Know. It was a nasty
     Scheming ting cook up by
     Evil godless men . . .

SAMUEL Naomi why yuh talk so much?
     Hush up and look. Yuh don't
     See like a light around
     De two of dem? Yuh don't
     See how de air get bright
     Look like it full of men
     On fire, flying and floating,
     Settling round madda and son?
     Oh Massa God take time

Me begging yuh . . . Take time
Wid sinners. Jesus help.
Naomi answer me. Yuh ever
See a angel yet?

1995

My sister gets married

It is dark

At five she is stirring
catarrhd in wet coughs
of old whiskered wives
assembled for rites
black bumps on fat boxes
knees knitted together
heel out and toe in
securing the bride for
them brazen can't finish
these days . . .

My sister gets up and
she walks to the window
in an ocean of sky
sees the crazy old crabs

She opens the window
and smiles clouds feel bad
embarrass like how them
dress drab and bedraggle

Crabs curl into their backs
wrap shawls gainst cool breeze
gainst the pride of the mornin
pat safe in them bosom
nuff thread bag containing
queen gold and king silver
for blood is the sign them can
lef go dead quiet

Beyond in the yard is
the one she will mate with
she measures his limbs feels
the stems of his arms as
they wrap her slight body
his trunk as it tumbles
cut down by her eyes

My sister is wise

she will give herself
to him little by little
he'll pole up the stream
of her hauling so patient
work his craft to the river
head feeling the way
then reckless on rapids
run with the river

Crabs bless the new blood
left di money for wares
bedsheet with embroidery
new ewer and basin
big enamel chimney
coal pot some flat iron
a plaque for declaring
di Lord is di head of

dis house breaking bread
with the household
eavesdropper divine
every God time
you open you mouth . . .

My sister looks down at
her small sturdy body
she knows long years later
she'll gather to marry
daughter and daughter
black bump of a crab with
a threadbag of silver and
rheum in her eyes.

1997

➤ ◄

ALTHEA PRINCE

Ladies of the Night

Miss Peggy had been whoring ever since she could remember and she felt no shame about it. "It takes one to know one," she said whenever anybody called her a whore.

She was not certain, but she had a feeling that she did her first whoring when she was maybe less than twelve years old. Her mother, Miss Olive, always pretended she could not remember how old her daughter had been when she lost her cherry. Eventually Miss Peggy got tired of asking Miss Olive about it. She got tired because her mother's only answer would be, "Me doan member dose tings." Then she would suck her teeth, going "choopse" in disgust at being asked such a question.

Miss Peggy knew her mother was lying, knew she just did not want to admit anything. Maybe it was the way Miss Olive darted her eyes whenever her daughter asked her that question that made the lies so obvious. Deciding that it was best to leave the topic alone, Miss Peggy could see her mother's embarrassment behind the shifting eyes and angry voice. Embarrassment was not a feeling Miss Olive showed often to her daughter, but Miss Peggy knew her mother so well that there was nothing she could hide from her.

Miss Olive could have admitted the truth because it would have made no difference to Miss Peggy who enjoyed whoring and felt a certain pride at how early she began to have power over men. She remembered her mother calling out to her as she played with some stones in the yard, "Peggy, come child, come go wid dis man. He have money to give you." Peggy had thrown away her stones and had gone inside their little house with the man.

She had not realised what was expected of her until the weight of the man was on her thin body and she found herself pressed into the sagging bed. She had screamed as he entered her and he had put a big hand over her mouth. When the man had put his pants back on and left the house, Peggy had got up. Feeling ragged inside herself, she had crept outside to her mother. The man was nowhere in sight and she had run to her mother, tears streaming down her face, a five-dollar bill clutched in her hand.

"Is no big ting, chile. You have to do it sometime, so take it easy. I going wash you off."

Then she had looked at the money that her daughter still clutched in her hand. "How much money he give you?" she had asked. Peggy had extended her hand and opened her fist to reveal the five-dollar bill. Miss Olive had smiled. "Five dollars! And is you first time. Well, well!"

Peggy had felt a little better at having made her mother smile at her. She did not really understand how she had managed to secure so much money, but she was happy she had pleased her mother. Pleasing her mother was her major task in life at the time. Mostly she failed at it and waited for the shower of blows that always came with Miss Olive's disapproval. Little Peggy had watched as her mother added the five-dollar bill to a twenty-dollar bill in her purse but did not know that her mother had also been rewarded by the man.

Now Peggy was grown up and was called "Miss" just like her mother. She felt stronger than Miss Olive for she knew that she was better at getting money from men than her mother had ever been. She only dealt with men of High Society, men who were from the upper classes and who were mostly light-skinned. She also serviced calypsonians from Trinidad when they came to Antigua to put on shows at Carnival time.

Her customers and the goods Miss Peggy bought with her body made her the envy of the neighbourhood. Her neighbours were not prepared, however, to pay what she paid, and they would insult Miss Peggy when they saw her and call out at her as she walked down the street, "Whoring Miss Peggy!" That was when she would retort, "It takes one to know one!"

Now that Miss Olive was old and could no longer ply her trade Miss Peggy looked after her. She set her up with a tray and Miss Olive sat outside of their little house on a chair with the tray on a box and sold snacks to people as they passed down the street. The tray held sweets, cigarettes and chocolates. Sometimes when Miss Peggy was in the mood she would even parch peanuts in hot sand in a doving pot and package them in little brown paper bags for the tray. Or she would make "suck-a-bubbies" – sweetened, flavoured milk squares – in the freezer of her refrigerator.

Miss Olive felt proud of Miss Peggy but would curse her at the slightest provocation and there was never a day that went by when she did not find reason to be provoked. The surrounding area would ring with her harsh voice and sometimes people would stop and listen on their way to the market or to town, but they would soon become bored and move on because Miss Olive always cursed her daughter about the same topics: Miss Peggy's love of men and her love of money. Everyone in the neighbourhood found it strange that Miss Peggy, the biggest curser in the area, never ever answered her mother.

One day everything changed.

It started off like any other day. Everything went as usual until the early part of the afternoon. Miss Olive was sitting outside at the front of the house, minding her tray and brushing flies with a whisk brush. As the flies circled the tray she would switch the whisk from one hand to the other, the tail of the whisk making a massaging sound as she kept the flies on the move.

Miss Peggy was inside the house with a regular, twice-a-week customer . . . the only customer that Miss Peggy ever fed. He was eating goat-water and the smell of the stewed goat meat filled the street. He was the same man who had paid her five dollars to have sex when she was a little girl.

Miss Peggy went outside and asked Miss Olive for a cigarette from the open package on the tray. Miss Olive's answer was sharp and immediate: "You not tired feed dat man and give him me cigarette? Why he don't go home to his wife and ask she for cigarette and food?" Then she sucked her teeth with a resounding "choopse," still brushing at the flies throughout.

Miss Peggy stood in front of the tray, watching her mother for a full minute. Then she asked again for a cigarette and Miss Olive went "choopse" again, ignoring her. She switched her whisk brush from one hand to the other, indicating she was busy and was not going to give Miss Peggy the cigarette. The nonchalant swoosh, swoosh of the whisk meant Miss Peggy was dismissed.

Miss Peggy charged into Miss Olive and her tray. She bit her and punched her and slapped her. The man ran out of the house and tried to hold Miss Peggy, but there was no stopping her. She picked up a stone and used it to beat Miss Olive's back. A neighbour left his tailor shop and ran, his tape measure swinging around his neck, to call the police. Nobody could stop Miss Peggy and everybody knew it. Neighbours came and tried and gave up, standing by helplessly while Miss Peggy beat her mother to the ground.

Some people were laughing and passing comments as the beating continued: "Lord me God, is what happen to dis woman?" "But dis is a crazy woman!"

One woman said to Miss Peggy, "Miss Peggy, you is a advantage-taker. You is a young woman to you mother. How you beat she so?" She said it over and over as if the repetition would make Miss Peggy stop. It was no use. Miss Peggy continued to beat away at Miss Olive as if she were tenderizing conchs. Then she sat on Miss Olive's legs and ripped off her clothes. As the old woman lay naked on the ground Miss Peggy scratched at her and slapped her. Miss Olive moaned loudly while she tried to cover her nakedness and protect her face from her daughter's nails.

The neighbours found it doubly strange that Miss Olive, known for her fighting skills, did so little to defend herself from Miss Peggy's blows. She could not have done much anyway, but she did not even try; she just moaned or grunted at each blow and tried to dodge them. And Miss Peggy, known for her talk, did not say anything at all while she was beating her mother. She grunted like a wild pig and just kept on hitting her, sometimes holding on to Miss Olive and digging her teeth into her arm or her shoulder. She drew blood, spat it out and dug her teeth into another part of her mother's body. It was the worst beating the neighbourhood had ever seen. It was also the first time they had seen a woman bite someone. It was unusual for a daughter to beat her mother, let alone bite her.

As the beating continued Miss Peggy began to tire. She then switched to using only her head on her mother. She butted her in the stomach and Miss Olive made a sound like a live lobster in a pot of boiling water. Then she fainted.

Still Miss Peggy beat her mother, only now she cried as she beat her. When the police came it took three burly policemen and four of the men standing in the street to pull Miss Peggy off her now unconscious mother. Miss Olive was taken to the hospital in shock and Miss Peggy was locked up for the night in the police station. The next day, when the police took Miss Olive home from the hospital, they asked her if she wanted to lay a charge against her daughter. Miss Olive refused and Miss Peggy was charged only with causing a disturbance.

After the fight Miss Peggy and Miss Olive stopped speaking to each other, but they continued to live together. Miss Olive started to cook Miss Peggy's favourite foods on Sundays. And during the week, Miss Peggy did all the cooking so Miss Olive could mind her tray. Before the fight Miss Peggy would insist that Miss Olive could cook and mind the tray at the same time. She claimed that she did not have time to cook as she was busy with her clients. She brought in most of the money and could not be expected to interrupt her work to cook.

Now Miss Peggy cooked willingly every morning before she began to work, and if Miss Olive tried to make a meal, Miss Peggy would firmly take the pot from her without a word and do the cooking herself. Miss Olive would look pleased but would say nothing as she went about setting out her tray on the ground outside.

After the fight Miss Olive began to do all the ironing. Before the beating she used to insist that Miss Peggy had to look after her own clothes. Miss Olive even washed all the clothes on some days although the soap powder gave her a rash on her hands. Without a murmur of complaint she would rub her hands with Vaseline after she did the washing. One day Miss Peggy brought home a bottle of sweet-smelling hand cream and wordlessly handed it to her mother. Miss Olive's face softened as she took the gift, but she said nothing. It was, said the neighbours, some kind of peace.

Two or three months after the fight Miss Peggy and Miss Olive began to go to church and take Communion every Sunday. They did this with no discussion between them. People in the neighbourhood knew that although they were going to church together they were still not speaking to each other. The first Sunday they left the house at the same time, each dressed to kill. Neighbours came to their windows to watch Miss Peggy and Miss Olive walk up the street. As the two women passed the little Sunday market on the corner, all heads turned and people stopped haggling over prices to watch.

"Is what church coming to?" Miss Tiny said loudly as Miss Peggy and Miss Olive walked past her tray of mangoes, "Lord have mercy!"

Everyone laughed at Miss Tiny's comment and Miss Olive and Miss Peggy edged closer to each other as they heard the laughter, but still they did not speak to each other. Their arrival at the church caused as much stir as the walk through the neighbourhood had done. The minister was very disturbed by the presence of the two best-known whores in Antigua at his Communion rail and had several long talks with God in private during the service. But neither the minister nor God seemed to be able to do anything about Miss Olive and Miss Peggy being in church that Sunday morning or any other Sunday morning. Worse yet, neither could do anything about them walking up to the Communion rail, heads held high.

Miss Olive and Miss Peggy continued to present themselves at the eight o'clock service every Sunday. Piously they would walk up the aisle for the body and blood of the Lord, opening their mouths wide as the minister concluded, "which was given for you." After they took their sip of wine the minister would surreptitiously wipe the chalice most carefully and then spin it to a fresh spot before presenting it to his more respectable communicants.

Things went on like this for many years. Then Miss Olive died. One morning Miss Peggy noticed her mother had not got up at her usual time and she went over to her bed and shook her. Miss Peggy screamed and started crying and when a neighbour came running to see what was wrong, she sobbed, "Me mother dead. Lord me belly, me belly. Me mother dead an ah never tell her ah sorry."

After her mother's death Miss Peggy would struggle to find her speech, then sigh and drop her shoulders and say nothing. She did not even speak to the men she serviced regularly. With Miss Peggy the men felt as if they were taking advantage of her. Eventually they left her and moved on to the new houses where the new whores from the Dominican Republic lived. At least they spoke to their clients, even though it was in Spanish. They laughed too, and sang along with the music on the juke box.

Only one man continued to come to see Miss Peggy and he gave her money every week though he no longer touched her. He was the man she cooked for at least twice a week, the five-dollar man at the centre of the fight between Miss Peggy and Miss Olive. Over the years he came to see Miss Peggy every day. When he got old and could hardly walk he still visited her, leaning heavily on a cane as he shuffled down the street to Miss Peggy's house. He no longer went inside when he visited but would sit outside on the little bench where Miss Olive used to sit and mind her tray.

Miss Peggy now relied on selling from the tray to earn her livelihood. While she tended her tray her friend would sit on the bench and watch people passing by. Miss Peggy would sit on the steps silently, happy in his company. The man seemed very comfortable sitting there with Miss Peggy. He did not seem to need to speak.

Miss Peggy would look happier when the man came to visit her and she would fuss over him and cook for him and go to the shop and hold up two fingers to indicate to the shopkeeper that she wanted two cigarettes. After the man had eaten she would offer him the cigarettes and while he smoked she sipped her cup of chocolate tea. It was an easy, comfortable friendship between the old man and Miss Peggy, still a young woman in her thirties.

Several years later the man died. Miss Peggy found out about it when his death was announced on the radio. All his children and grandchildren were listed in the death announcement and Miss Peggy wondered how it was that a man who had so much family used to be so lonely that he would come and spend every evening with her. She cried sadly when she heard the radio announcement and could not even bring herself to eat her lunch. She went back into her bed and kept her windows closed. Late in the afternoon, there was a knock on Miss Peggy's door and she jumped up from her sleep, almost expecting it to be her friend. She had been dreaming about him and it was around the time of afternoon that he used to visit her. Then she remembered he had died. Her heart felt heavy with grief as she came fully awake.

She went to her door to answer the persistent knocking and saw a man wearing a suit standing on her step. He asked to come in and speak with her, telling her that he was her friend's lawyer. Miss Peggy let him into her little house, wondering what he could want with her. The lawyer explained that she had been named in the man's will. She was to receive money to look after her for the rest of her life. That part of the will, he said, was very clear. He gave Miss Peggy a strange look and began to read from the paper in his hand: "And for my beloved daughter whom I sired with Olive Barnabus, who is called: Peggy Sheila Barnabus, I bequeath the following . . ."

Miss Peggy went back in her mind to the first day she lay in a bed with the man whom she had come to call her friend. She remembered how he left her ragged inside. She remembered, too, how her mother had rejoiced at the five dollars he had given Miss Peggy. She had known deep down inside that her mother had been jealous of her friendship with him and Miss Peggy had secretly enjoyed her jealousy. "My beloved daughter whom I sired with Olive Barnabus." Miss Peggy's mind went over the words again and again while the lawyer continued to read the terms and conditions of the will. She did not understand all that he said and could not find her voice to ask any questions she might have had.

At the funeral Miss Peggy stood on the sidelines listening to the hymns. In her hand she clutched a bouquet of ladies of the night she had begged from Mrs. Sebastian on her way up the street to the cathedral. Some people in the funeral party knew her and knew of her friendship with the dead man. Others assumed her to be one of the family's servants. The few dark-skinned people at the funeral could be accounted for so Miss Peggy stood out. She noticed some questioning looks and became uncomfortable. It was not a big funeral so there was no buffering crowd Miss Peggy could melt into. When the first sod was thrown on the coffin she left quietly, hoping that no one would notice her departure.

As she left the grave she passed a handkerchief she had wet with bay rum over her forehead, then she held it to her nose and her mouth. She felt faint, but she walked with determination to another part of the cemetery where she searched the headstones until she found her mother's grave buried among weeds and grass. She bent down and pulled up the weeds crowding the lilies of the valley she had planted there after the last rainy season. She pulled one blossom from the bouquet of flowers in her hand and gently pressed it into the sod at the place she knew her mother's head rested.

"He dead, mother. He dead," Miss Peggy said, bending to pull a weed. She sat by her mother's grave until the mourners had left the cemetery, then walked to the other grave where she sat down. Laying her bouquet of flowers at the head of the grave, she kissed her fingers and pressed them into the soft sod.

"Goodbye," she said softly, then got up and brushed the graveyard dirt off her dress and her shoes and set off for home. She unlocked the padlock and threw open the wooden door, letting the soft evening sun into the little house. Then drawing back the curtains and opening the windows she threw open the shutters to let in more sun. Her voice was strong and lilting as she sang, *Why should I feel discouraged / Why should the shadows fall / Why should my heart be lonely*. She paused only to change into her home clothes before continuing, *For Jesus is my potion / My constant friend is He / I sing because I'm happy / I sing because I'm free / His eyes are on the sparrow / And I know He watches me*.

She finished changing her clothes and put her tray outside next to the bench that first her mother and then her father used to sit on as she sang, *Whenever I am tempted / Whenever clouds I see. . . .* Then Miss Peggy laughed a sweet joyous laugh. She sat on the little bench and took up her mother's whisk brush as a group of children walked past. One threw a little pebble at the house and shouted "Whoring Miss Peggy!" before the group raced down the street. Miss Peggy set down her whisk brush carefully. She got up from the bench and walked into the street. Putting her arms on her hips, she bellowed, "Whore like you mothers! It takes one to know one!"

1993

➤ ◄

M. NOURBESE PHILIP

And Over Every Land and Sea

Meanwhile Proserpine's mother Ceres, with panic in her heart, vainly sought her daughter over all lands and over all the sea.[*]

QUESTIONS! QUESTIONS!

Where she, where she, where she
be, where she gone?
Where high and low meet I search,
find can't, way down the islands' way
I gone – south:
day-time and night-time living with she,
down by the just-down-the-way sea
she friending fish and crab with alone,
in the bay-blue morning she does wake
with kiskeedee and crow-cock –
skin green like lime, hair indigo-blue,
eyes hot like sunshine-time;
grief gone mad with crazy – so them say.

---

[*] Quotations are from Ovid, *The Metamorphoses*, translated by Mary M. Innes.

Before the questions too late,
before I forget how they stay,
crazy or no crazy I must find she.

->- -<-

As for Cyane, she lamented the rape of the goddess . . . nursing silently
in her heart a wound that none could heal . . .

ADOPTION BUREAU

Watch my talk-words stride,
like her smile the listening
breadth of my walk – on mine
her skin of lime casts a glow
of green, around my head indigo
of halo – tell me, do
I smell like her?
To the north comes the sometimes
blow of the North East trades –
skin   hair   heart   beat
and I recognize the salt
sea   the   yet   else   and . . . something
again knows sweat   earth
the smell-like of I and she
the perhaps blood lost –

She whom they call mother, I seek.

->- -<-

It would take a long time to name the lands and seas over which the goddess wandered. She searched the whole world – in vain . . .

CLUES

She gone – gone to where and don't know
looking for me looking for she;
is pinch somebody pinch and tell me,
up where north marry cold I could find she –
Stateside, England, Canada – somewhere about,
"she still looking for you –
try the Black Bottom – Bathurst above Bloor,
Oakwood and Eglinton – even the suburbs them,
but don't look for indigo hair and
skin of lime at Ontario Place,
or even the reggae shops;
stop looking for don't see and can't –
you bind she up tight tight with hope,
she own and yours knot up in together;
although she tight with nowhere and gone
she going find you, if you keep looking."

➤➤ ◄◄

When kindly day had dimmed the stars, still she sought her daughter from the rising to the setting sun. She grew weary with her efforts and thirsty too . . .

THE SEARCH

Up in the humpback whereabouts-is-that hills,
someone tell me she living – up
there in the up-alone cocoa hills of Woodlands,
Moriah, with the sky, and self, and the bad bad of grieving;
all day long she dreaming about wide black nights,
how lose stay, what find look like.

A four-day night of walk bring me
to where never see she:
is "come child, come," and "welcome" I looking –
the how in lost between She
and I, call and response in tongue and
word that buck up in strange;
all that leave is seven dream-skin:
sea-shell, sea-lace, feather-skin and rainbow-flower,
afterbirth, foreskin and blood-cloth –
seven dream-skin and crazy find me.

→→ ◄◄

*. . . the earth opened up a way for me and, after passing deep down
through its lowest caverns, I lifted up my head again in these regions,
and saw the stars which had grown strange to me.*

DREAM-SKINS

Dream-skins dream the dream dreaming:
(in two languages)

Sea-shell

                low low over the hills
                        she flying
                up up from the green of sea
                she rise emerald
                      skin
                      fish belt
                weed of sea crown she

Feather-skin

                lizard-headed
                  i suckle her
                  suckling me
                      flat

thin like the
host
round and white
she swells enormous with
milk and child

Sea-lace

in one hand the sun
the moon in the other
round and round
she swing them from chains
let fly till they come
to the horizon
of rest

Rainbow-flower

six-limbed
my body dances
flight
from her giant promises
she reaches down
gently
snaps my head
a blooded hibiscus
from its body
crooning
she cradles the broken parts

Afterbirth

one breast
white
the other black
headless
in a womb-black night
a choosing —

one breast
neither black
nor white

Foreskin

a plant sprouts there —
from the mouth
mine
wise black and fat she laughs
reaching in for the tree
frees the butterfly
in-lodged
circles of iridescence
silence

Blood-cloth

wide wide
i open my mouth
to call
the blood-rush come up
finish
write she name
in the up-above sky
with some clean white rag
she band up my mouth
nice nice

Blood-cloths
(dream in a different language)

sand
silence
desert
sun
the wide of open mouth
blood of rush

hieroglyphs
her red
inscriptions
her name
up-above sky
                      sudden
clean of white
                      cloths
    wounded mouth
broad back
                hers
to tie
  carry
  bear

"the voice, the voice, the voice"
      she whispers
      she walks
      she whispers
              ceaselessly

⇸ ⇷

Ceres knew it (Proserpine's girdle) well, and as soon as she recognized it, tore her dishevelled hair, as if she had only then learned of her loss: again and again she beat her breast.

SIGHTINGS

Nose to ground – on all fours – I did once
smell that smell,
on a day of once –
upon a time, tropic with blue
when the new, newer and newest of leaves compete,
in the season of suspicion she passed,
then and ago trailed the wet and lost of smell;

was it a *trompe-l'oeil* —
the voice of her sound, or didn't I once
see her song, hear her image call
me by name — my name — another sound, a song,
the name of me we knew she named
the sound of song sung long past time,
as I cracked from her shell —
the surf of surge
the song of birth.

⤜ ⤙

For behold, the daughter I have sought so long has now at last been found — if you call it "finding" to be more certain that I have lost her, or if knowing where she is is finding her.

ADOPTION BUREAU REVISITED

blood-spoored
the trail follows
            me
following her
            north
                  as far as not-known
                  I trace it
                        dream-skins dream
                              the loss
                        ours and ancient
                              unfelled tears
                              harden
                        in the sun's attention
                              diamond
                  the many-voiced one of one voice
                              ours
                        betrayal and birth-blood
                              unearthed

Something! Anything! of her.
She came, you say, from where
she went – to her loss:
"the need of your need"
in her groin

                              the oozing wound
                            would only be healed
                              on sacred ground
                              blood-spoored

              the trail . . .
                              following
              she
                          follows . . .

                                                      1989

Meditations on the Declension of Beauty by the Girl with the Flying Cheek-bones

If not   If not   If

Not

If not in yours

   In whose

In whose language

Am I

If not in yours

   In whose

In whose language

Am I   I am

   If not in yours

In whose

  Am I

(if not in yours)

  I am yours

In whose language

   Am I not

Am I not   I am yours

If not in yours

If not in yours

   In whose

In whose language

   Am I . . .

Girl with the flying cheek-bones:
She is
I am
Woman with the behind that drives men mad
And if not in yours
Where is the woman with a nose broad
As her strength
If not in yours
In whose language
Is the man with the full-moon lips
Carrying the midnight of colour
Split by the stars – a smile
If not in yours

       In whose

In whose language

          Am I

          Am I not

          Am I   I am yours

          Am I not   I am yours

          Am I   I am

If not in yours

       In whose

In whose language

          Am I

If not in yours

          Beautiful

1989

Commitment to Hardness

Diah lay on her back staring out into the darkness of the room; she had come awake suddenly with the feeling that something had awakened her, but all was still. There was no difference between the blackness in the room and that which she saw out the open window. It was the stars that helped her to recognize where the room ended and the window began. Ben breathed softly next to her. The physical longing for him was as sudden as it was strong: she felt her stomach muscles contract and tighten – the desire for him seemed to begin there and spread down through her cunt, where she felt the familiar sensation of waves moving through her as those muscles contracted and relaxed with him. She touched her clitoris – it was firm while the lips of her cunt vibrated ever so gently. She was wet for him – along her thighs, down her legs and up her body to her nipples, which were now tingling – the feeling for him spread, sometimes it ran slow like molasses creeping down her legs, at other times it would leap from one part of her body to another – clitoris to breast, to mouth – even her tongue felt desire, and she felt that each area of her body was feeling its own unique type of desire. The wanting of her cunt was different from the wanting of her lips, but altogether the different desires meshed until she felt herself one concentrated point of desire and want. She reached out to touch Ben where he lay on his back. She placed her hand on his cock and she began stroking it gently as it lay curled to one side; as she stroked she felt it first shudder and then harden ever so gently. She continued to stroke, keeping up a slow rhythm, and soon what she held in her hand was the hardness – of his cock. It was a hardness that was like no other hardness – all other expressions used in calypsos, and blues songs, and what people call dirty jokes came to mind – ramrod, big big bamboo, pole, driving shaft – all these were accurate and yet not accurate – those things were all lifeless in their hardness. This hardness she now held, running her fingers up and down its surface, was a living hardness with a commitment to be hard, to be nothing but hard, and that commitment had to do with something else – something larger than her or Ben. That commitment to hardness belonged to the race – making Ben's cock a part of him and yet not a part of him. It was like a woman's stomach when it was enlarged with child – she had seen people pat a woman's pregnant stomach with a familiarity that they would never presume in ordinary circumstances. She herself had done this when her friends had been pregnant, rubbing the stomach and predicting the sex of the baby. Pregnant stomachs belonged to the race, the tribe, not in the sense that right-to-lifers and anti-abortionists said, giving them the right to dictate to a woman – it was more a sense of the stomach allowing others to share in a moment of time common to them all – that they all needed to remind themselves of. So this lance she now held in her hand belonged to the race in its commitment to hardness, but no lance was ever so soft-tipped, crowned by such a velvet head. Diah's hand continued its gentle but firm stroking; she imagined going up to a man and patting his dick and suggesting it belonged to the race. She had to stop herself from laughing out loud, as she saw the obvious limits to her analogy between women's pregnant stomachs and men's dicks. Diah's hand moved more swiftly over Ben's cock, which now trembled and shuddered with every touch as he lay there breathing softly letting her keep him hard while she grew wetter still with the wanting of him. She stopped stroking now, pushed herself up, and throwing a leg over Ben, she rolled over so that she now lay on him. She sat up and felt his cock rubbing against her buttocks, and then she raised her hips, shifted her weight back, and slowly began lowering herself on him – he groaned softly – a small sound from the base of his throat. She wanted to feel every inch of him as she lowered herself and so at times she would raise herself again so that she covered the same distance twice – three times – over and over again. She wanted him to do nothing, just lie there offering himself to her – the commitment of himself and the race present in the unbearable hardness she felt between her legs. He seemed to sense what she wanted, because unlike their usual lovemaking he made no attempt to be more active. She moved herself on him, first in circular movements making small tight sounds, then up and down, and still Ben lay there, a willing partner offering his cock and its goodness. Diah didn't know why but it was important that Ben not respond for the moment; maybe it equalized relations between them. Diah reached out to the bedside table for her tobacco and cigarette papers – Ben remained hard within her as she rolled and lit up. Every so often she moved her hips, feeling Ben pulse in response inside her. She took long slow drags on her cigarette – she had never thought that sameness could be erotic, but the first time she and a female friend had made love, the shock of the absence of power – the sameness between them – was what turned her on; no matter how gentle, loving, and non-sexist a man her lover happened to be, there was still this marker of difference – that was now inside her – so attractive yet to be feared. As if to emphasize that difference and so maybe go past it, Diah now ground herself into Ben's crotch, feeling the soft tip of his penis stroking deep inside her; she heard herself make soft moaning sounds. Quickly she butted out her cigarette, now she was jealous, she wanted to taste herself – to taste her goodness; she rolled off him and told him she wanted to suck him, to suck her juices off his cock, and she closed her mouth over his commitment to hardness. His sounds joined the rhythm of hers, she was tasting herself salt and tangy along the length of him, and when she had sucked him clean of her, he entered her again. This time they began to laugh and laugh as they rode home together, she gripping his buttocks and every so often stroking the back of his balls to make him groan with pleasure, he bracing himself on his arms as he slammed himself into her, each urging the other on and on, their mutual laughter and shouts becoming like some boisterous call and response until Diah saw herself as if separate from her body, observing Diah and Ben light up the darkness with a robust joy. As they lay together afterwards, she was grateful for the cool breeze that came through the window drying the sweat on their bodies. Thank god for commitment to hardness, she thought, and chuckled to herself; her fingers were intertwined with his and she lifted them to her lips and kissed them. He returned the gesture. She reached across him for her cigarettes.

"Stay with me, Diah – don't go back to Canada. It's not fair that you're leaving when we have this together – how can you leave?"

"I don't know – let's talk about it tomorrow."

"Yes, tomorrow."

1992

H. NIGEL THOMAS

Spirits in the Dark

3

Going to high school meant that he had to live in the capital. The buses that went to town returned long before school was out. It was a distance of thirty miles and during the rainy season mud-slides sometimes blocked the road. He had been to town a few times before that. The first time must have been when he was four. His second trip was when he was seven. It was during the time that the police came to their house to question his father about the whereabouts of Butler, a man the government wanted. Old Mr. Manchester came with the police. His father and other people said Butler was for poor people. He was fighting so that everybody, not just those who owned plenty land, could vote. They said the government put Butler in jail, in a wet cell, because they wanted him to catch consumption and die. *Butler did not die. He became prime minister.*

When he and his mother got to town they saw a man dressed in a gown that looked like it was made of animal hair. The man was talking to a large crowd. His mother pulled him away from the crowd but he resisted her long enough to see the man pull at something that released a tail bearing a flyer. It read, "England, kiss this monkey's black arse." The crowd clapped. His mother pulled at him more fiercely and half dragged him away. A little way down they met about thirty policemen heading toward the crowd with their clubs swinging. A few days later he heard his father and the other men talking about what the police had done to Boysie. Boysie, he later found out, had been trying to organize workers' unions on the large plantations.

He thought he had seen Boysie a few years ago, dressed in the colours of the Ethiopian flag, selling African trinkets to passersby near the post office building. But that was probably another of the illusions and hallucinations he had been having off and on during the first two years of his madness.

He boarded with an acquaintance of his father's family. Miss Dellimore was about forty-five. She lived in a three-room shack on a hill overlooking Hanovertown. Her four children lived with her. The oldest, a woman of twenty-eight, shared a bedroom with her mother. The second, Alfred, a man of twenty-five, worked sporadically on a road-mending gang. Alfred and his mother were always quarrelling. She accused him of spending "alla yo' morney 'pon poussey"; and he countered, "Yo' only jehlous cause no man spending nur-ting 'pon a dustbag like you." She threatened constantly to put his clothes in the street and he dared her to so he could knock out what remained of her teeth, but neither ever got around to carrying out the threat. He shared a bedroom with this fellow. The other two children, boys fifteen and twenty, slept on mattresses in the general room: kitchen, sitting room, storeroom, and, at night, bedroom.

He paid Miss Dellimore fifty of the seventy-five dollars he received monthly, and each week, his mother sent her bags of ground provisions and baskets of fruit. But Miss Dellimore still complained. His mother would laugh and say, "Town naigger will dig out yo' eye if yo' let them." Miss Dellimore always wanted to know what the neighbours were telling him and would conclude her questioning with, "I don't trust those blasted people; town naigger will thief bread out o' them own pickney mouth."

It was a new experience. Instead of the large plains of sugar cane, sometimes green, sometimes brown, he now looked at the buildings crowded upon one another. Most times the people's faces seemed as blank as the asphalt streets on which they were standing or walking. The sea, too, was so calm, almost like water in a tub. Not like the Atlantic where he came from. It shouted, it pounded the shore, it made you know it was there. The people did not speak to anyone they did not know and they didn't seem to have feelings. It was the first time he heard the expression "nothing for nothing."

He used the public library a lot and usually stayed there until it closed at eight. He did his homework there. He read books other than his textbooks and copies of *Time*, *Newsweek*, and *The Manchester Guardian* that Mr. Bunyan loaned him. When he finished at the library he sometimes walked to various points in town. The first night he came upon the sidewalk beggars, not yet asleep, quarrelling with one another over their favourite politicians – their unwashed bodies and festering sores blending with the odours of stale fish and rotting fruit rinds. Occasionally he walked onto the jetty and surprised someone shitting in the sea, or into the sheds where bananas were piled before being shipped to England. People made love there on the days they weren't used. He liked when he got home to find the Dellimore family asleep.

It was shortly after he moved to town that he began to think a lot about the relationships between men and women. He noticed the number of Black men in the capital who had White wives. He heard people say that all the Black doctors and lawyers liked "milk in their coffee."

People told all sorts of stories about these marriages. You couldn't hang around the market women for very long without hearing one. One White woman was said to have given her husband strict orders not to talk to Black women, but she had missed a little detail: he was interested mostly in Black men. They clapped whenever they heard that one.

These relationships forced him to think about the people in Compton. One night when he was seated near the lily pond in the Botanic Gardens, images of barefooted people walking on hot asphalt, the stinking beggars quarrelling with one another, naked children with snot running over their lips, women bent from too many pregnancies, men beating their women, preoccupied him. Why?

His father did not beat his mother and he brought his wages home. One time his mother worked in the fields. One day Mrs. Manchester saw her and told her a woman of her colour shouldn't be out in the sun like that and promised to take her on to nurse her daughter. His father forbade it. He heard then the story of his maternal grandmother, who used to be a housekeeper with the Montagues. Mr. Montague slept with the household help. He hired them himself and with his sexual tastes in mind. That was why his mother looked almost White. Many of the children around were the sons and daughters of the White plantation owners. So his father had stopped his mother from working completely.

He had never heard his father say please to his mother. "Get me a basin of water!" "Press my blue shirt!" "Bring my dinner outside." She stopped whatever she was doing to do whatever he'd asked — whether she was kneading flour, mending a dress, or washing her feet. She said so many pleases whenever she asked him for anything and would stand there like a child expecting to hear him say no. When he said yes, she was so full of gratitude. Sometimes he wanted to scream at her. One day he started to say to her, "Aren't you tired being a towel for daddy to dry his hands with?" But he thought better of it. She bragged to the neighbours that "Henry never once raise his hand fo' hit me." *He realized now that that was a part of his mother's strategy for handling his father. Unquestionably she was the stronger of the two — and she probably knew it, too. But he did not understand it then.*

He preferred Roly-Poly Richard. On Sundays in Compton, he used to watch him, his fat belly hanging over his trousers and his "coolie" hair falling on his shoulders, rocking from side to side along the canal road, his three youngest sons, his grandson, and his wife — a fat, brown-skinned woman — accompanying him. One of the boys would be carrying a pingwing basket with food. They picnicked and bathed at Bellevue River. He would have liked his father and mother to do the same thing. Roly-Poly taught his boys to wrestle and they lived like brothers. The men said Roly-Poly was soft in the head, that he spoiled his children, and that his wife wore the pants.

Roly-Poly died while he was recovering from his first breakdown. He went to the funeral. There were hundreds of people. An ordinary person didn't bring out that many people. Secretly, they must have admired him.

Barslow was another case altogether. He was String's father. String was sixteen but looked twelve. The older boys joked that in elementary school they used to tease String that they would use him for fish bait. String's father left his mother because she would not drop a case against him. Jerome was around ten when it happened. He had seen only part of it but had constructed the story from various things his mother and others said.

Barslow had stopped giving Eunice money. One morning she asked him for some and he told her she should try whoring. At lunchtime when he came in expecting food, there was none.

After he finished beating her an ambulance took her to the hospital and she aborted a pregnancy on account of it. A group of women from Hanovertown urged her to take Barslow to court. The villagers advised her against it. The townswomen promised to take care of her, and she prosecuted him. The judge found him guilty but let him go unpunished because he had a clean record. The townswomen were outraged but soon forgot about Eunice, and Barslow never again gave her a penny. Eventually she began wasting away from consumption, and String had to leave school to work in the fields to take care of the two of them.

➤➤ ◄◄

On Saturday mornings, when it wasn't raining, he walked to the edge of the promontory a little distance out to the coast to watch the sunrise. He still had the scrapbook in which he'd written a description of it.

He stayed long enough to see the sea become its usual royal blue, the land green, and the mountains grey.

The sea had always fascinated him. Since he was around eight he'd often climb the hill a hundred yards outside his village to look at its corrugated blue, white-flecked surface. When it pounded the shore on windy nights it left him with a vague haunting fear. In August, when it was calmest, he would go into the shallow parts because there were whirlpools just outside the shore and bury his body in it and enjoy the sac-like feeling of the water around him.

The farthest he had ever got when he ran away from the hospital was the Olgay Beach. He did not have time to take off his johnny shirt because the police had been chasing him. He'd only wanted to get that feeling of the water. They were sure he'd gone there to commit suicide and had afterwards put him in seclusion and on heavy medication.

He never quite saw the full effect of a sunset because the sun always set over the mountains. True, it was lovely to look at, with the ridges standing there like they were walls blocking a flaming sky, but he would have liked to have seen the sunset from the mountain top, watch the sun dip into the sea. It would have meant walking at least five miles up into the mountains. But to have to walk back alone in the dark did not appeal to him. *A few years later, when he and Peter were friends, he had thought of asking him to go with him. But after he'd had his dream about Peter, he became a little afraid each time he was alone with him.*

By the time he got to the Coastal Highway that fronted Miss Dellimore's house, the country buses would be already streaming into town with food and shoppers. There were the women laden with huge bamboo baskets ringed and crowned with vegetables too. They'd already walked six or seven miles, had already lifted down their baskets, sold from them, and repacked them many times. A dozen or so shoppers waited for specific vendors. There were friendships between the vendors and shoppers. Occasionally a vendor brought a gift for a shopper and vice versa, and during the transaction they spoke of children and illnesses and brothers and sisters and relatives overseas. Then the baskets would be hoisted onto the cloth pads that cushioned the scalp, the arms again plop down the women's sides, and the trek resumed down to the valley floor where the capital lay in as yet unheated asphalt and concrete.

Later, when he got down to the market, which occupied the quadrangle in the commercial heart of the city, the women would be seated like queens on wooden crates surveying their heaps of tannias, dasheens, yams, sweet peppers, carrots, string beans . . . and the potential customers. They served several customers all at once, never closing a transaction without trying to convince the buyer that she needed something else: "No tannias fo' the Sunday soup? Smell this thyme. Yo' must want lettuce! Them sweet peppers! Ain't they juicy?" Often the contradictions were glaring. But they broke off when they saw another potential customer or when the shopper, usually smiling, left. The plaid heads, fat arms in short-sleeve dresses protected by dungaree aprons with arm-deep pockets – where wads of dollar bills lay, coming out only to engulf other dollar bills – created a carnival of colour. He loved to meander among them, hear their enticing talk, and picture their lives at home.

The open-air market was flanked by the indoor markets – grey barrack-like structures with iron grids for windows. In one of them everything except fish and meat was sold. There, the professional market women, who bought wholesale from growers, reigned, sometimes cursing, sometimes fearing, sometimes threatening to poison, their competitors. Country lore abounded with tales of them, of the sorcery spells they'd put on other market women, causing them to go crazy or to produce deformed babies. He knew an albino child who was said to be the product of such *maljeu*.

They boasted about their children in secondary schools, over-seas, in nursing school, in the civil service. They were proud their children didn't speak "bad." That was why they slaved day in and day out to make a better life for them. "Is only them what don' got no ambition what going foller in we footsteps." Over the years, as he understood what was going on, he found it funnier and funnier that these women spoke dialect and their children replied in stan-dard English – were expected to reply in standard English. He wondered how they felt about their parents. He knew how the parents felt about them.

The rear wall of the fish and meat market was in contact with the sea. It had an external extension, an enclosure of chicken wire with a floor of beach sand – it was actually an enclosed part of the beach – littered with candy wrappings and fruit rinds. Here the fishermen sold their catch, first to the indoor vendors, and the leavings to the outdoor ones. The outdoor ones, depending on the season, bought a hundredweight bamboo basket of fish and sat on the street outside the wire mesh and sold to the passersby. Outside the mesh, at a spot where the sea lapped the land, little boys scaled, gutted, and salted the fish of the customers for a small fee.

On slow days the outdoor vendors put the baskets on their heads, slung a conch shell over a shoulder, and leaving an odour that ought to have discouraged buyers, wandered into the suburban communities, announcing their presence with the conch shell. On the slowest of days they hired taxis and took the fish all the way into the country where on arrival it stank and the price tripled.

People in the villages didn't have that kind of pluck. They took orders. He liked the market women. They owned some of the biggest houses on Isabella Island. The villagers said they were robbers.

The food vendors intrigued him most. They operated from the sidewalk beside the fish and meat market, very close to the public latrines. He had heard numerous stories about them. The first time he began observing them, they were talking about some market woman's son who had done well in school, was employed in the civil service, and had the gall to want to marry into an establishment family.

"He want fo' hang he hat too high."

"Education must be turn him stupit."

"Them say the old man come out with a gun and tell him fo' scatter. Jesus Christ! He knock the flowers off the steps, and run through the flowers garden, and over the hedge. Lawd, the servant gal say she laugh till she piss she drawers."

"Good fo' him. He class not good enough fo' him."

"Missah Blizzard should o' shoot him."

Most of the food was contained in four-gallon biscuit tins. Invariably there were pots of fish in a thick, brown sauce; rice and peas; and sliced ground provisions, plantain, and breadfruit. It was all covered with sauce-stained towels to discourage the swarms of buzzing flies.

Country people looked down on people who ate this food. "Is town food what got yo' so." They liked to pick on one or two of the vendors who, they were sure, put shit in the sauce to bewitch the eaters. How else could people in their "right head" return to buy food from them? "You don' see is witchcraft!" Others, they were convinced, spat in the food. And they all put piss in the drinks they sold to accompany the food (a woman who sold coconut-sugar cakes under the gallery of a bookstore made them from coconut her children had chewed). "Town naigger, them nasty anyhow. They don' wash they pot." Convinced of their stories, they would spit in disgust.

One Saturday Jerome bought food from one of the women, after looking around to make sure that no one he knew was in sight. The lady served him sitting on a wooden crate hunched over the biscuit tins. She ladled a scoop of rice and peas onto a tin plate. To that she added a slice of tannia, a slice of plantain, and a slice of breadfruit; onto that she put a slice of fish and a full ladle of sauce. He ate it and liked it. The lady asked him how it was, and he said good, and she smiled, pleased.

She came to him in the hospital, opened her thighs and tried to swallow him, mixed food with her faeces, opened his mouth and forced it down his throat, quacking like a duck all the while and changing faces – his mother's, Miss Anderson's, Miss Dellimore's, Olivia's, Hetty's, but mostly keeping her own – and left him only after he had swallowed it all.

The food vendors quarrelled frequently among themselves. Among the six women was a man whom the buyers and non-buyers said was the biggest woman of the lot. They called him Sprat. He had an enormous frame and was over six feet tall. He was not fat. His face was broad and the colour of fresh asphalt. His huge red, bulbous lips resembled Sambo's. He arched forward slightly, was pigeon-toed, and had a big, projecting backside.

He got more customers than the women. While Jerome was

eating, a customer approached one of the female vendors, began to order from her, but changed her mind and bought from Sprat. The disappointed woman pouted, and fidgeted with her headtie, and cut her eye at Sprat.

"Melia, is not me fault if me cooking better than yo's," he told her, laughing.

"Go long, woman, yo' pussy bigger than mines," she shot back.

"Is yo' husband that tell yo' so."

"Me husband don' sleep with man."

"But you does sleep with 'oman."

The other women paid no attention.

Another customer came, renewing the competitive spirit and ending the row.

He bought food from them on numerous occasions. One day he was around when Sprat loaned Melia ten dollars to buy some ground provisions somebody was selling at a bargain. Another time, a big-hipped, big-breasted food vendor had it out with a thin, light-skinned one. He did not know what had started it.

The big-hipped one said, "This 'oman without no drawers always taking 'way me customers."

The light-skinned one lifted her dress to disprove the accusation and told the big-hipped one to do the same.

This time everyone laughed.

"Anyway," the light-skinned one continued, "is flour bag drawers you does wear."

Eventually they got around to whose nightgown had a red rooster on the front, from a popular brand of flour. One was unable to keep a man because she never cleaned herself. The other kept one only because she had given him something to drink that turned him *dotish*. One had eaten some of her children and was therefore a cemetery; the other who had none was a mule. One was a whore by day, the other by night.

It wasn't ten minutes after they'd stopped quarrelling when the big-hipped woman discovered she was out of pepper sauce and the light-skinned one gave her some.

On another occasion when he went Sprat wasn't there. While

he ate people came and asked for him. Sprat had the flu and three of the women had been to see him. One said he would be out the next week and she was buying supplies for him that day.

→► ◄←

When he returned to Compton that first July–August vacation, he found that it was not the same village. The canefields, in full growth then, even the mountains in the distance, didn't give the serenity they'd previously given. Neither the booming billows of the Atlantic nor its occasional flat surface stirred him. He could no longer imagine the monsters of the deep, changing their shapes like the waves, or shipwrecked sailors crying for help, their powerful arms threshing the billows – as he had done in earlier times.

Now he was aware of history. The fields reminded him of the whips in slavery. He fancied he could still hear the lashes and cries in the wind sweeping through the cane blades. The low pay of the villagers and their fear of White people told him that slavery hadn't quite ended.

Several years after he had joined the civil service, he'd reflected on how unhappy he was although he did not have to worry about the basic things that bothered the majority of Isabellans; and he'd written in his journal that "all emancipation ends in slavery / too subtle for the emancipated to see."

A great deal was festering there. Butler had been chief minister for some time, and some of the estates had unions; many, probably most, of the union organizers were in jail or in hiding. The police were under the control of the British administrator. Six policemen were on permanent duty in Compton, with orders to arrest anyone who came around to talk union activity. The administrator had been quoted in *The Isabellan* as saying that he agreed with the planters that where the workers were squatters, union organizers were trespassers. A few of his villagers had gone to public meetings Butler's men organized and had been fired by Mr. Manchester and ordered to remove their shacks from his land.

A lot had changed in thirty years! In the last election Butler's party lost every seat. They found out that he had two houses in New York and a fat bank account in Switzerland. His finance minister fled to England of all places the day after the election. The British did not extradite him for the trial. Beggars on horseback flogging beggars on foot. The beggars change places but the lash goes on. Butler was crippled now. His cronies didn't even visit him, it was said. At least they named the Trans-Island Highway after him. The workers he fought so hard for in the early days when he wanted to hold on to power were still struggling. Very few earned a living or even half a living on the estate now. Much of it had been turned into a golf course and very little was cultivated elsewhere. It was the party of the middle class that had passed the law giving squatters on the estates the land their shacks were on. Immediately they'd begun tearing them down to build small wooden and concrete houses. Not enough land though. Their two-bedroom house was surrounded on three sides. Three feet from the back wall of their house was the front door to their neighbour's house. He had seen his mother stretch across a window and hand something to Millicent over in her house.

He did well in school that first year. Except for algebra and science, he got the highest marks in his classes. He was a year older than the other boys. They decided to let him skip a form because of his performance. His mother insisted he take his report to show his elementary school teachers. That embarrassed him. He was no six-year-old showing off the toy he had got for Christmas.

One evening his father was sitting on the steps. He had just come in from the fields. He looked at Jerome and shook his head. "Don' think cause yo' head getting full o' what White man know, yo' better than we. I sure o' one thing: White man not teaching yo' the most important things what yo' supposed to know." He wanted him to talk on, but his father was a one-sentence man.

1993

ARCHIBALD J. CRAIL

The New Order

The guerrillas were here again last night. As usual, the soldiers arrived only this morning. Along the footpaths and between the shrubs, the eighteen-year-old conscripts snaked, rolled and ran from cover to cover – seemingly bent on surprising an unseen enemy.

I hang about the mission station entrance most of the time. This way everyone can see me and neither side can mistake me for the enemy. Sometimes the wind brings the sounds of gunfire and explosions but it doesn't matter to me who is winning or who is losing because I have neither friends nor enemies.

As for the guerrillas, I know most of them by name as I grew up with them. But we don't speak. To them, as to their enemy, I am merely a fixture of this abandoned institution. My insanity is taken for granted and no questions are asked or greetings exchanged. I am completely ignored.

I suppose if I had been an insane woman, the most degenerate among the soldiers would have gang-raped me. In their quest to conquer all things living, there would have been my womanness to defile. But as an insane man I have ceased to exist: a nonentity through which they stare in their search for hidden enemies. Perhaps the psychologists among them, hidden in their camouflaged uniforms, are able to detect through my body language the presence or absence of the enemy. Maybe that is why they let me live. I can see no other reason for my continued existence or for the case of bully beef the army chaplain leaves at the gate once a month.

These abandoned buildings with green moss on the roofs, walls cracked and scarred by mortars and bullets, were once a centre of activity for the entire area. From miles around, the villagers came for medical treatment and education and to find God. And I was part of life here. Now the only permanent inhabitants are a few cats, the odd snake and myself.

I remember growing up with many white people about the place. Even in my tenth year the director and his assistants were all from overseas. My mother told me they came from many parts of Europe and North America, but the ones she liked most were from Britain. These people occupied all the mission houses and singles' quarters and had exclusive use of the bathrooms and toilets. I never found it strange that my mother and all the other black teachers went home for meals while the white teachers, nurses and priests went to the mission mess hall. In my childhood this mission was a huge place. There was an elementary and a high school, a Bible college and a hospital. The hospital was always the busiest place during daytime, with people coming from all over because of snakebite, broken legs, sleeping sickness, or the myriad of other misfortunes people can suffer. Our two-roomed house was at the back of the principal's house. He always called on my mother to do translation work at night.

Life was not too difficult. As a teacher's child I wore shoes, a shirt, and pants. Children from the villages often came to school without shirts and always barefoot. Looking back now, I sometimes think my life was too protected. I never had to look after goats or scare the birds from the grain fields. My whole life revolved about our little corner in this foreign outpost. After school, when I had done my chores of carrying water and chopping kindling, Meme would allow me to watch the white children play. Although I was not allowed to join them, at least I could improve my English by listening to their shrill voices. Of course I can only speak now with the wisdom of hindsight. Nevertheless, for what little I gained, my loss was greater. The village children avoided me and soon I could not express myself in the language of the Oshikwanyama. But as Meme said, I was growing up for better things than the life of the villager.

In my twelfth year there were some problems. A few villagers refused to pay the cattle tax. The mission director had them flogged. Later, the police were called in because some of the black teachers refused to teach. They said they could not teach when they were refused permission to use the toilets or the mess hall. Meme said they were all Communists trying to change things. The teachers were also flogged. Although the principal told them to stay on as an example to others, they disappeared into the bush without waiting for their paycheques. In the weeks that followed, some of the grade twelve students were not seen any more. By the end of that school term, the senior classes were so empty that the few students remaining were told to go home and wait for the following year.

On my thirteenth birthday the guerrillas came. They were not strangers at all.

There was Father Haidimbi's son, David, who used to be head altar boy. Now he was a commander, carried a grenade launcher and addressed everybody as "comrade." Both men and women, young and old were shown the same militant respect. Only when he met his father's eyes did David falter in his commanding attitude. For the briefest of moments, the eighteen-year-old in battle fatigues was reduced by his own awareness to a mere son meeting his father after a long absence.

"*Walelepo?*" David asked. Are you well?

"*Eheh,*" his father answered. Yes.

"*Nawatu?*" Did you sleep well?

"*Eheh.*"

"*Umpiri?*" Is there peace?

"*Eheh.*"

It was almost as if David had shown traditional respect to all his people and not merely exchanged greetings with his father. The earlier scowl on Father Haidimbi's face was replaced by intense pride.

Then there was Hambalaleni. As a religious instruction teacher, she had driven the fear of God into us. Now, with her camouflaged uniform and combat boots, she seemed ten feet tall. We children were herded into the assembly hall and told to be proud of our country, our people and ourselves. Instead of hellfire and brimstone, she told us about the revolution and how we were all going to be free. We did not even have to wait for heaven to enjoy it. It would be right here once the country was liberated. I feared for the question period which never came. Instead she asked if we had understood what she had said.

"Yes, miss!" we chorused in unison.

"I am not your miss!" she shouted back at us. "I am your comrade!"

Some of us tried to catch the eyes of the former senior students. However, their attention was elsewhere. With their brand-new AK-47s, they stood guard all over the mission station and stopped the mission staff from going anywhere.

Afterwards they disappeared into the bushes as quietly as they had come.

Later still, everybody was called to the director's house. Red-faced with anger and embarrassment (he had been forced to kneel in a corner of his office during the entire visit), he told us in his clipped English voice to guard against evil influences. In the middle of his speech he suddenly instructed the principal to phone both the soldiers and the police. "Tell them to hurry, Dusting. They may still be able to catch these . . . eh, misfits." Then he instructed my mother to speak. She did:

"We must forget about what these wayward children said. If we do not obey the director, all these good things will come to an end. This mission will be closed and all you people will be living in the villages again. The soldiers and the police will be here soon to take statements from everybody." She turned to the parents. "Father

Haidimbi, why did you not tell that boy of yours to throw away the gun and come back to school?"

To this Father Haidimbi said nothing. Some of the other parents, who also had children among the guerrillas, just shifted about and stared at their feet.

After the guerrillas' visit, some of the whites left. They were mostly the old nuns and nurses who said they did not want to become "involved." Father Thomas mentioned Malaysia, where trouble also started in such a way and his brother had had his head chopped off. Now there were soldiers at the mission every day. With their guns, tanks and uniforms, they looked very smart and didn't appear particularly threatening. Trying to look detached from their surroundings, they seemed very bored. They always withdrew in the late afternoon to their base five miles south.

When Sister Eileen told my mother they might meet in heaven, she was broken-hearted. My mother had tended Sister Eileen in sickness, washed her clothes and cleaned her house; now she did not even think of taking us with her to England, the place she had spoken so much of. "You would have no problem in London, Khomotso," Sister Eileen had said. "There are many people from Africa. Besides, this is no place for you as you are very much English. You certainly must meet my two nieces. Jane and Jenny are always asking about you when I go home on furlough." And then she would show us some pictures of her youth and the rosy-cheeked girls. I would have liked to meet them myself and show them how well I could walk and talk like an Englishman.

Now she was gone. We were left with pictures of an English countryside and ornaments depicting lords and ladies relaxing near ponds and lakes. Perhaps that's what heaven looks like.

When David Haidimbi's band came again six months later, they were very rough. The director, principal and all the white staff were gagged and tied up in the office. As for the rest, we were herded into the assembly hall. Now he wanted volunteers to join the people's army. The whole grade twelve class stepped forward. David then called my mother to the front of the gathering. "You have been warned to leave this place, comrade," he told her.

This, of course, was news to me.

"You come here with your guns and things like new toys trying to scare us," Meme answered. "Now you tell me to leave the mission. How will I feed my son when I have no work?"

"We are fighting a revolutionary war, comrade," David said. "You are either with us or against us. Why are you telling people we are just a band of thieves out to destroy the things which the white people built? Today I tell you that we are creating a new order. The mission can continue to operate but do not speak against us. We are here to liberate you from your oppression."

My mother's voice was beginning to grow shrill. "What oppression are you talking about? Here we are trying to give the children an education so they do not have to herd goats and live as their fathers lived."

David was now becoming angry. "This mission station, comrade, is only one small part of our country." He continued in his all-knowing adolescent voice. "And you are only one person in a nation of people. You have been teaching here for fifteen years. Within all that time, you have not used a toilet or the mess hall here. For all that time, you've earned a fraction of what the white employees get paid. Why is it all of our young men do not get any further education after this place but have to work for slave wages on the richest diamond deposits in all of Africa? Even there they are not allowed to use the little education they've gained in order to work as clerks or bookkeepers. Do you not long for the day when you can be fully in charge of this mission? That day will never come if we do not throw off this yoke of foreign oppression. Comrade, please believe that what we are doing is in the interest of our country and yourself." This long speech left him quite breathless. For a minute I thought he was just dragging on because he did not know how to stop.

Meme tried to speak to David Haidimbi again but he simply

ignored her. "Please, David," she begged him. "Please, Comrade David, will you allow me one more chance to stay here?"

He gave her such a sharp look that she visibly shrank into herself. The seniors were allowed to pick up an extra change of clothing, and they all left in the darkness.

That night, Meme was very quiet. When the principal called for her to do translation work, she did not go.

The next day my mother disappeared. Someone had seen her leaving the school building on the way to the library. No one saw her arriving at the library, though. For me there was no goodbye, no farewell. She was just gone. I tried to remember the last words we had spoken and how she had looked at me. I can remember the words but they had no particular significance. It was simply that I had to remember to wash my ears thoroughly. Could this have been a code? But then we'd never spoken in code before.

The two-room house was unbearably quiet. The pots, pans and furniture and her clothes in the closet were so familiar and yet so strange. Where did I start to make myself a meal? It was easy enough to make a sandwich but cooking was an entirely different thing. All day long I sat at the kitchen table and stared at the open doorway. Toward supper time, one of my mother's friends brought me a bowl of soup. She said she felt sorry for me and perhaps my mother would come back soon. It was not my mother I missed but the order of my day: To be able to wake up and know there was someone to regulate my life. That was what my life was missing: To have these utensils used and the sounds of their usage bring life to this utter silence. At some distance I could hear the white children playing in the compound.

The next day was Monday. I started getting my school uniform ready. Meme would have been disappointed if I had gone to school in a wrinkled shirt. While ironing, I suddenly caught myself humming her favourite hymn, "Rock of Ages."

On Tuesday the history teacher approached me. "Son, you seem to be working hard these days," he said. "Please take it easy, my boy. Most of us have also lost a dear one during these times of trouble. Are you making out okay at home?"

"Yes, sir."

The schoolwork provided an escape from my mother's loss. I realized this part of the day provided me with a semblance of order I desperately needed. Into this I threw myself with fervour. I drank in all information with a thirst hitherto unknown to myself. Except when I was called by the neighbours for meals, my time was spent with school books. In the evenings, I would read until I fell asleep with Bismarck or Napoleon on my mind. I even dreamt of them. If they were alive today, then surely they would have sorted out this mess of fighting in my country with no problem at all. Marching across the country with so many thousands of footsoldiers and cavalry, they would restore peace in just a short time. They would leave in their wake beautiful buildings and bridges with a hard-working population forever thankful for this release from uncertainty. They would leave in their wake order.

Two months before my grade ten final examination the principal came to tell me he had found a job for me on the copper mines. I thought it was because of my low marks in mathematics that he wanted me to quit school and start working.

"Please, Father," I begged. "I promise to study even harder now."

"You are a good student," he said, "but we can't go on supporting you forever you know. A man must grow up and face the responsibilities of life."

"But I only want to finish my final examination."

"If you do not take the job opportunity now," he said, "it will be months before the recruiting officer from the mines comes around. Who is going to feed you in the meantime? Besides, we need your mother's house for another family."

The pictures of the English countryside and peaceful strollers receded further and further in my mind. I could not tell him I feared the unknown; instead I asked to be a teacher's aide.

"No, we can't afford to pay you. Better start packing your things for tomorrow. Here's some money for the bus fare, which you can pay back once you start working."

"But what will I eat, Father?"

"Don't worry, the mine company will feed you."
He put the money on the table and left.

There is an exhilarating experience, unparalleled by any other, in descending into the bowels of the earth. Perhaps death is as exciting but I still have to experience it. Climbing into the wire-mesh cage suspended from overhead cables was my first physical step towards mining. I boarded with nervous anxiety. Experienced workers smoked their pipes while others leaned against the seemingly fragile structure with looks of boredom on their dusty faces. I felt a sweat breaking out on my body. Perhaps it showed on my face, for suddenly I saw the others grinning at me. The operator released the handbrake and, with a woosh of air, we descended. The walls of the mine shaft seemed to rush in to us and the air became increasingly warm.

The cage stopped at various tunnel entrances. People came on, got off. Some had heavy, important-looking equipment all covered in dust. A few times, young white men in neat white dust coats came on board holding clipboards and pencils like badges of office. They rarely spoke to anyone or each other. When we finally stopped at our tunnel entrance, I was surprised to see the cage going down even farther. The deafening roar of jackhammers came from the well-lit tunnel. Even though it was unbearably hot, I broke into a cold sweat.

The work was back-breaking. However, I felt a new strength developing within myself. Swinging the pick or pushing the jackhammer, I worked with the frenzy of a man possessed. Afterward, showering in the cement cubicles, I would feel a quiet sense of fulfilment enveloping me. At first I was anxious to display my knowledge of the world and the people and things in it. Later it became a burden which I soon learned to abandon lest people avoid me because they thought I was trying to be different from them. Sometimes older men would ask me to read or write a letter for them. Otherwise my education was like a beautiful teapot which gathers dust on the shelf and is only taken down for the benefit of visitors. Slowly and imperceptibly the stories of Napoleon, Waterloo, spyrogyra and the annual rainfall of the Amazon basin receded from my memory. I no longer even thought of Sister Eileen and her English countryside. Only sometimes did the memory of my mother appear. One day I was startled by the thought I could no longer remember what she looked like. I simply couldn't remember her face. Sometimes, before I fell asleep, I would see her face vaguely but, try as I did, I could not bring her features into sharp focus. On other occasions, there would be the outline of her dress hem and her gnarled, swollen feet in fashionable shoes. But like an aging conjurer, I could not bring her full picture into view.

And then, two years later, the shift boss told me I would be laid off at the end of the month.

I pleaded with him to let me stay. I told him there was no work at the mission station; I had no relatives living. All to no avail. My passbook was stamped to say I was no longer employed in the area and had to leave within twenty-four hours. Thrown out of the company hostel, I had nowhere to sleep.

There was no one living at the mission station. The principal's house was empty. The classrooms that once were alive with children reciting math tables were now as quiet as death. Desks upended, papers and books strewn on the floor and a dried puddle of blood in a corner – these were the only signs of a hasty, violent escape.

Later the soldiers came. They frisked, arrested and interrogated me. The two hundred Rands I had saved was taken. After six months of beatings and imprisonment, I was released. What else could I do but come back here?

David Haidimbi has asked me to join the guerrillas but I cannot go into another unknown. Their slogans of freedom, equality and justice are strange words in my ears. This is where I make my last stand. From this place I will not leave; somebody will have to kill me first.

There is an order to my life now. While all is still dark outside, I get up from my sleeping place behind the altar and await the arrival of the soldiers. I pick up every shred of paper and stuff it into the neck of my shirt. My trouser pockets are too full now. One day, when I have time, I will read all these pieces of newspaper, hymn books, letters and bills brought here by the wind. Perhaps they will give an answer to my life and the meaning for my continued existence.

1992

➤ ◄

DIONNE BRAND

Winter Epigrams

4

they think it's pretty,
this falling of leaves.
something is dying!

1983

I am not that strong woman

I am not that strong woman on the mountain
at Castle Bruce
the mountain squarely below her feet
the flesh bursting under her skin
I cannot hold a mountain under my feet,
she dug yams and birthed a cow
I am not the old one
boxes on her head in Roseau
the metred street, she made one hundred turns in it

the pee streaming from her straddled legs
she stood over the gutter,
the hot yellow stream wet her ankles
and the street,
nor the other one on church street
skirt tied around her waist
mad
some aged song shared her lips
for many years with a clay pipe.

I am the one with no place to live
I want no husband
I want nothing inside of me
that hates me
these are walls and niches
park benches and iron spikes
I want nothing that enters me
screaming
claiming to be history,
my skin hangs out on a clothes line
drying and eaten by the harsh sun
and the wind threatens to blow my belly
into a balloon
to hold more confusions,
alone is my only rescue
alone is the only thing I chose.

I'll gather my skin like a washerwoman
her hand insisting the wind out,
I will bare my teeth to the sun
let it feel
how it is to be dazzled.

1984

Hard Against the Soul

X

Then it is this simple. I felt the unordinary romance of
women who love women for the first time. It burst in
my mouth. Someone said this is your first lover, you
will never want to leave her. I had it in mind that I
would be an old woman with you. But perhaps I
always had it in mind simply to be an old woman,
darkening, somewhere with another old woman,
then, I decided it was you when you found me in that
apartment drinking whisky for breakfast. When I came
back from Grenada and went crazy for two years, that
time when I could hear anything and my skin was
flaming like a nerve and the walls were like paper
and my eyes could not close. I suddenly sensed you
at the end of my room waiting. I saw your back arched
against this city we inhabit like guerillas, I brushed my
hand, conscious, against your soft belly, waking up.

➤➤ ◄◄

It's true, you spend the years after thirty turning over
the suggestion that you have been an imbecile,
hearing finally all the words that passed you like air,
like so much fun, or all the words that must have
existed while you were listening to others. What
would I want with this sentence you say flinging it
aside . . . and then again sometimes you were duped,
poems placed deliberately in your way. At eleven, the
strophe of a yellow dress sat me crosslegged in my
sex. It was a boy's abrupt birthday party. A yellow
dress for a tomboy, the ritual stab of womanly gathers

at the waist. S*he look like a boy in a dress*, my big
sister say, a lyric and feminine correction from a
watchful aunt, *don't say that, she look nice and pretty*.
Nice and pretty, laid out to splinter you, so that never,
until it is almost so late as not to matter do you grasp
some part, something missing like a wing, some
fragment of your real self.

1990

Just Rain, Bacolet

Back. Here in Bacolet one night when the rain falls and falls and
falls and we swing the door wide open and watch the rainy season
arrive I think that I am always travelling back. When the chacalaca
bird screams coarse as stones in a tin bucket, signalling rain across
this valley, when lightning strafes a blue-black sky, when rain as
thick as shale beats the xora to arrowed red tears, when squat Julie
trees kneel to the ground with the wind and I am not afraid but
laugh and laugh and laugh I know that I am travelling back. "Are
you sure that this is not a hurricane?" Faith and Filo ask. "No," I
say, with certainty, "it's just rain. I know this, it's just rain . . . just
rain, rain is like this here. You can see it running toward you. And
this too: don't fight the sea and don't play with it either; that shell
blowing means there's fish in the market and, yes, I'd forgotten the
water from young green coconuts is good for settling the stomach
– you have to cut or scrape the skin off shark before you cook it,
otherwise it's too oily – and this prickly bush, susumba, the seed is
good for fever, and the bark of that tree is poison . . ." Knowing
is always a mixed bag of tricks and so is travelling back.

On one side of this island is the Atlantic and on the other the
Caribbean Sea, and sometimes, very often if you drive up, up

the sibilances of Signal Hill to a place called Patience, yes, Patience Hill, you can see both. There are few places you can go to without seeing the sea or the ocean and I know the reason. It is a comfort to look at either one. If something hard is on your mind and you are deep in it, if you lift your head you will see the sea and your trouble will become irrelevant because the sea is so much bigger than you, so much more striking and magnificent, that you will feel presumptuous.

Magnificent frigate drapes the sea sky, magnificent frigate. Bird is not enough word for this . . . nor is it enough for the first day just on the top of the hill at Bacolet that red could draw flamboyant against such blue and hill and cloud and the front end of the car float between them. . . .

. . . At first I went alone, was brought, arrived, came, was carried, was there, here. The verb is such an intrusive part of speech, like travelling, suggesting all the time invasion or intention not to leave things alone, so insistent you want to have a sentence without a verb, you want to banish the verb.

Anyway, I was carried by the way they'd cut the road, fast and narrow, and with magic because always it was impossible for two cars to pass each other but it happened, and magic because one afternoon cutting through the rain forest on Parlatuvier Road to Roxborough but right in the middle of the rain forest a woman, soft in the eyes and old like water and gentle like dust and hand clasped over the hand of her granddaughter, a little girl, appeared, walking to Roxborough. So we stopped, seeing no house nearby that she may have come from or be going to. The road was treed and bushed on all sides, epiphytes hung from the palmiste and immortelle, and we stopped to talk to her. "Thank you, darling, thank you. What a sweet set of children! I going just down the road. Thank you, darling." To be called darling and child, we knew it was magic because no one, no stranger in the last twenty-four years of my life and in all of Faith's living in the city we had left, had called us child and darling. We stared, grinning at her. We settled into her darling and child just like her granddaughter settled into her lap. Magic because she had appeared on the road with her own hope, a hope that willed a rain forest to send a car with some women from North America eager for her darling, her child, or perhaps she wasn't thinking of us at all but of walking to Roxborough with her granddaughter to buy sugar or rice and her darling and child were not special but ordinary, what she would say to any stranger, anyone, only we were so starved for someone to call us a name we would recognise that we loved her instantly.

One day we are standing in a windmill – no, standing in a windmill, trying to avoid the verb to meet, which is not enough for things that exist already and shadow your face like a horizon. We climbed to the top of the windmill at Courland Bay with S. The wooden banisters have been eaten away by termites. They've eaten the inside of the wood, ever existing, trying to avoid the verb to meet, as I, we try. We learn that you cannot hold on to the banisters though the outside looks as it might have looked long ago. She had told us what year, some year in another century, 1650, or perhaps 1730. We climbed to the top, passing through the bedrooms the windmill now holds, the bats' droppings in the abandoned rooms, then outside to the top, up the iron stairs. That is when she said that the mill had been here – a sugar mill, a plantation – and there were the old buildings, traces of them, here since then. That is when she showed us the old building, near the caretaker's house, near the cow roaming on her thick chain, near the governor plum tree, tangled up in mimosa and razor grass, but not covered and not all of it there. We learn that you cannot come upon yourself so suddenly, so roughly, so matter of factly. You cannot simply go to a place, to visit friends, to pick mangoes on your way to the beach and count on that being all. You cannot meet yourself without being shaken, taken apart. You are not a tourist, you must understand. You must walk more carefully because you are always walking in ruins and because at the top of a windmill one afternoon on your way to the beach near Courland Bay you can tremble. At the top of a windmill one afternoon on your way to bathe in the sea when you stop off to pick some mangoes you might melt into your own eyes. I was there at the top of the windmill taken apart, crying for someone back then, for things which exist already and exist simply and still. Things you meet. I am afraid of breaking something coming down. Something separates us.

We leave the top of the windmill and the owner, who is still talking about carving it up and selling it in American dollars, and go to talk to the caretaker who feels more like home, more like people. He knows the kind of talk we need, talk about the rich and the poor, talk about why you can weep when looking at this place, talk that sounds quiet in the trembling and razor grass, as if he understands that there are spirits here, listening, and we must wait our turn to speak, or perhaps what they are saying is so unspeakable that our own voices cut back in the throat to quietness. This is where it happened and all we can do is weep when our turn comes, when we meet. Most likely that is the task of our generation: to look and to weep, to be taken hold of by them, to be used in our flesh to encounter their silence. All over there are sugar mills even older, filled with earth and grass. Now everything underfoot is something broken.

Faith went to the Rex last night. It was Friday, the latest Robert Redford movie was on. Not because she likes Robert Redford but because it's the only cinema and she loves the movies. She loves the Rex with its hand-painted sign, freshly painted every Wednesday when the movie changes. I am scared of the movies, scared since I was small. Scared because I was afraid of people and because the movies were new and something you had to learn to go to and to take care of yourself when you were there. Going to the cinema, you needed money and you needed to dress up and you were in public where people could see if you were dressed up or had the money. And if you didn't have enough money, you had to sit in Pit where there were a lot of rough boys who made rude remarks about girls and tried to touch you and went to the cinema just to do this and to heckle the screen or imitate the star boy if it was a western. I was fearful, too, that what I would see on the screen would confirm the place we occupied in the world. We were going to see how much better white people lived than we did and how far away the reach to that living was because we would have to reach into white skin to live it. The re-enactments always came up slightly short. The lipsticked white beauties and the slicked-back white macho twisted us into odd shapes on tropical streets, made us long for black turtle-necked sweaters, blue jeans and leather jackets and cowboy hats. So having only this memory of cinema in the Caribbean, I didn't go to the Rex with Faith to see *Indecent Proposal*, and she went because she didn't believe me, being much more adventurous than I and having grown up when film wasn't new or scary but the first primer of the culture, as much as the primary text of mine was the British canon. When she came back she said it was lovely, yes lovely, that the whole cinema heckled Robert Redford and Demi Moore and the guy from *White Men Can't Jump*. They laughed and jeered at American romanticism. Perhaps something in a Black cinema in a Third World country makes a screen full of white patriarchy and desire as money seem silly, unlikely and grotesque – unbelievable. Nobody was buying it and not just because it was a silly-ass movie in any terms but because nobody was buying the general screen. She said she finally felt a whole audience feeling like her and more: outside the screen and critical, belonging to another intellectual cosmos, one that was not craziness but sense. And nothing that ever came on the screen at the Rex would be seen with anything other than this sense. She had spent so much of her life in the lonely deconstruction of the American movie text that the Rex was home, the true meeting of the hegemonic and the counter-hegemonic, and the counter-hegemonic made more than sense; it was normal, but deeper – they were laughing. The crowd, probably blue-jeaned and longing in every other way for America, found America laughable. So I changed my mind about the Rex, but I still never went, still so fearful that Faith went every Friday by herself or with a woman we'd met who was waiting tables in a restaurant. One Friday night I met her on the street in between a double bill. She was looking for coffee; the street that circled the harbour was packed brightly with young women and men, liming, hanging. Her face came luminous and teary in the crowd. I went to meet her. I thought that she might have been lonely because I hadn't gone with her, but it wasn't loneliness, it was ordinariness that moved her.

She wanted to keep walking in the crowd on Friday night and going to the Rex.

Travelling is a constant state. You do not leave things behind or take them with you, everything is always moving; you are not the centre of your own movement, everything sticks, makes you more heavy or more light as you lurch, everything changes your direction. We were born thinking of travelling back. It is our singular preoccupation, we think of nothing else. I am convinced. We are continually uncomfortable where we are. We do not sleep easily, not without dreaming of travelling back. This must be the code written on the lining of my brain: go back, go back, like a fever, a pandemic scourging the Diaspora. Go back, the call words waiting for an answer. How complicated they can get: all the journeys to the answer, all the journeys, physical and imaginary, on airplanes, on foot, in the heart and drying on the tongue. Faith and I glimpse it here. When we first get off the airplane and slip into our skin, the gravity of racial difference disappears. But it is this and more: a knowledge we slip into, a kind of understanding of the world which will get us through. Here we only have to pay attention to what we do. One night Vi called, said, "Do you want to see a leather-back turtle? She's laying her eggs on Turtle Beach." We went. I felt called as I do for every event here. Surrounded so by spirits, history, ancestors, I give over to their direction. I realise that I live differently in Canada. I live without connection to this world with its obligations, homage, significances, with how you are in the soul.

A woman told me a story last week of how a man from Quebec who had laid floors for a living had all his money stolen on the beach by thugs. "He show me his knees from working and he knees mash up," she said. "And when I look at them knees I say to myself if that man ever kneel down on them knees and pray for that thief, put a light on that thief, god help him. Is so people does look for trouble." She understood the power in his knees in ways that the man from Quebec could not. Knees like that were a weakness where he came from.

So I was called to a great thing. The leather-back turtle came up on the beach like this that night. Every May they come up on Turtle Beach to lay hundreds of eggs. I had forgotten. And when the eggs hatch after six weeks, tiny turtles scramble to the sea under the predaceous swooping of pelicans and frigates. The hotel, its light and customers intrude on this beach, but this part of the sea is inscribed on all the generations of leather-backs, so they come even as investment and real-estate brokers gobble up the sand and water. One came making circles and digging her back fins into the sand and then she left without laying. The sand there was too hot, Vi said. So she went back into the sea waiting for another time. Later, down the beach, we came on another. When my eyes became accustomed to the dark I saw her. She was ancient, her head larger than a human's but somehow human-like and her eyes full of silver tears, her skin, black with tiny white spots, wrinkled. She dug a nest in the sand behind her, measuring, measuring with the length of her fin. Then I heard her sigh, a sound like an old woman working a field, a sound more human than human, and old, like so much life or so much trouble and needing so much rest. This is how old I'd like to be: so old I'll cry silver, sigh human. But I must say here truly how I felt: as if she was more than I or more than human, higher on the evolutionary ladder, beyond all surmising or calculation, nothing that we could experience, greater than us not because we had said so but because she was. I watched her for over an hour, dig and measure, dig and measure, and then lay her eggs. I went closer to see them and remembered eating one as a child on another beach. "I've seen this before," I told Vi. "When I was little," eating something it had taken the leather-back fifty or sometimes seventy years to make, delicate and soft after more than half a century. I remembered the torch lights cutting shadow along that other beach and my grandfather digging for the eggs of this now-endangered species. She was seventy by her size, broad as the span of my arms and as tall as I lying down, and when she was done and had sighed again she covered the hole in the sand and began circling, camouflaging the place she had lain her eggs, making other places looking the same until I could not tell where she had laid them. A leather-back turtle cries on a night like this; her tears are silver and when she is done circling, having done all that she can do, she heads laboriously for the sea. She seemed tired. She spun down to the shore, waited for a wave and then plunged, washed, splendid, rode into the sea.

We are so eager to return, our powers of recognition isolate only the evidence in support of a place. So I did not mention the unnecessary clutter of tourists and cameras which had to be policed and . . . I took this as a gift, this intimacy I intruded on at Turtle Beach, with the tourists, the ones we had to shush, and the lights and the hotel and the cigarette-smoking man Vi told to "have a little respect." I measured only the space that the leather-back and I occupied. I took it as part if not all the answer to going back.

We drank Carib up to the last drinking spot on the Northside Road to Moriah, Castara and Parlatuvier. We stopped, asking for my grandmother's people in Moriah. She was born in Moriah to Angelina Noray and a man named Bobb. I asked an old, big, gentle man coming down the road where the Norays lived, knowing that all I needed to do was mention a last name and whether they had vanished or were still alive the name would conjure them. "Well, the ones on the hill or on the flat?" he asked. "I'm looking for my grandmother's people, she leave here long, long ago. She had a brother name Dan." "A long time ago. Daniel. Well, is the ones on the flat you want then." We looked to where he pointed in the high lush valley that is Moriah. I did not go to the shelf in the hill to see them, just said thank you, comforted, and pointed the car up Northside Road, remembering his arm pointing to the luxuriant bamboo where my people came from.

"See, see Moriah, Moriah, Moriah. See, see Moriah, Moriah, Moriah. Dingolay lay lay lay lay oh . . ." See Moriah. This children's song comes back to us, and Vi and I speculate as to what it might have meant. We hope it was a place to escape to. We know that they do a wedding dance here, only ceremonial now, dating back to the nineteenth century: "See, see Moriah, Moriah, Moriah. See see Moriah, Moriah Moriah Moriah. Dingolay lay lay lay lay oh dingolay one boy one girl . . ." Marriages not being allowed to property, we speculate that perhaps the enslaved ran to this high valley to dance the wedding dance as a sign of revolt and self-affirmation.

Just last night in the Scarborough public library we listened to an architectural anthropologist from the University of Florida talk about the way the French built sugar mills and the way the British built sugar mills and the way the Spanish built sugar mills, how they used the wind and the water, their drains and ditches, the proximity of their great houses to the mills. . . . He said nothing about the people who built them and worked them because he was an architectural anthropologist and not concerned with people, but he did make an attempt to appease us by saying that the Moriah wedding was a blend of the European and the African cultures. It never occurred to him that it was in poor taste and perhaps even foolhardy to stand before us and call European conquest and African enslavement a "blend." It didn't occur to him to think of the Moriah wedding as a mask, a more-than-simple duality suggesting mockery, irony, picong, self-affirmation, absence, change, recognition and antimony. Later, he introduced his protégé, also from the University of Florida, who was a social anthropologist who said that he in fact was interested in the people who worked in the mills and that at Courland Bay he had found English crockery in a place that he had identified as slave quarters. This suggested to him that the slaves and the master had a relationship of cordiality. He would have had us believe that at Courland Bay, which used to be one of the largest slave plantations, and boasting hundreds of acres and hundreds of slaves, the master let his slaves drink in imported English teacups. He beamed in a kind of self-absolution, a kind of brotherhood, and sat down to the grateful applause of the representatives of the local and the island government and the historical society.

"That is what does happen when you let people into your business."

Parlatuvier, Parlatuvier, Parlatuvier, old talk, old talk or furnace pipe, what is the meaning? Castara, Castara, cast away, cast away, next to Englishman's Bay. I'd rather the mystery of names, and I'll keep to myself all the women on the island and where we met them. These maps are for passing word of mouth, the way to another place like Moriah for purposes of dancing and lovemaking. And we left some conversations for lesbian anthropologists who also read looks and movement and the inclination of figures and the shortness and silence of this passage as cryptic as the signals for escape.

A long time ago I think I fled this place because flight is as strong as return; it is the same often. One is not the end of the other or the beginning of the next, and often when we go back all we can think of is flight. And in flight . . . But this time I wanted to stay. We wanted to stay. This ease we slip into leaves us stranded once we have to disappear again. The closer we get to home the more we disappear, contemplating immigration lines and police lines and bank lines and just bullshit lines.

"I know why we don't want to go home. What we have to deal with is not understandable, it's crude and mean-spirited."

"We live with hatred all around us, don't we? Exploding the skin."

"It damages us. Damages every part of us but mostly your soul."

"We have to live so small there; here at least there is the simple, simple assumption of goodwill."

1994

→→ ←←

DANY LAFERRIÈRE

Dining with the Dictator

(translated by David Homel)

SCENE XVIII: NEITHER LORD NOR MASTER

Accept this offering of necklaces,
my mournful fandango – M.S.-A.[1]

The sun reached the sofa. I picked up Saint-Aude's poetry and read:

> In the bard's tent
> sleeps the gold of my lamp.

I closed the book and sat in motionless meditation. My senses open. I wanted the air to yield up the multiple meanings of these lines. A good line of poetry lives at room temperature. You begin by conjuring up its special smell that fills your being. The smell of the poet when he wrote the line. In this case, the line smells of cat piss, lime and human salt. Its taste is that of the Host, bread without leavening. A good line will burn your fingers. Its average speed is three hundred and sixty kilometres an hour. You don't need more than one good line a day.

---

[1] Magloire Saint-Aude (1912–1971), a Haitian poet.

I got up to make a sandwich in the kitchen. Miki had fixed me a bowl of chocolate. The girls' underwear was scattered through the house.

I went to wash my face in the sink. The combined smell of perfume, sweat and sperm almost knocked me off my feet. I lingered there a minute or two to breathe it all in.

Outside, a car horn sounded a dozen times. I wanted to tell them that everyone was gone, and that they'd all headed for the beach. I stopped; I'd almost forgotten I was a wanted man. Where could Gégé be? No doubt cooking up some new trouble. Knowing him, he was probably on a fresh scent. He would change shirts, and no one would know who he was. Gégé was always on the move. It's hard to hit a moving target. Meanwhile, I was waiting here, nailed to the spot, waiting like a fool for them to come and pick me up. Like a cow hiding in a slaughterhouse. Maybe that *was* the right place to hide. No one would ever think of looking for a cow in a slaughterhouse. Sharks come and go at Miki's place and never even look at me.

"Where's Miki?" Choupette asked abruptly as she stormed into the house.

I knew all of them. They didn't know who I was, but I'd seen them plenty of times, in every possible position. I can see everything in Miki's house from my window.

"She left."

The other girls came in behind Choupette. Papa must have stayed in the car. ·

"Miki went to the beach with Pasqualine," I repeated.

Marie-Erna waved her hand in the air as if to say she knew that and didn't give a damn. The girls fanned out through the house. They took everything: clothes, food, perfume, records, a bottle of Chanel No. 5 and Cover Girl make-up. A regular raid. I couldn't do anything about it. I didn't know the code. Miki had asked me to look after the house, but what did she really mean? Was she serious? Had she anticipated this horde of pillagers? Was this the normal thing to do? What was really going on? Miki was their friend, wasn't she? But these girls would devour anyone – including each other.

A fight broke out over a scarf.

"Keep you hands off that," Choupette ordered.

"How come?" Marie-Erna asked.

"It belongs to me, shit. I lent it to Miki last week."

"I don't believe you," said Marie-Erna and put the scarf in her black leather purse.

"Give it to me!" Choupette raged.

"Hey, girls, calm down," said Papa, who had just walked into the room.

"Shut your face," Choupette shot back, turning on him.

Papa cut a quick look in my direction. I didn't lower my eyes. He wasn't Frank, after all.

"You're a real bitch," Marie-Erna told Choupette.

I watched the tennis game. Balls were flying over the net from both sides. Smashes from all corners. Real professionals. Papa wouldn't be asked to umpire. Marie-Erna was sexier than Choupette, in a certain way. Though I was probably the only one who held that opinion. Choupette was so absolutely physical. Her mere presence was enough to make you surrender. When you saw her, you could think of only one thing. Her mouth was made for it. Her lips, her teeth (glistening white), her wrists, her ankles, everything about her was designed to push men (and women, too) to the edge of despair, madness and murder. Marie-Erna was more subtle. When you first cast your eyes on her, she seemed almost ordinary. But one look and you were caught, hopelessly trapped. With Pasqualine as their princess, these girls were the *crème de la crème* of man-killers in this town.

"All right, you can have it," Marie-Erna said, this time, about a blouse.

"No, you keep it," Choupette said casually. "I don't want it any more."

"I don't want it either," Marie-Erna told her. "I don't really like Miki's stuff."

Choupette took the blouse from Marie-Erna's hands and threw it on top of the record player.

"Come on, let's go," she ordered.

"If you don't really need it, then I think I will take it," Marie-Erna decided, stuffing the blouse into her bag.

"You're a walking garbage can," Choupette told her.

Papa got to his feet. Did he understand the girls' secret code? I didn't think so. He was only following along. But then again, you never know.

"Let's go, Marie-Michèle," Choupette called out.

Marie-Michèle had stayed by the window the entire time, not moving, with her back turned. Obviously, she didn't agree with the proceedings.

"Go on without me," she said through tight lips.

"Come on," Marie-Erna urged, "it'll be fun out there."

"No. I don't feel like it any more."

"Leave her alone," said Choupette, "we're going to have a ball without her."

"That's right, go ahead and have fun," said Marie-Michèle.

"Come on," Marie-Erna begged from the door.

"Don't worry about me. . . . I'm having my period."

"So what?"

"I just started, and I hate the smell of blood on me."

"Bye-bye," said Choupette drily.

The two girls went out, making the most of their departure. Papa followed behind.

"I'm sure she's got something going," Choupette said.

"That bitch!" Marie-Erna agreed.

The Buick pulled off in a cloud of dust. The beach was less than an hour away.

SCENE XXII: LA PETITE MORT

The gallop of the Antinea — M.S.-A.

A taxi pulled into the yard and a girl stepped out. She walked around the car to the driver's window. Instead of paying, she stroked his cheek. The man laughed and backed his car out of the yard. The entire notion of money was being challenged.

She knocked at the door. I opened it. Halfway.

"You're out of luck," I told her. "They've all gone to the beach."

She looked at me coolly, then slipped through the doorway.

"Who said I wanted to go to the beach?"

"Everybody else . . ."

Casually, she tossed her bag on the floor; she wasn't interested in my explanations.

"I just got the hell out of my place."

I've always dreamed of being able to make that declaration.

"Why?" I asked, after a minute.

She looked at me as if I were dumber than a cockroach. That wasn't the right question to ask. At times like this, you're better off talking about the weather.

"Do you know Miki?" she asked.

"I'm her neighbour. I live across the street."

With a girl like her, you couldn't make up just any old kind of story.

"I'm her cousin, Marie-Flore."

I'd seen her from my window. She must have been fourteen years old, and not a day more. From across the way, she looked older. I would have said sixteen.

"My mother's a slut."

Fighting words.

"Oh? Why's that?" I asked stupidly.

"Because she screws with that bastard."

"Who?"

She paused, but not for very long.

"My father."

"Oh, I see . . ."

"The bastard did everything he could to screw me."

This time, the pause was longer.

"Ever since I've been eight years old, every man wants to screw me. Funny, isn't it?"

I didn't know if it was funny or not. I looked at her and waited.

"You're like all the rest. That's all they care about. Though God only knows why."

There was rage in her heart as she considered me. Rage and courage.

"Do you know why?"

"No, I don't."

"You don't know?"

She flew into blind fury.

"What are you talking about?" I stammered.

"You don't know why every man wants to screw me?"

Suddenly she began taking off her clothes. She ripped open her blouse. Her breasts emerged into the open air like drowned men coming to the surface. She took a step closer. I retreated towards the sofa. She put her breasts in front of my face, where I could lick them. It was like having two .38s pointed at me. All she had to do was pull the trigger.

"Go ahead, tell me!" her voice boiled with anger.

I tried to avert my eyes and escape.

"How do you like my breasts?"

I didn't answer the question.

"Say it! Say you want to suck them!"

I didn't say it.

"That's all you want, right?"

"Leave me out of this."

Finally, I took my chances and stole a look. It was worse than I thought. The breasts of a virgin.

"I want to know what makes all of you so damn crazy."

I had no answer to that painful question. Just a hard-on as stiff as a poker. She lifted her skirt, took my hand and put it between her legs.

"What's that?"

"Your vagina."

"No," she told me. "It's your mother."

Good God! Fourteen years old, and she knows that already. But she wasn't through yet.

"What does your mother say?"

"I don't know."

Definitely, I didn't know very much today.

"My vagina says, *corruption!*"

"What?"

"*Corruption! Corruption! Corruption and more corruption!*"

She pushed me backwards. I fell onto my back. Down into hell. She was the angel of death. I lost consciousness. The room turned into an enormous, living uterus. I was being sucked up by the great womb. The medusa, the mother, the mucous membranes. The sea, the secretions. The great vulva. The bottom of the ocean. I swam against the current to escape. Everything was pulling me back into the belly. Fighting the waters. I saw a feeble glow at the end of the tunnel of flesh and secretions. I heard the great waterfall. I used my shoulders to wriggle free. Head first. I heard the water. I opened my eyes. A green shoe was sitting in the middle of the room. No one will ever know all the power contained in a green shoe, alone, in the middle of a room.

SCENE XXXVI: ON SHEETS OF SILK

Last lieder – M. S.-A.

The girls returned in a storm of laughter.

"Did you see the look on the driver's face when Choupette kissed him?" Marie-Erna said.

"I thought," Pasqualine answered, "that his eyes would pop out of his head."

"Did you really kiss him?" Miki asked.

"I've got no prejudices," Choupette told her. "I kiss who I want, when I want, where I want. And if I don't want to kiss someone, all the tea in China won't make me change my mind."

"I'm that way, too," Marie-Erna insisted.

"Ha! You," Choupette said, "a good meal will change your mind."

"In a restaurant of my choice, of course," Marie-Erna replied. Everyone dissolved in laughter.

"I'm not a whore," Marie-Erna announced. "I won't take a man's money."

"Tell it to the Marines," Choupette scoffed.

"It's true," Marie-Erna said. "Remember that guy who had loads of cash and wanted to open a bank account for me?"

"Sure, but you were too dumb back then," Choupette told her. "You were just fourteen."

"Don't insult me," Marie-Flore laughed. "I'm only fourteen."

"And you're dumb, too," Choupette said.

"It's simple as pie," Marie-Erna stated. "I don't want money. I only want what money can buy. Get it?"

"Actually, I don't," Miki admitted.

"The guy's got to take me out to eat at a good restaurant, then afterwards we go swimming in the pool at the Sans Souci, then we go dancing at a fancy discotheque, and if he wants to screw me, it has to be on silk sheets. Get the picture, Miki?"

"You're expensive, girl," Choupette told her.

"If the guy wants to save money, he should take his wife out."

"It all sounds good," Miki admitted, "but you have to pay somewhere."

"On sheets of silk," Choupette giggled.

"I don't understand you," Marie-Erna said. "I'd expect it from a chick fresh out of diapers, like Marie-Flore. Sex doesn't interest those guys, Miki, and you know it, so don't try to fool me. They just want to show off. I can't tell you how many times the guy's begged me to let him get a little sleep – on those silk sheets. They all want to be with a girl who has that tigress look. That way, it looks like they've got something between their legs. All I want is to live on a pedestal, like my mother used to say, every day of my life. He who lives like a rich man *is* a rich man – that's my motto."

"They're not all millionaires," Marie-Michèle pointed out.

"Of course they're not," Marie-Erna retorted. "But when one runs out of money, there's always another. There's no shortage of men who want to spend their money. Besides, I'm doing them a favour."

Marie-Erna began strutting around the room like a marquess, fanning herself with an imaginary fan.

"But in the end, there won't be anything left," Miki said seriously.

"What end?" Marie-Erna wanted to know.

"When you're not young any more."

"I'm not philosopher enough, Miki. Life'll take care of the rest."

"I used to think that way," said Miki, "but that was before I met Max."

"Of course," Marie-Erna agreed, "it's not the same thing. You hit the jackpot: a handsome guy, sexy, who probably knows how to fuck, who's rich and never even there. Everybody can't be lucky like you."

"If I were you, Miki," Choupette laughed, "I'd even consider being faithful."

"That's one luxury I can't afford," said Miki with a smile.

The girls burst out laughing.

"I was afraid you'd say the opposite," Choupette said, in the midst of a laughing fit. "That's my policy. I take it all: money, presents, fancy restaurants, hotel swimming pools, dresses, jewellery. I take it all, even things that don't belong to me. I don't give a shit about men. I plunder them, and that's it. I plunder the handsome ones, they're the easiest marks, the ugly ones drive a harder bargain, life hasn't been kind to them, but I plunder them in the end, too. I plunder the big ones and the little ones, the rich and the poor, the handicapped and the nice guys and the torturers. I ask only one thing of them, and that's to be a man. They can never hate me as much as I hate them. I am a plunderess!"

"Why do you hate them so much?" Marie-Michèle asked with fear in her voice.

"I suppose you love them?"

"I do. Well, maybe not . . . I don't know."

"I hate them for everything they put my mother through. My mother was a saintly woman, and they took advantage of her for all the years she was on this earth. Try to understand, Marie-Michèle. I spent my childhood watching her wait for a man who never showed up. She gave them everything, everything she had. Now I'm going to get it all back, with interest. Down to the last penny. It'll be a thirty-year mortgage."

"All men aren't that way."

"You think I give a shit? They should have been paying attention, those bastards, they should have watched their step instead of crushing that poor woman like a snail. My mother was a saint. She never had an evil thought, let alone did an evil deed. A real saint. Even when they stepped all over her face, she went on defending them, loving them, worshipping them. My mother worshipped men, they were her gods. They kicked her in the butt and she went on loving them. They don't know what love is. They're animals, and that's exactly the way I treat them."

"I didn't know you were such a romantic," Marie-Michèle said, her voice breaking.

"Go fuck yourself."

1992/1994

CECIL FOSTER

The Rum

Her eyes, dark and hurting from lack of sleep, focused tenaciously on the bottle as he tipped some of its reddish liquid into a transparent plastic container with no ice. Even without a word from her, Gerald knew what she was thinking, the same as what he, too, was pondering that moment. He placed the bottle with the rum in the centre of the table, on top of the unopened envelope with the Visa bill, right beside the half-full box of Corn Flakes, in front of the bowl with Olga's breakfast.

"So early?" she finally asked, not raising her eyes or head from her own bowl of cereal. Not sniffing this time. "Starting to drink so early?"

"Just a nip," Gerald mumbled apologetically, out of habit. "For the cold outside," he added, pointing his head in the direction of the back yard.

"Oh," she said with a tone suggesting she didn't buy his explanation. "Becoming like the old men at home, eh! Drinking so early in the morning and alone, too."

He didn't answer but watched as she almost absent-mindedly looked through the glass door into the back yard to where the bundles of snow were still piling up on the already high mounds. They had left smaller drifts before the Christmas vacation to go back home. Gerald thought he saw his wife shudder, if ever so imperceptibly. Obviously, more than the winter weather was on her mind, on her face. He knew it wasn't just her wish to protest that he was becoming so much like the men back home, people who had become so reliant on the alcohol, that he had seen two of them buried from sclerosis of the liver on this trip alone. But apart from the deaths and funerals, he felt like telling her, if only he could be so lucky to be like the old men at home: to be among friends; to drink rum and water in fellowship and comradeship; to be at home growing old, mellow and forgiving of the unexpected turns in life, but to be in the company of and sharing the spirituality of lifelong companions. To sit with trusted buddies and to argue, debate, or console one another. To reason it is perfectly understandable that in one lifetime nobody should ever attain all the dreams born in their youth. And to drink rum and water in peaceful acceptance. To smack their lips after each drink, to ritually wipe their mouths with the back of their hands in celebration of spirituality gained from aging gracefully and together.

Other matters were troubling her. The same things that were eating at him and which he, too, found so unspeakable. Why for years now, he and his wife could never really talk, except when exchanging a few civil commands, a result of simply having to share the same physical space and trying to get along somehow, or when swapping emotion-starved pleasantries. Except for the un-written rule of always making time and effort for any discussions, even if so formal and matter of fact, about the children. In this case, there was no need for words to explain the obvious. From the adjoining room, he heard the sounds of the three children redis-covering their toys after the three-week vacation, the noises ampli-fied by the nascent silence in the house. The sounds confirmed the kids were really back home and obviously happy to be back in a comfortably secure and familiar environment; happy, at least, until they, too, would have to fight their own battles.

Gerald wished he could be like them: innocent, naive, and so totally accepting that this hostile and so-difficult place in which he now lived was in fact home; that Olga could be like them, too.

Instead, he felt the heaviness of the psychological and emotional oppressiveness symbolized by the room's silence of their deep thoughts. And he smelled the mustiness so prevalent in a house and life in which nobody had lived for some time. Gerald could feel the same mustiness in his heart. The lingering taste of this distasteful odour in his mouth from when, on this trip back home, he was lulled into opening so many rooms in his heart. Chambers that had been closed for so long and the keys placed on some ledge with cobwebs.

Now, he was faced with the task, like a true Canadian boarding up his cottage for the winter after an enjoyable season, of hammering long spikes and nails into his heart to reclose all those rooms. The same doors and windows that, unlike those of the cottages, would not be reopened automatically with the inevitable arrival of the next summer's sun. His self-imposed shutters could only come down in the heat of the tropical sun. And until now he had believed that would happen only if he should allow those strong, revitalizing rays from back home to sting his skin and awaken him. If he should ever try to be at home again. If he should open the doors and windows to let in the streams of sun rays. If he would dare to allow the sun and the strong winds he knew as a boy to come in and drive out the mustiness, to make the rooms fresh and liveable, as it used to be in his dreams. But that was until now. Unfortunately, now he knows better. Sometimes it takes more than the strongest rays, more than even the tropical sun.

His eyes returned to the bottle of rum on the table, the same type of bottle he had seen in virtually every home over the Christmas and New Year's holidays in his native land. The same type of bottle his old friends, now mere acquaintances and fading further, and family worshipped. When they talked and rejoiced and tried to overcome the lost years that had put such a damper on every conversation. If not for the bottles, and their contents, he wondered, what would have saved the day when all other conversation pieces bombed so quickly, like a meteor trapped in the hostile Earth-atmosphere and forced to self-ignite, leaving only a stream of ashes and smoke?

And there were other bottles, too. Like the one on the counter, where Olga had put it only moments earlier. The bottle he is to take to his buddies at work. Everyone had asked him to bring back a bottle of rum for them, not knowing the importance he was now attaching to each bottle.

He was taking one forty-ounce bottle for the entire group. Maybe not much in terms of volume for so many, but certainly enough in terms of the kick from the alcoholic proof exceeding the 40-per-cent limit allowable for bottlers in Canada. And it would be so symbolic of all his thoughts and hopes, withering so fast even 150-per-cent-proof alcohol could not preserve them.

Gerald looked at the bottle on the counter. Its very presence was telling him something. No matter how long he put it off, eventually he would have to get up, take the bottle, place it in his bag, and head out into the cold. But before that, he would have his drink, even if it was so early in the morning. For it was already very late in the day, too.

He could never accept the deep, heart-wrenching uneasiness of knowing he was firmly caught between two cultures. Perhaps, for the rest of his life, he would find himself in the awkward position of never really feeling welcomed in this country. And of now knowing he could not return to the home in his past. It was not as easy as reading a book and facing the option of going on to a new page and its unknown challenges or turning back to read what he already knew and liked. He could not return home. And yet, he was not at home in Toronto.

In the past ten years, he had gone back to the Caribbean island three times. The first was just after one year in Canada, when the home fires were burning strongest in his heart. He simply had to rush back to quench them, if only to prove to everyone at home he was successfully adapting and settling in a new country.

That was perhaps mistake number one: of dashing home when he had not really adjusted. He had unreasonably set up the expectations at home that he was doing well. He made them feel he could only continue to climb the ladder of success. The same expectations that had later forced him not to be honest with himself or others. Especially when he felt like pleading for those that remained behind to understand the alienation and separation he was experiencing. When he felt like confessing to them experiences they would not want to endure if they knew the truth.

But the first year is always so deceptive for an immigrant and the host country, like two boxers elusively feeling out each other in the first round before launching the later onslaught. Hence, it took him another three years before he was on his feet, financially and mentally, after the early knockdowns, three years for Olga, on whom he was totally dependent, to save enough money for them to make the trip back home, this time looking less pretentious and certainly not bragging of success as much as before. That was why it took another six years before he could screw up the courage to go back. Every time, going home was tougher than the previous. Every time, he had to face up to how much he was losing, how he had aged and slowed. How he had lost touch with the people he really knew and loved. How he had failed to cement any genuinely long-lasting relationships in the new country. If only the folks at home knew he was too busy surviving and adjusting to be concerned with making friends. If only someone had told them that, in any case, Canadians, so unlike the people back home, were basically cold and unfriendly. If only his folks knew how lonely and scared he was.

On this last trip, he had visited the homes of friends, people who used to be friends, close friends. The same people with whom he used to laugh and cry, scheme and brag, fight and compete. But this time his visits were only to discover there was now nothing to talk about. Awkward conversations simmered around events ten or fifteen years ago, which thousands of miles away in Toronto were so fresh in his mind, but when discussed back there seemed so tame and stupid he wondered why he even remembered them. From the look on the faces of his hosts, he could tell they felt the same way.

They, too, were gladly attempting to cross the gulf separating them. Time, distance, and different experiences had made the chasm too deep and the current too strong.

That was when they sought refuge in the rum bottle and its effects. When they pretended they still had something in common, that they were still friends, perhaps showing their first signs of growing old, like the people in the hospital Olga talked about, those with the faulty memories capable of recalling minute details of a generation earlier but unable to say what they had had for the last meal. It was almost like nothing worthwhile had happened since he left the shores. And yet, time did not stand still, except for the memories of people, places, and things frozen in his mind.

He did not have to suffer through this painful experience alone. He saw how the same reactions took hold of Olga. How when she was with her best friend there was nothing to really talk about after they had quickly exhausted the nervous laughter, the ritualistic praises for having such big children, and the comments of how time had been kind to them and had flown so quickly from when they had been young women.

And the children, absolute strangers among their closest relatives, among their very blood. He recalled the three of them standing so stiffly, hands behind their backs or nervously cleaning their nails or their arms hanging loosely at their sides, in front of these perfect strangers claiming to be their Grandma and Grandpa. Knowing they shouldn't be afraid of these people mommy and daddy had talked so much about and claimed to love so much, as much as they loved their own mommy and daddy, feeling they should similarly love these people and be thankful to them for giving them a mommy and daddy. The children forcing the smiles, answering in one-syllable words and obviously wishing someone would rescue them, until mommy or daddy stepped in with some inane statement for the children to tell Grandma and Grandpa about school, or about their bicycle or some such thing.

The children's stiffness changed after the first couple of meetings, after the children had talked to the strangers for a while, but never disappeared totally. No matter what, these Canadian-born children always looked and acted out of place on the island, particularly in the company of their relatives. They did not look natural or at ease playing with all the other kids who introduced themselves as cousins and nephews. Who prompted them to say anything so they could hear the foreign accent, so they could laugh and giggle, even while some of them set traps for the unsuspecting visitors. He and Olga could never relax. They always had to be on the look-out to protect these trusting, foreign-born kids. And when they played, the Canadian-born members of the family had no idea what they were doing, had to be taught by kids many years their junior, had to be told that, in cricket, a batter is set up differently from when playing baseball, and that the batter did not have to run even if he hit a fair ball. No, these kids were better off back in Canada, hopefully a place they would call home. For they had no other place to call such, even if, because of their parents, they automatically qualified for citizenship elsewhere. This was no vacation for the individual members of this Canadian family, not with all that stress.

Gerald looked across at Olga. She didn't have to say anything for him to know how she felt: how she wasn't looking forward to cleaning those bed pans at the hospital; how she wished she could somehow step from one culture into another as easily as she put aside the tropical swimsuit for the heavy winter coat.

When they came to Canada, she had bigger dreams than to be just a nursing aide. She wanted to be more, to make some money and to go back home, and enjoy a better life. But the pieces never came together. Perhaps they married too soon. Before they really got to know and understand each other. Or, they should have waited longer before having children. Maybe it was his fault he didn't find a proper job soon enough. So that, because of him, Olga couldn't afford to quit her job to go to nursing school and get her RN. She could not get the status and money, as she had planned. Maybe it was none of these things individually, but all of them conspiring. So many things had gone wrong, had not jelled as planned, and as immigrants they had no choice, no money, and no control of their future.

Gerald thought of these things and how, as recent as on this trip, he had reassured his cousins and friends who had asked how he could help them to get to Canada. And he had felt like asking why they wanted to give up everything so precious, to cut all those ties, simply to become a stranger in a strange land. He felt like asking them to look at him, a man forty-two years old. He wanted to ask them to read between the lines of every boast from his lips. A foreigner with no real friends, no links to his youth or his history. A man whose children would grow up in a hostile land. They would have only some vague notions of having other relatives somewhere over the ocean, but knowing that he and Olga would be the only family and friends for them. These children were entitled to so much more than what he and Olga could offer.

But he couldn't. He couldn't destroy the myths, couldn't destroy any legitimacy he still had. He couldn't face the possibility of confronting the painful questions of why he didn't want others to live in this Promised Land, too. Of why so selfishly he didn't want others to have the same opportunities as he, to take chances just as he had. There were no honest answers to these questions, or to truthfully ask, is it better to live poor among lifelong friends and common traditions or to be lonely, badly in debt, in a new land?

Olga had her answers, that like him, she wouldn't share with anyone, not even Gerald. But after twelve years of marriage, a time when their bonds were truly tested so at times divorce seemed so attractive, he knew her. He knew how she felt when, as soon as the aircraft lifted into the air on the return trip, the tears rolled out the sides of her eyes. The way she folded her bottom lip so tightly and bit into it, the way she cried so silently all the way to Toronto, all the time being an attentive mother pretending not to cry, not to show hurt. The way only mothers know how to hide these things from children.

He knew it so well from all the years with her. From the way she squeezed his hand as if to say that despite their mutual misgivings they had only each other and the kids; that she needed to draw strength from him and she would give him what she could. That the next time they returned to this place of their birth, the situation might be worse – they would be even more alienated. Their children, grown older, wouldn't even want to go back to see the old houses where mommy and daddy lived as kids. Not when they can go camping among the mosquitoes and black flies in the various parts of Canada in which their parents won't be caught dead. Or when they drive across North America with their friends, or . . . when they do all those things that Canadians do as rites of passage. And it wouldn't be any better for them in the country of their children's birth. As parents and foreigners in what should now be their home, they would be growing old, alone and by themselves. Life for Olga and Gerald would not be what they had hoped. They would not become what they thought they wanted when they were as young as their children, when their parents back home had started teaching them how to dream. They would be old, alone, and failures. What else was there to look forward to? Gerald understood why she cried. Why as soon as the flight attendants wheeled the trolley with the drinks down the aisle of the aircraft, he ordered two big rum and cokes, with generous helpings of the rum. One of the drinks was supposedly for Olga, even though he knew she would not touch it. By the time they nodded off in the darkness over the Atlantic Ocean – when the lights inside the aircraft had dimmed so softly and peacefully, the only noises of people snoring or occasionally coughing, of the plane hurtling through the air and time – the flight attendants had refilled the two glasses three times. Olga had started to get distant from him and to murmur something about his trying to drink the airplane out of all the rum on board. Maybe she still didn't understand. Not quite. Perhaps that was what was wrong with their relationship – just like what was wrong with their dreams in Canada. They were unsuited for each other. They were drags on each other; one holding back the other. One never really helping to propel the other mate to higher levels of satisfaction, if to any satisfaction at all. Neither of them strong enough to give up on the other. To accept failure and to try starting all over again. So they compromise. They settle for less and what few comforts they had. They make the best of what they have and silently wonder, if they had a chance to live their lives over again, would they inflict themselves on each other? Or would they have the good sense to recognize that no matter how much they are attracted to each other, they are unsuited and would end up dissatisfying each other.

Just like Canada: the same way that as youths they had felt that mutual attraction; the same way they had felt as young, bright people that there was a future with each other. Now, at the point of midlife crisis, they realize how such early promises had long ago dried up. It was almost as if it had happened when they were not even looking. The same way that Canada had turned so sour for so many immigrants like them. For as they headed back to what should have been their home, why did something tingle in them and make them wish the plane was headed in the opposite direction, although they knew that, too, would not be a solution? So that secretly they wished they were in a plane stuck in a vortex, hoping neither to go back nor to go forward. Hoping to keep spinning over the Atlantic, just stuck animatedly, going nowhere. So he kept reaching for the glasses: for if this plane could not spin and remain suspended, maybe he could. Maybe his head could become light. He could airily drift off, spinning, spinning, and going nowhere. So that when he got home, he was still spinning, even when he got into the cold bed and inhaled deeply the mustiness of being away.

Gerald had heard Olga groan in her sleep throughout the night. He knew it wasn't only from the cold, for the heater laboured to warm up the house after three weeks of bitter cold. They had switched off the heating to save money they had needed to pay for the holiday, to the bank for the Visa card. But it wasn't the cold in the room that caused her to cling to him and forced him to be strong, or to at least appear to be strong. Women had it so easy, they could cry and show their feelings. A man had to put up a brave face. Especially a macho Caribbean man. A man so macho that he dared not run away from everything; he dared not to be free, for fear others, especially ignorant people back home, laughed at him.

Gerald looked into the glass and swished the rum around the inside. His eyes dropped on the unopened envelope with the Visa bill he would be taking to work. They had not bothered opening it, had just picked it out of the Christmas cards. They didn't need to look at an itemized bill to be shocked: they had known before they left for Barbados the damages that would result from purchasing all those clothes, gifts, food, and whatever they felt the others at home wanted. The previous year's tax refund, with which they had planned this trip, didn't nearly cover all the bills, not even the airline tickets for five travelling at the peak Christmas period. Such was the reality beyond the alluring grip of the rum.

"Do you have on your boots yet?" Olga shouted at the children. For a moment it was hard for Gerald to be sure whether she was a bit angry or just jaded and already acting mechanically. "I don't want you getting to school late the very first day back."

"Maybe we shouldn't have cut it so fine, coming back only the night before school," he said.

"Maybe we shouldn't be doing a lot of different and stupid *things*," she responded. "And not so early in the damn morning."

Gerald looked at the brown liquid in the glass. She was both angry and jaded. And yes, he knew it was too early to start drinking. But what's the use of arguing, or even agreeing with her? They knew the ways of the world and the repercussions. His bosses might smell the alcohol on his breath and disapprove – or worse. Only the alcoholics at home started so early and took as a trade-off the funerals and alcoholism. Maybe he had become alcoholic in three weeks. The trade-off: his job?

He put the glass on the table and stretched out his legs. The clock on the side wall was ticking loudly. Time was getting away. They'd be late for school, for back at the office, for the hospital. They'd be late for colleagues to ask them what good times they had had at home, to talk about pictures to be printed, about the rum, and the inevitable, teasing question about why they had even bothered coming back to this Godforsaken country so bitterly cold in the winter. They'd be late all right and, perhaps, were it not for the children, he and Olga would prefer to be even later to avoid these questions. For, ironically, only the children would be free to tell their schoolmates the real truth, the full truth. They would not have to pretend. They could say they prefer to be back in Toronto. Or, should they really feel that way, they could admit they had enjoyed the Christmas respite, the brief reprieve in the islands. They could do and say whatever they wished and felt. They were young, free, and at home. No obvious compromises, no trade-offs.

Outside, the snow was falling heavier. The car in the garage would be cold and might not even start. Gerald felt old. The rum, perhaps because of the small sips, wasn't even stinging his mouth any more. At least it caused him to belch, reminding him that he should take a cup of coffee to break the overnight gas in his stomach. After all, he should not rely on the rum for everything; the same way he should not have expected so much from Olga; the same way he should not have wanted so much from Canada.

Across from him, Olga was just as tense, not prepared to face the world outside. The look on her face, the sloping shoulders, told him the truth. And he knew her well enough to just read her body language. So that they didn't need to talk. So that he only had to hear her sniffing loudly at the fumes of the rum escaping from his nose. Instantly, he would know that at any moment she would be brassing him up for drinking too much, for drinking so early. Except, that at this moment she wasn't sniffing, just sighing and sitting, hunched over the cereal bowl. Gerald's eyes shifted to the bottle of rum on the counter, the one for his friends at the office. He had to think. Perhaps for the first time, he felt he should say something to his wife. Mentally, she seemed to be willing him to show the strength to make a move. So they would all follow. So they wouldn't jeopardize their jobs by seeking refuge in this house, by becoming recluses, by being permanently transfixed in some twilight zone between these two cultures. She wanted him to go out and just clear the driveway of three weeks of snow and to start the engine, warming the interior of the car for his family, just like any other working day. Just like a father and husband who dared not shirk his responsibilities.

"Mom, we got to go," the voice called. Olga and Gerald looked in the direction of the family room, the look on their faces appearing to ask if, from now on, this was from whom and where they would have to draw their strength and inspiration. From now on, the people who would start talking for them. "It's getting late and I want to give my gift to the teacher before class starts. Otherwise, she might ask me to give a report for show and tell and I wouldn't know what to say, except that the sun was so hot, the food different, and the mosquitoes kept biting me at night."

Olga put down the spoon which had been suspended in the air over the bowl as they had listened to the voice. She glanced up at Gerald, who had automatically picked up his glass again, with more urgency swirling the contents under his nose, as if sniffing it. As if he dared not delay acting on an important command, he quickly put the glass to his lips. Taking the opportunity, he made it appear not so obvious that he knew Olga was silently crying again. The tears oozed out of her eyes. She wiped them away. At the same time, Gerald gulped down the rum and wiped his lips clean with the back of his hand – just like the old men back home over all the years.

"Let's go," Olga said. Quickly, she was her old self, the one from whom he drew so much. The same person who, resolutely, went through the doors to the outside knowing her only chore for eight unrelenting hours would be to face those filthy bed pans. "Let's go."

Gerald gulped another grog, a bigger one. It burned. His mouth, his throat, his stomach, everything – all the way down to his guts. Even his eyes. The liquor went down like deceptively sweet fire. The sting was so great, he squeezed shut his eyes and blinked several times to clear them of whatever was causing his vision to blur. Olga carefully put on her coat. She turned to face him. As if reading his mind, to know how much he needed it, she gently reached out and squeezed his hand. Then, she handed him the keys to the car.

"Let's go," she repeated softly. In some way, he knew she was freer than him. She didn't have to pretend that it was only the rum causing him to blink so much. She didn't have to hide from the truth. She had cried openly at the funerals and at the trade-offs and was at peace with herself. Olga knew they were back in Canada, probably for good. She was getting ready to accept this outcome. But not Gerald. As a man, he would not, could not, accept this fate. "The kids are waiting. Let's go."

1997

MAKEDA SILVERA

No Beating Like Dis One

"No beating like dis one, a sorry fi yuh!" My cousin, Elithia, taunt-
ing me as I waited for Auntie Maggie to get dressed to deliver me
personally to Mama. She was taking no chance in sending a note
with me. No, this news was too important, too juicy, to give me to
deliver. Auntie Maggie wanted to be there to dramatise, to show
me up like some piece of dutty cloth.

I spent two weekends out of every month at Auntie Maggie's
house. I can't say I enjoyed them very much, except for the company of Winnifred, my other cousin, who also spent weekends with
Auntie Maggie. Her house was larger and had more rooms than our
two houses combined. And there was Lloydie. He was thirteen
years old and lived next door with his mother in a rented room.

Auntie Maggie's daughter, Elithia, was nine. She was short and
chubby, with equally short, stubby hair parted in countless plaits.
She hated them, especially the way Auntie Maggie always tied
pieces of ribbons at the end. Whenever Auntie Maggie was out of
earshot we would chant, "Picky-picky head, go buy new head."

Friday and Saturday evenings we would play games. I was not
very good at marbles, but I loved to watch Winnifred play with
Lloydie. Winnifred was good. We played hopscotch and jacks, but

my favourites were baseball and dandy-shandy. Elithia liked these two games best. I was always eager to include Elithia, because she wasn't a good player and I would drive the ball into her back or belly, laughing wickedly when she bent over in pain.

Elithia was Auntie Maggie's only daughter. Her mouth was as big and loud as a petchary bird and she loved to take news to Auntie Maggie. If we excluded her from a game, she would threaten to tell Auntie Maggie about something that happened weeks ago that the rest of us had long forgotten. We would then be banned from playing with Lloydie or from sitting on the verandah in the evenings.

"No beating like dis one." Elithia's mean voice sing-songing behind my ears. I tried not to cry, not because I was thinking about the beating I would get when I got home, but because I couldn't hit blabbermouth Elithia right where she deserved it. I couldn't even promise her, Auntie Maggie was right beside me. "Come we ready, mek we go."

I burned with embarrassment. I would have to take the bus with Auntie Maggie. Auntie Maggie was fat. Very fat. The few times I'd ridden the bus with Auntie Maggie she'd used up all of two seats. Everyone would stare at us. I loved Auntie Maggie, despite her exaggerated accounts of what I did. I just didn't like taking the bus with her. And today Uncle Blue, her husband, was not around to take us in his car.

I reached the bus stop with Auntie Maggie, with Elithia's soppy voice still singing in my ear. "No beating like dis one. No beating like dis one."

I remembered the last time I got a beating. . . .

Congregational Hall School was about six miles from home, in downtown Kingston and close to the higglers and their guava cheese and grater cakes. We would spend our bus fare on sweets and then beg from people at the bus stop. Who could resist, "Come buy piece a guava cheese, only trupence!" "Nice girl wid de pretty ribbon, greater cake fi only a treepence. And dem fresh!" "Paradise plums fi sale. Pretty girl wid de nice hair – over here!"

Almost every evening I spent my bus fare on one of those tempting sweets. After sucking the last taste from my tongue, I would set out to get threepence to get me home on the bus. Two days a week I also visited my father at his barbershop on East Queen Street, not far from Parade Station. Papa rarely came to our avenue and he was always glad to see me. He would greet me with a big hug and boast to his customers, "Yes man, dis is my daughter from my second marriage. Four from de first marriage and two little outside one. And dem all look like me."

The customers in turn would express their admiration. Then my father would give me an ice cream cone or sometimes bun and cheese. After eating, I would ask for threepence to pay my bus fare. I had to be careful about this because he was always quick to blame Mama. "She didn't give yuh enough fi yuh bus fare? I'll have to come up dat avenue and have a good talk wid her." When Papa was in that mood I would say goodbye and head for Parade Station.

Mama knew I visited him sometimes but certainly not as often as twice a week. If she'd known I visited him to beg bus fare, she would have beat the living daylights out of me. It happened before: "From de day dat man walk out, he never even try to find out if ah have nuff to feed you. Never ask about money fi school uniform and yuh gone to beg him trupence, gal?"

"Please m'am, beg yuh a trupence to tek de bus home." Or "Good evening, mama. Beg yuh a bus fare please?" Sorrowful and lost.

The lady would ask, "What 'appen to yuh money?" And I would whimper, "Ah lost it, m'am," or "Someone tek it out of my school bag, m'am." If it seemed she was undecided, I would continue, "What time is it, m'am? Jesus! Ah didn't know it was so late! Ah should have been home to pick up my little sister, poor ting. She must be still out at de piazza hungry and waiting fi me."

I was a loner at this and if I came down to Parade with a friend from school, we would be very careful to do our begging in separate directions. Some days I would get the threepence on my first try. Some days it took a long time to get the money or I would only get twopence. Those evenings I walked home, always following the bus route, the long way home, but the only one I knew. Walk up Parade, past the big Coronation Market, on to Spanish Town Road, past deserted and burned-down buildings, past shacks, burial grounds, madman, madwoman, children in tear-up clothes, on to Waltham Park Road, then finally Chisholm Avenue, and then the turn onto our little avenue.

The day I got the beating of my life was a Friday evening. I begged and begged at Parade but couldn't come up with three-pence. I decided not to go to Papa, afraid he would accompany me home. That Friday I begged for hours. When the last lady I tried told me it was six o'clock I knew it was time to start walking home. I began the long walk, munching on my guava cheese and thinking about what excuse to give Mama for being so late.

Mama greeted me at the gate, "Weh yuh deh since school let out?" As I opened my mouth to answer, her right hand came down on my face. I fell on the ground, then got to my feet quick and ran to the shed in the back of the yard. Mama sat waiting on the veran-dah. It was dark by then and I was hungry and frightened. Why didn't she call me or shout at me? I tried to slip by her into the house. Tamarind switch came down on my back and Mama gripped the collar of my blouse.

"Yuh won't stop eat off yuh bus fare? Yuh won't stop beg 'pon street? Yuh love call down disgrace 'pon me? Tek dis."

The tamarind switch danced all over my back. I was shaking and screaming. The next-door neighbours opened their windows to hear better. Some came to the fence to get a better look. Mama didn't let up. "Yuh want to call down de whole avenue?"

"No, Mama."

"Well shut yuh mout. Yuh no have no shame, gal?"

Throughout all the talking, Mama did not miss a beat. My back was the African drum she never knew. I continued to scream, yell-ing for the police. This was a sign of disrespect. "Is show yuh want to show me up, gal? Is scandal yuh want to call down on de yard?"

I don't remember when it ended. What stayed with me for a long time were the welts and cuts on my back and behind. It was a long, long time before I begged at Parade again.

Auntie Maggie and I sat at the very back of the bus. "When ah done tell Lulu what yuh going on wid, yuh going to be sorry! What dat yuh doing at your age, eh? Eleven years old and yuh looking man already!"

The whole bus-load of people turned round to look at me. Auntie Maggie had a full house for the dress rehearsal and when we got home she would give a perfect performance.

Soon the entire bus was taking part. "Yuh have to watch dem pickney nowadays. Dem get big before dem time," a red, freckle-faced woman offered.

Another nudged the young girl seated next to her, "Yuh hear dat? Yuh watch yuh step. Cause anyhow yuh do a ting like dat, a bruk yuh foot."

An old woman announced, "She need a good beating."

From the front a hard-faced woman was quick to add, "Yuh have to stop dem tings before dem reach higher proportion. 'Fore yuh know it, she bring in belly." They talked around me like flies swarming a plate of food.

People got off the bus, new people came on. Auntie Maggie continued her recitation and the new people on the bus took up the chorus.

"Yes m'am, me know a girl who start out jus' like dat, de same womanish style. She now sixteen and is tree pickney she have fi tree different man."

"She start see her menstruation, yet?" a tall man with glasses asked.

"No not yet. Ah tekking her home to talk to my sister. Mek sure she get a real beating." One man in the bus eyed me up and down.

By now I was crying. The voices went on. "And look 'pon her eye. See how dem bright. Yuh can tell she bad."

More agreement. "Yes, especially when dem start fi cry, dat is a sure sign of badness." Another time I hadn't cried and the public complaint was that I was dried-eyed and womanish.

I had everyone's attention. Nobody was paying attention to Auntie Maggie's size. Even I forgot that Auntie Maggie took up two entire seats at the back of the bus.

"Chisholm Avenue," the conductress called out. Auntie Maggie said goodbye to the crowd and pushed me to the front. Everybody I knew was on the street that evening. I put on my don't-talk-to-me face as I passed my friends, but that didn't help.

"What 'appen?"

"How come yuh Auntie holding on to yuh so tight?"

"Yuh going to get a beating?"

"Yuh coming to Tony birthday party tomorrow?"

Auntie Maggie didn't miss that. "She not coming to nobody party. De only party she going to is de one in her bed. Yuh wait till ah tell her mother what a good-for-nutting daughter she have. She won't see de light of de day fi de rest of her life."

"What she do, m'am?" a fat, round-faced girl named Joy asked. My heart jumping all over my chest and sweat covering my face, I waited for Auntie Maggie to go on and on as she had in the bus, but she didn't seem to hear Joy's question.

"Yuh wait till yuh go home and Lulu hear about your carrying on. All dis shame a little pickney like yuh bring down on yuh mother. Want to turn big 'oman before yuh time."

What would it be? Worse than the Parade beating? Mama's heavy hands? The tamarind switch?

Joy, Tony, Babes, Petal, Rowan, Glory and two boys I didn't know were now trailing behind us. A tall, heavy-set boy joined the procession. It was Joy's older brother, singing, "Fatty walking down de road with a skinny girl in hand. Little girl, where yuh going to run to, oh yeah."

Auntie Maggie stopped to give him a big cut eye. He added more verses and followed us straight to the gate of my yard. Auntie

Maggie, grabbing on to my wrist, commanded me to walk faster. When I protested, "Auntie, ah walking as fast as ah can," she gave me one cuff on my forehead and told me not to backtalk.

The procession laughed and danced behind us. Joy's brother added new verses. Auntie Maggie's face was purpling up. Despite her fingernails digging into my wrist, I had to bite my lips not to laugh.

"Girl, yuh auntie fat, eh. Hey mama, what should ah eat to have a nice round figure like yuh, mama?" The others laughed and applauded.

Auntie turned on me, "Is where yuh know dem hooligans from?" With this she let go of my wrist to twist my right ear until I was sure she'd torn it off. I was beyond shame. I screamed and cried and I didn't care who saw me.

By the time we turned off Chisholm and onto my avenue the crowd had doubled. I no longer cared about any beating. So what if Mama tied me up with a rope against the tamarind tree and beat me till the next day?

Mama was sitting on the verandah, reading the newspaper when we reached the house. Auntie Maggie pushed me forward, stopping to latch the gate behind her. Part of the crowd waited at the gate, others ran next door to Joy's yard.

"Lulu, dis girl of yours going to mek yuh shame before she turn thirteen, yuh nuh. Ah don't know what yuh going to do with her."

Mama picked up her knitting. I stood in front of them, my knees wobbling.

"Sit down." Mama motioned to me.

"Is dese tings mek her tink she is a big woman, yuh know. Yuh should let her stand still until we finish talking."

Mama ignored Auntie Maggie and told her to start at the beginning.

"Lulu, ah don't even know where to start. Ah know yuh going to shame, my dear sister, but dis girl of yours don't have any of dat. Ah in de backyard dis morning washing clothes and beg her to go buy some soapsud at de shop fi me. Ah wait and ah wait and she don't come back. Anyway, ah give her de benefit of de doubt. Yuh know dat is Saturday and de line-up at de shop long. Winnifred and Freddy was inside dusting de furniture, so ah send little Elithia to put her head out de gate and look if she see dis one coming."

With this Auntie Maggie paused, took out her handkerchief, wiped her big round face. "Girl, go and get me a glass of water. Put nuff ice in it." She stopped the story while I went to get her ice water.

"Well, little Elithia come go out to de gate and look up and down de road and no sight of dis one. She come and tell me dis. Ah wait a while longer and ah worried now, so ah send her back to look again. When she come back, ah say to her, 'Elithia, go cross de road and knock on Lloydie mother gate and find out if dey see her.'"

Auntie Maggie stopped to fan her face with a piece of Mama's newspaper and continued, "Lulu, ah hear de gate bang loud and say, 'What 'appen, Elithia?' Not a word come from de little girl mout."

Auntie Maggie got up, stretched her legs and commented on the tree laden with ackees. "As ah was saying, Lulu, not a word from Elithia mout. So ah say to her, 'Yuh find her?' and she say, 'Yes, Mommy.' Ah say, 'Where?' and she say, 'She and Lloydie on Lloydie mother verandah.'"

Auntie Maggie stopped again. By now I was getting tired of the story, tired of Auntie Maggie. I felt like grabbing the story out her mouth and telling it myself, getting my beating and going to bed.

Mama kept knitting. I couldn't read her face. Waiting for Mama to say something, Auntie Maggie took a sip of water and wiped her face again with her handkerchief.

Mama looked up. "Maggie, ah don't know de story so tell me what 'appen. It must be important if yuh tek bus all de way here to tell me."

Auntie Maggie got up from her chair and, arms akimbo, looked at me and then at Mama. "Sister, ah don't know what yuh going to do wid girl."

"Maggie, yuh already say dat. Continue with de story," Mama cut in, this time a slight edge to her voice.

Auntie Maggie ignored that and went on, "By de time she catch twelve is living trouble yuh going to have on yuh hand. Dis girl is a risk. When she start to menstruate yuh will have to keep her tie up to avoid shame an disgrace on dis avenue."

Mama kept knitting, looking directly at the centrepiece she was working on for the dining table. The zinc fence separating our yard from Joy's sagged with people waiting to hear what Auntie Maggie would say next.

"Well, me sister. Elithia went over de yard and when she see what she see on de verandah she run and come tell me. She didn't let dis one know she see her."

"Maggie, me daughter have a name. Use it. She don't name 'Dis One.'"

"Lord, it hot." Auntie Maggie fanned the air viciously. "When Elithia tell me what she see ah couldn't believe it. Ah nearly box her mout, but ah know my Elithia don't tell lies, and she wouldn't mek up someting like dat. She don't have dat dirtiness in her mind to tink up dose kind of ting.

"Jesus, it hot," she went on to no one in particular. "Ah hope it rain. We need it, everyting so dry."

I thought the fence was about to fall as people jostled for a better view. "Yuh ackee tree full, eh Lulu," Auntie Maggie said. "A wouldn't mind a dozen or so to tek home. B really like ackee. Your yard really blessed, all dese fruitful trees. Ah have a big yard and. . . ."

Mama cut in, "Ah just pick a few dozens off de tree dis morning. Yuh can tek dem home with yuh."

"God bless you, Lulu. Now where was I in de story? Oh yes. Little Elithia carry me to de spot on de verandah where she and Lloydie was. When ah come and look ah frighten. As dere is a heaven and a God, Lulu, ah never know dis girl so ripe, so womanish."

Auntie Maggie stopped her account and kicked off her shoes. The smell from her feet was overpowering, but she didn't seem to notice and Mama didn't comment. I tried to breathe through my mouth.

"Yes, Lulu, as ah was saying, when ah see dem it was a sight dat would mek even Satan blush." She got up and spit in one of the flowerpots on the verandah. I looked at Mama. Mama's face was the same. The only response was more shuffling against the zinc fence.

"Lulu, when ah tiptoe and look on de verandah, on de cold concrete, ah see dis shameface girl lie down and dutty right on top of her. Her skirt lift high over her face." Auntie Maggie looked at Mama in amazement.

Mama was still knitting. She hadn't said a word. "Wait, Lulu, yuh don't hear what ah just say to you. Dutty bwoy Lloydie was laying down on top of dis one, in de broad daylight on de verandah, on de cold concrete tiles."

The zinc fence swayed back and forth.

Finally Mama spoke. "So dem was naked?"

Auntie Maggie looked at her in disbelief. "Yuh wasn't listening to me, Lulu? Ah say her frock was over her head. Him still had him pants and shoes on, but de fact of de matter is dat dem know what dem was doing. And who knows, if ah didn't catch dem in time, dey would be stark naked.

"Is no example fi little Elithia, yuh know. Dis chile is evil and is no good fi a girl chile to be growing up with so much woman-ness in her already."

"Well," said Mama, "Ah going to mek sure she don't corrupt Elithia any more."

"How dat?" Auntie Maggie asked, totally confused.

"Ah won't send her around any more."

Mama motioned to me to go have a bath. It was almost night though the sun was still out. I didn't hear any more of the conversation and Auntie Maggie finally left with her ackees.

I sat in my bath wondering what would it be? A piece of wire from the electric light pole? The big leather belt that hung behind the bedroom door? Mama called "come eat." I finished everything on my plate.

Mama spoke again, "Clean your teeth when yuh finish eat, come kiss mi goodnight and say yuh prayers before yuh go to bed."

The sun was slowly going to sleep.

1991

Old Habits Die Hard

Old man, skin scaly tree bark to touch. Rust eyes, water hazy. The iron is gone. Legs, arms, ready kindling. Bedbug. Bedridden. Bedlam. Bedpan. Bedraggled. Bedfast.

Faeces don't give ear to him any more. Old man in diapers. Old man in white gown. Mashed potatoes with milk is all he can eat. Old man needs steady hand to feed him. Out of habit, old woman folds clean, neatly ironed pyjamas. Clean towel. Wash rag. Enamel carrier filled with mashed potatoes.

Disordered eyes. Looks past visitors. Old man recollects just one, old woman. The others bear no memory. Disappointed, you can see it on their faces, the tight turn of the lips, the begging in the eyes. Talk to us. Touch us. Remember us. He only sits, no teeth to his grin. Old man looks and looks. Memory escapes. No longer father, husband, grandfather, uncle, brother, friend.

Old man pulls towards old woman. Grab him, he'll shit, piss on the floors, run around like a madman, a bedlamite. The visitors approve of the restraint. We love him, they say. Old man wants to run, old man wants to go home. The visitors go. Room too depressing: some stringy flowers in a mug, a plastic balloon the only grace, a heavy curtain shuts out the light.

Old woman stays behind. She feeds him potatoes, eggs, milk through a straw. She talks to him. He cannot answer. She tells him things, answers for him. His hands are cool. She pulls the blankets closer to his body. His face sweet like dark plums. Time to leave. Keepers in white come to lead her out. She kisses old man. Water in his eyes. He stares. He stares. Night is a black sheet. Old man pass away, old man dead, old man gone. She had felt it. Hands cool, getting cold, heat leaving the face, purple turning black, eyes turning.

The mourners come, eat, sing, cry, drink, help to bury him. They go home. Old woman must bury him a second time: clothes to give away – Salvation Army, Goodwill; mattress to turn over; bank account to settle; pension to straighten out. One pot to cook, one mouth to feed. Out of habit, old woman does the wash, folds her nightgown. She always irons it. Washes towels, washes rags, folds them. Those go into the suitcase. Changes her bed sheets. Best pillowcase; lovely lace, that. Lies down. Pulls up the black sheet of night.

1994

PAUL TIYAMBE ZELEZA

The Rocking Chair

Everything about him was frail and haggard. His body was bent like a hunchback, and his twitching face was a collection of sagging skin. His legs and arms were wobbly. His eyesight was failing. But he still had good hearing. He would sit in his rocking chair watching and listening to the outside world as it moved along in its cold, uncaring, and superficial ways.

The chair was all he had. It was a true friend. Predictable and undemanding. It never complained, moved, or got tired. It was always there, squeaking in autumn, squealing in winter, creaking in spring, and crackling in summer. It comforted and kept him company without expecting anything in return. It accepted him unconditionally.

It was probably as old as he was, although he could not be sure, for he did not remember his age. The varnish had long peeled off, exposing the original grains of the wood, now stretched out in dull, irregular strokes, spirals, and circles. The seat was made of leather straps and covered by a cushion padded with feathers. He knew every part of the chair, its texture, veins, and pimples, better than the back of his own hand.

He called it Magdalene. Every morning and before retiring he would dust her inch by inch with a tattered black cloth that had once been felt and white, while singing a medley of half-forgotten hymns, ballads, and love songs. He would swing her as he tap-danced with his cane. In turn Magdalene would rock and grate, as if she were overcome with excitement. He tired easily, and before long he would slump into Magdalene's lap, tightly holding on to her arms. She would embrace him and rock him to sleep. Like a baby, he slept several times a day. Night and day became artificial interludes in a relentless slide to timelessness and nothingness. He slipped from sleep to awakening, dreams to reality, with the ease of a sleepwalker. Memory lost its power to intervene, to impose order and meaning, to mediate the past, the present, and the future.

Only Magdalene remained real, a permanent link to something outside himself. He had outlived friends and his wife. And the children, afraid of the curse of age, had abandoned him. The whole world had forsaken him. It worshipped the shallowness of youth over the endurance of age, material possessions over the sanctity of human relations.

Once a month an old lady came and brought him food and cleaned his place. She never said anything beyond "Hello." The night before she came he would take his only bath for the month, and early the next morning he would wear his favourite blue shirt over which he hung a striped tie. She always banged the door instead of knocking. He would watch her from Magdalene's lap, a smile oozing out of his toothless mouth.

Every day he prepared for this moment. Without her, one moment was like the next in its interminable monotony. When she came, he was animated by the warmth of her presence. He felt human, complete. But on such days Magdalene looked sad.

"You are in love with her, aren't you?" she asked him one day.

"Love? How can I love anybody else? It's you I love." But Magdalene did not believe him. She had seen how he perspired and breathed hard when she came. He would not take his eyes off her as she cleaned the room. He would stiffen and wet himself.

When she stopped coming, he quit taking his monthly bath. He would slouch into Magdalene's lap and stare listlessly out of the window.

Magdalene squatted in the middle of the bare room, facing long glass windows lined by streaks of dust and soot, cobwebs and bird droppings. The outside world steadily shrank from view as the grime gradually enveloped the window. Step by step, as time progressed, he pulled the fading curtains aside until the entire window was almost laid bare, except for some bird's-foot violet shrivelling in dry and sterile potted soil.

All he could see and hear were trucks. They droned incessantly from dawn to dusk. At first the noise rankled him and he would try to plug his ears with his fingers. But he soon gave up and started mimicking the sound. Gradually he came to like it and grunted and rumbled like a truck. So good did he become that sometimes he was not sure whether he was hearing the trucks or his own voice.

He watched the garbage dump grow from a deep empty crater in the ground into an ugly mountain of waste. Trucks came every moment of the day. They would stop by the edge of the dump and manoeuvre into the right position, then belch while releasing their forklifts and finally defecate the refuse of affluence – stacks of paper, piles of plastic objects, heaps of broken glass, worn tires, and mangled metal, mounds of rotten food and masses of toxic substances.

His eyes would follow a particular truck, observing every movement it made. He would stretch his arms, fold his shaky hands, and steer the air while jerking his head sideways and forward like the driver. And as the truck hoisted its forklifts and dropped its load, he would rock excitedly up and down, back and forth, farting, to Magdalene's eternal annoyance. Occasionally, she would push him away. But she always felt bad when he fell and would gently pick him up so he could resume his watch.

The truck he liked most was long and articulated. It was painted green. Instead of droning, it thundered and whistled like a train. Manoeuvring it required dexterity and grit. The steering was sometimes slippery and the gears occasionally locked. On several occasions it hung perilously close to the edge of the dump, gawking at the abyss. But he always managed to steer it away to safety. And he would pull the lever of the forklifts and the bowels of the truck would open and discharge their debris.

By the time the sun woke from its slumber and began ascending, the dump would already be swarmed by birds. There were the long-legged, long-billed herons and storks in their soft plumages of blue, grey, and white, grunting and clattering as they waded through the garbage. In addition there were the brightly marked, aggressive woodpeckers with their stiffened tails and chisel-like bills, rattling and trilling as they hopped in search of insects. And finally there were the predatory falcons and hawks with their hooked beaks and long, curved talons, flapping, gliding, and diving from one perch to another in search of smaller birds and other prey.

The garbage dump transmitted a rainbow of colours and a cacophony of noise. He marvelled at the birds as they stretched and shook their wings and tails in order to keep fit. He laughed at their elaborate courtship displays. The male herons would erect their feathers, extend their heads and necks forward and downward, and clap their mandibles. The willing females would sputter and shake suggestively. And the mates would cement their bond by building nests together and carving their own territory.

Everything seemed to centre around territory, acquiring and defending it. The birds fought over it all the time. Fights erupted frequently, especially as a result of the predatory intentions of the falcons and hawks, which subsisted on devouring weaker and smaller birds. When they saw hawks, the defenceless birds would cry with alarm and try to run away, but often unsuccessfully. The mighty hawks would soar above them, then dive and dip toward the cowering creatures and wrap them under their wings and tails before strangling them with their feet, after which they would tear the smaller birds' flesh with hungry beaks.

There were two birds he particularly liked. They were both blue herons. He named them Marty and Jane. He watched them grow, court, incubate, and have three offspring. Their nest lay in the oldest and most crowded part of the dump, where fights for territory were normal and fierce. It was during one such fight that their first child was killed. Then Jane fell sick after nibbling from a toxic bag and died soon after.

Marty looked after the remaining children as well as he could. Food in that part of the dump was scarce, and when he fell ill, the children did not have enough to eat. In fact, one eventually died from hunger, while the last one decided to leave. He went to the newer part of the dump, which was sparsely populated and had fresh supplies of garbage. Marty never heard from him again, for he was ambushed and gobbled up by a hawk shortly after arrival.

Old and dejected, Marty crouched alone in his crumbling nest. He was too old to do the snap dance and court a new mate. The other herons were too busy carving and protecting their turfs. And he did not understand the language and habits of the other species of birds. Nobody talked to him, and he talked to no one, so that he lost the ability to communicate with others.

Each day Marty got up reluctantly, afraid to face another long day of waiting. He did not wait for anything special, since everything that happened was banal and predictable. All everybody did was work, eat, mate, and sleep. He waited for the end. Only death could have real meaning, for it was final, the consummation of all that was possible.

Marty died one cold winter morning. All the other herons had migrated to warmer southern climes before the start of winter. The trucks continued to come, filling the dump and desecrating the landscape now covered with the frozen tears of the gods. Among them was the green articulated truck, puffing its way to and from the sordid dump.

He wept for Marty and waited for the birds to return.

"Why, Magdalene? Why?"

Magdalene squealed with great sadness. "That's the way things are."

"It shouldn't be like that. Please promise me you will be with me till the end."

"Which end?"

"The end of my life."

"What makes you so sure your life has an end?"

"But it has to. Look at Marty."

"How do you know his soul did not go somewhere else?"

He shook his head. That night he did not sleep, wondering about his life and his death. Why had he been born? Why had he come all the way across the great turbulent seas as a young man? Where was the dream of a happy future? What had he to show for his efforts now? Was this all his life had been about? Was it all part of some macabre plot?

It was a harsh winter. The days were awfully short and the nights unbearably long. Magdalene squealed continuously. It was biting cold outside, but insufferably hot inside. Waves of dry hot air streamed from the heater. The heat was so debilitating that he sweated and dozed most of the time. He lapsed into a kind of stupor, neither fully awake nor asleep. His motionless body, curled in a fetal position, was clasped and swung by an increasingly weary and tired Magdalene.

As time slowly went by, the potted plant by the window looked more frazzled than ever as it shed its dead leaves. One day he picked up one of the leaves. Burrowed there was a small spherical egg. A few weeks later it hatched into a larva. The larva spun silk threads with which it constructed its cocoon. After some time the larva turned into a caterpillar. The caterpillar had irregular shapes and resembled the colour of the leaf so that it was sometimes difficult to see. He never saw it move except when he tried to caress its loose hairs and slippery scales. It would coil and make a faint grating sound and give off a strong smell. So he rarely touched it.

Many weeks later it split and shed the larval skin and began turning into a butterfly. Tiny wings, folded flat along the ventral surface, could be seen, together with the legs, head, eyes, and antennae. The butterfly remained in its pupal case for several more weeks. It was not until the beginning of spring that it finally emerged into a mature butterfly of exquisite and fragile beauty. Its wings were marked with brilliant colours, shades, and dots. He named it Bill.

He almost forgot about the dump site and the birds, which

returned in droves at the beginning of spring. The number of trucks seemed to increase, as well. The garbage mountain climbed higher. The hot sun worked wonders on the refuse so that putrid smells once again suffocated the air. And the insects, rodents, and worms multiplied and grew fat, while some mutated as they ate the entrails collected from gluttonous households and factories.

Magdalene, too, appeared rejuvenated by Bill. She lost her dejected look and smiled a lot. The three of them spent a lot of time together. But as he grew up, Bill preferred sitting by the window to the companionship of the old man. Each time the latter tried to touch him, he would dart away and hang near the roof, where he would remain immobile for some time. Invariably the old man would give up and slump back into Magdalene's lap, watching Bill's antics until he could no longer keep his eyes open. So frustrated was he that once he jumped up and tried to hit the roof with his cane. But he fell and injured his hip.

His annoyance with Bill increased considerably when another butterfly began appearing outside the window. As soon as Bill spotted his friend, his antennae would stiffen, his wings would stretch, and his mysterious underside would flash contrasting bands of splendid colours. The two butterflies would try to stroke each other with their antennae as they flapped their wings in a wild dance, their bodies clinging desperately to the window. Then suddenly they would make angry, screeching noises.

The old man got tired of Bill's behaviour and made meticulous plans to catch him. But none of them worked. He noticed that when the butterfly was not hanging on the window it rested on the potted plant. He decided to move the plant and bring it closer to Magdalene's spot. Bill resisted the bait for a while and avoided coming near the plant. However, hunger soon forced him to come. But he made sure to move only when the old man was asleep. The latter soon discovered the ploy and one day he feigned sleep. Bill gingerly approached the plant and began nibbling the leaves. Suddenly he was pounced on and enveloped in darkness.

"At last I have got you!" the old man exclaimed. Bill struggled in vain, trying to flee.

"No, please don't!" Magdalene screamed. The old man was trying to break one of Bill's wings. Magdalene left her usual spot and followed him. "Leave the poor butterfly alone."

"He's mine. I brought him up and now he thinks he can desert me," he protested.

"You don't own me," Bill cried.

"Oh, yes, I do. I brought you into this world," he said in a cracked voice.

"He is right. You don't own him, just as you don't own me."

"I do. I own you. I bought you at a flea market. I spent my whole life working so I could own something."

"You don't own anything, not even your life. You didn't give yourself your life, did you? And lest you forget, you were born without possessions and you will also leave without possessions. You worked to live, that's all. To live!"

"There has to be something more. To live for what? To live to die?"

"To experience the sweet mysteries of life. Isn't that enough?"

"But how can I experience these mysteries when everybody has forsaken me?"

"But I am still here."

"Yes, Magdalene, you have been kind to me. But you are not enough. Where is my family? Where are my friends? I have nobody. Even Bill doesn't want me now."

"Wounding him may make him stay with you, but it won't make him love you. Let Bill go and find his own kind."

"But where is my own kind?"

"Everywhere and nowhere. Like air. Invisible."

"There are people everywhere, but nobody to relate to. You and I sit here every day, hearing and watching people all the time. They are always in a hurry, always preoccupied, disconnected. It was not like that where I come from and in my youth. I was alive then. People lived. Now they go through the motions of living, but they are dead inside. Dead like me."

"But you aren't dead," Magdalene protested affectionately.

"What's the difference?" he sighed deeply as he wobbled to the window and opened it for the first time. He unfolded his palm, stroked and kissed Bill, and let him out of the oppressive room into the open air. Bill looked at him for a while. His fear and anger melted into sadness tinged with joy. He hobbled, then soared and glided like a bird. The old man's failing eyesight soon lost track of him. He felt a sense of hollowness, shame, and guilt. How could he have contemplated hurting Bill?

As Bill headed for the garbage dump and was welcomed into the gregarious colony of butterflies, the old man began closing the window.

"Leave it open," Magdalene said. "It's been stuffy in here for too long. We need fresh air!" She moved back to her regular spot and began swinging. He turned back, leaving the window open, and threw himself into Magdalene's welcoming embrace. She started chuckling and rocked him excitedly. And he went into a deep slumber. Streams of fresh air gushed in, caressed his face, and drifted out with odours hanging around the room. Magdalene rocked him gently through the night, the following day, and the days after that.

Once in a while swarms of butterflies and birds came through the open window to peek at him, or entertain him and pay their respects. Even dragonflies came. Their numbers grew larger and larger. Hovering over him, they would sing and dance. Capering at his feet were worms, maggots, and fleas of all colours, sizes, and shapes. They also crawled out of his nose, ears, mouth, eyes, and from every crevice and pore in his body.

Then they all started to choke as fumes filtered through the door and the window. The buzzing and singing died, replaced by sirens and the anguished cries of people from the other parts of the building. The grounds below were thronged with a terrified crowd. Water hoses splashed and soaked the building, but they could not reach the thirty-third floor. Some petrified residents jumped out of their windows.

The crowd surged forward as it saw a man rocking by a window. People screamed themselves hoarse with words of encouragement and love, imploring him not to jump and assuring him that rescue was at hand. And, indeed, it was. A helicopter was flying above the building. The crowd sighed audibly as two rescuers, strapped to the helicopter, jumped out and made for the window. They all held their breath. Everything came to a complete standstill.

Then a thunderous uproar erupted as one of the rescuers reached the window. The crowd jostled as everyone tried to get a better view of the rescue operation. Suddenly the sky turned dark as the rescuer lost his grip and the man he had pulled from the rocking chair fell apart and his remains showered the anticipating crowd. The cries of the rescuer were soon drowned by shrieks of horror from the crowd.

There was utter chaos as the crowd dispersed in panic, leaving behind terrified firefighters. The flames gathered force as they lapped their way up the massive apartment block. Presently the fire reached the last floor and jumped into the open window where the rocking chair was still swinging. In a flash it was no more.

The severed head was later recovered and the man's family eventually traced. The three children came from their scattered homes. They buried him quickly and turned to the long and more rewarding battle of distributing the fortune he had left behind, which was quite considerable.

After the landlord was reimbursed for the fire by the insurance companies, he erected a new apartment block on the same plot. In fact, the new block resembled the old one. It faced the same dump and it was packed with the same lonely souls.

1994

ANDRÉ ALEXIS

Despair: Five Stories of Ottawa

1.

There was a man named Martin Bjornson who lived, precisely, at 128 MacLaren. He lived with his mother (whom he knew as Mrs. Bjornson) and a fifty-year-old parakeet named Knut. The parakeet had learned to cough and spit like a tubercular old man, sounding much as Martin's father, Frederic, had sounded, but it was otherwise unremarkable.

One night, while the Bjornsons were at home playing a game of two-handed *whist*, Knut coughed, spit up and then said, quite distinctly it seemed to Martin, "Jesus, Maria, my corns are killing me." These were Knut's first and last words. After pronouncing them, he keeled over and died. The Bjornsons were as surprised by Knut's unexpected revelation as they were by the sudden death that followed it. It took them quite some time to finish their game of *whist* (won by Mrs. Bjornson with a flourish of trump). When they had finished, and when he discovered that his mother was *not* named Maria, Martin said:

– Did you understand what Knut meant, Mother?

– Did Knut speak? asked Mrs. Bjornson.

– Yes, he did, said Martin.

And he resolved to get to the bottom of the matter.

The day after Knut's demise, Martin began to wander the streets of the city repeating aloud the parakeet's final words – "Jesus, Maria, my corns are killing me" – in the hope that someone who recognized the phrase would unveil its mystery to him. The results were unpromising at first. After a week of wandering, the only people who had spoken to him were a panhandler named Morris and a dental assistant named Antoinette Lachapelle. Finally, Martin was heard by a pharmacist named Mario Prater who understood him to be saying "Jeez, Mario, my corns are hurting me." Mr. Prater, suppressing his disdain at such a blunt request for help, answered that adhesive pads were available for any foot. What he said was:

– You know, foot pads could help you there.

Which Martin mistook for a reference to a "Mr. Paz."

– Paz? Martin asked.

– Yes, answered Mr. Prater.

Martin thanked the pharmacist by pressing six or seven quarters into the palm of his hand and mentioning that, given enough notice, he and his mother would be pleased to have him dine with them.

– Smorgasbord! Martin said as he walked away.

Now, despite the cheerfully given invitation, this encounter was an unhappy one for the pharmacist, and it proved to be a tragic one for the Bjornsons. It was unhappy for the pharmacist because he felt ambivalent about being seen to take spare change from a passer-by. (He let the coins drop into his pocket, straightened his bow tie and whistled as he walked away.) It was an unlucky exchange for Martin because, although his mother did not know any "Paz," she did know a Mr. Prinz. (This particular *Prinz* had seduced her before her marriage to Mr. Bjornson, when she had been a girl in Carleton Place.) And when her son told her that Mr. Paz had had something to do with "Maria's corns," she understood him to say that Mr. Prinz had had something to do with them. Her heart began to palpitate. She had trouble breathing, and then she gave up the ghost. (She had kept her first name from Martin precisely because she feared he might one day discover her connection to Mr. *Prinz*, his biological father.)

Mrs. Bjornson's death left Martin without father, mother or family pet. In the face of such loss, it took real determination to carry on his search for the meaning of Knut's last words. But, after burying his mother in the clay behind their home, Martin carried on.

Mr. Paz, the only F. Paz in Ottawa, lived in the West End, behind the Merivale Shopping Centre. He was a blessèd man, devout and careful. He remembered all of his sins as though he had just committed them, and he suffered for them. So, when he saw Martin coming up his driveway, he thought he recognized the son of the only woman with whom he had committed fornication, a sin that was just then on his mind, and he rushed out to face him.

— I know what you're going to say, said Mr. Paz, and I'm not completely innocent, but your mother wasn't always . . . honest . . .

— What do you mean?

— She was a good woman, but she was just a little bit of a liar, said Mr. Paz humbly.

— Make that clear, Martin said.

— I'm afraid she told me she wasn't married when we met. And she mentioned that she had a parrot that could recite Leviticus backwards and forwards. . . .

— I didn't even know Knut could speak, said Martin.

— Knut? asked Mr. Paz. Was that the parrot? It couldn't say a word. She said that to seduce me, don't you know. . . .

Martin struck Mr. Paz with his fist and left him lying on the ground. Mr. Paz lay on the green grass with his arms out, like a man crucified. Soon Mr. Paz' body rose from the lawn; his body rose. It ascended. It floated above the houses in Merivale. It sailed over the thousands of freshly tarred roofs. It passed by tall buildings and from the ground it appeared to be a cross or a starfish, and then a speck in the sunlight.

Martin returned to his home angry and discouraged. He did not know that Mr. Paz was dead and that he had been the cause of his death. That night he kept his mother company, sitting by her grave. It was a summer evening and there was a slight, warm wind. The wind reminded Martin of silence, and the silence reminded him of Mrs. Bjornson. And he thought of the mysterious ways by which death enters the world.

2.

At precisely 128 Beausoleil, there lived a Russian translator named Leo Chung. He lived alone in a small apartment on the eleventh floor. He had few possessions, and what furniture there was had been passed over by the thieves who regularly entered and stole from the apartments in the building. It was well known that 128 was not a good address.

On a Saturday, Mr. Chung was laundering his shirt and tie in the building's basement laundry. He could hear people congregating in the meeting room beside him, and when it grew particularly noisy he looked in.

In the meeting room, tenants from all over the building sat in folding chairs before a large block of clear ice which stood beside a desk at the far end of the room. The building's superintendent stood on the desk. In the ice was the body of a certain Alfred Paradis, Mr. Chung's neighbour on the eleventh floor. Mr. Paradis' face was blue as powdered bleach. The superintendent was addressing the crowd.

– . . . Once again, he said, I'd like to thank you men for your good work. We'll never know, like Mrs. Korzinski said the other day, *why* Paradis here stole our things, but by golly we got him. . . . As I was saying to myself the other day, here's a man with so much stolen furniture in his place you couldn't get anywhere without climbing. . . .

– Are you going to bury him? Mr. Chung asked from his side of the room.

– He doesn't deserve it! someone shouted.

– C'était un monstre, said the widow Paradis.

– He'd be expensive to put under, said the superintendent.

– I'll pay, Mr. Chung said.

There was an anti-oriental silence.

– Well, said Mrs. Paradis, si c'est lui qui va payer I don't care.... (Mrs. Paradis thought: He was good to the kids. But, though the kids had climbed happily over the side tables, armchairs and love-seats to get at the bathroom, she couldn't count the number of times she had almost lost it on the furniture.)

– We bury him then, said the superintendent.

And he rapped on the block of ice with his gavel.

Almost two weeks later, Mr. Chung lay in bed, asleep. He was woken by the sound of dry coughing. When he turned on his bedside lamp, he found he was almost face to face with Alfred Paradis who sat in the chair beside his bed, and whose face was as baby blue as the last time Mr. Chung had seen it.

– Did I wake you? Mr. Paradis asked.

– Yes, said Mr. Chung.

– No problem. I just wanted to thank you. Hard to thank a man while he's asleep....

– Of course...

– It was a good thing you did, getting me a real burial.

Mr. Paradis scratched himself.

– I'll tell you, said Mr. Paradis, death doesn't cure psoriasis. I still scratch like a dog....

– Is there anything else? Mr. Chung asked.

– Yes, said Mr. Paradis. I give you three wishes, you know.

– Fine, said Mr. Chung. I'll think about it.

– Take your time....

Throughout the night, Mr. Paradis did indeed scratch like a dog. It sounded like someone shaking a bag full of leaves, and it kept Mr. Chung on the edge of sleep for hours. In the morning, Mr. Paradis sat at Mr. Chung's kitchen table blinking vigorously.

– You drink coffee? he asked.

– Yes, said Mr. Chung.

– Let me have some. It's not instant is it? Darned little brown things that melt in water. How do you know that's coffee? Could be cockroach dung for all you know. . . . So, do you have any wishes?

– I don't want anything, said Mr. Chung.

– Go on, said Mr. Paradis.

– World peace, said Mr. Chung.

– Make it something doable, said Mr. Paradis. You must be some kind of intellectual.

– Money, then.

– I can do that. I can get you money, but large amounts I'll have to steal.

– A raise?

– Three wishes and you want a raise? If it was me, I would go for good furniture, but a raise I can get you. You got a raise.

– A car.

– Buy it with the raise.

– There's nothing else.

– A new couch? A dining-room set? Something Moroccan?

– Whatever, said Mr. Chung.

And when he returned from work that night, his small apartment was lavishly decorated, filled with French furniture from the reign of one of the later Louis. There was scarcely room to manoeuvre. Mr. Paradis sat blinking on a red-velvet Louis XVI love-seat.

– Did you steal this? Mr. Chung asked.

– No chance, said Mr. Paradis. And seeing how well set up you are, what do you need me for, eh?

– Yes, said Mr. Chung.

– Good furniture at a good price, said Mr. Paradis. That's what Heaven's about.

Mr. Paradis began to fade away, scratching himself here and there as he went. The sound of dry leaves remained even after he was gone, and the apartment smelled of wet earth, a smell that hung about for days, as there were no windows that could be opened.

Later that night, when Mr. Paradis had disappeared for good, Mr. Chung gathered the lace antimacassars that were draped on the furniture and threw them down the garbage chute. Then, two hours before dawn, when he was certain he would not be seen, he cleared out every piece of furniture Mr. Paradis had left behind and put them in front of the apartment building for the garbage collectors. From that moment he felt confident his life would continue in peace until his death. And it did.

3.

In 1987 Mr. André Bennett of 128 Gloucester invented, or rather discovered, a solution to world hunger. He bred a plant that passes through the body as food does, but that, when defecated, reverts to its original colour, shape and consistency and can thus be replanted and harvested time and again. This was, to the majority of Ottawans, an interesting but unpalatable discovery. Very few could see how, without expert promotion, one might convince the poor and starving to eat what they had just expelled.

The plant itself was much like a Canadian Thistle, with smaller but more profuse spikes and a flower that was bright red against its lime-green stalk. It was lovely to behold, like something from a harsh world, but it had not been tested. It had never been given to human beings, though it had sustained a colony of rats for a year before Mr. Bennett made his discovery public.

As might be expected, Mr. Bennett's discovery attracted the attention of men of ambition throughout the city. And the first to promise him significant gain was Reed Marshall. Mr. Bennett surrendered his fate and the fate of his plant to Mr. Marshall forthwith.

Mr. Marshall had political ambitions, and his first act was to announce his candidacy for the office of mayor. His platform was "An end to hunger in the valley." With the help of his brother, Frederic, the owner of a local radio station, he quickly disseminated his ideas throughout the city. His first task was to end hunger in Ottawa, and through a radio contest the seven poorest families in town were discovered and given the privilege of being the first to eat what was now called "Bennett's Flower."

Food Day, as it was promoted, was a hot afternoon in July. A spruce rostrum was built in Minto Park, just wide enough to accommodate the ninety members of the city's seven poorest families. Mr. Marshall spoke to the small crowd that had gathered. He spoke into a microphone set before the rostrum. Several young boys pulled at the black electric wires that lay twisted on the pavement. At the end of his speech, he presented Mr. Bennett to the crowd, and Mr. Bennett pulled the long lime-green stalks from a plastic bag and handed them to the people on the rostrum. Thus, it was the Andrés, McKenzies, O'Briens, Lafleurs, Chaputs, Laflèches and St. Pierres who discovered that the plant did not grow *after* it had been consumed and defecated but *while* it was being digested. The plants grew in their stomachs, up through their esophagi and out of their mouths. The plants also grew downward into their intestines and out of their anuses.

Besides causing extreme discomfort, the growth of Bennett's Flower was phenomenal. Every hour, the family members had to bite off the tops of the plants as they grew from their mouths and cut off with secateurs the growth from their nether extremities. This meant they could not sleep, and when they did, as the children did, their agony was redoubled. The spikes along the stalks were, of course, a continual discomfort.

There was nothing to be done for them.

It was certain proof of Mr. Marshall's talent as a politician, however, that, acting quickly, he turned the disaster and the suffering of the poor to his own advantage. He personally saw to it that Mr. Bennett was reprimanded for his shoddy scientific methods. But he also spearheaded a campaign to ensure that funds be put aside for Bennett to continue his research on the plants, with a view to the discovery of a herbicide that might assuage the agonies of the humans from whom Bennett's Flower continued to grow.

– This research, he said, will surely be of comfort to the poor.

And it might have been, were it not that every member of the seven families died of starvation long before any balm was concocted. Still, it was ennobling to see the thin and naked poor, the Andrés, McKenzies, O'Briens, Lafleurs, Chaputs, Laflèches and St.

Pierres, snipping or trying to snip the plants from the mouths of their children, as they continued to do until their own last breaths.

4.

Nothing would give up life:
Even the dirt kept breathing a small breath.
— *Theodore Roethke*

When the cemetery on Montreal Road was dug up to make more room for the dead, there was a general outcry. A committee was formed to ensure that the bones and relics of our ancestors were treated with respect. To their dismay, they discovered that the cemetery was infested by a breed of worm until then unknown. The worms were lily-white, not more than an inch long, and narrow as pins. At their extremities, the worms had minute, bright-red spots. And, when they were touched or exposed to the light, they emitted short, sharp cries. The gravediggers, or Thanatory Engineers as they preferred, could not dig up a spadeful of earth without exhuming thousands of them. They made the soil look like contaminated faeces.

Shortly after they were discovered, the committee chairman, a distant relative of a distinguished corpse, Mr. Alan Thomas of 128 Wurtemberg, picked up one of the worms with his wife's tweezers and put it in a glass vial he had brought for the purpose. He took it home to study. He put the vial down on the low, glass-topped table in the family room, and it was there that his five-year-old son Edward discovered it. Edward opened the vial and swallowed the worm. Two weeks later, the boy began to speak with authority on aesthetic matters and to write poetry. He wrote beautiful poetry.

– It's like he swallowed Wallace Stevens, his father said.

– More like Eliot, scholars said, but not so neurotic.

– Still, an expert on child psychology remarked, there is no necessary connection between the worm and the poetry. The child was a prodigy with or without the Gravedigger's Worm.

To prove him wrong, Mr. Thomas swallowed one of the worms

himself. With the same results: after two weeks, he began to write accomplished poetry.

– The father writes like Baudelaire, scholars said, but not so neurotic.

– Worms have nothing to do with it, a psychologist remarked. The father was obviously a poet before this business with the graveyard.

In any case, within months both the father and the son began to acquire renown for their work. (That is, they were published and sometimes admired, but they were generally treated with the contempt professionals reserve for those to whom things come too easily. And then, so few people cared for poetry, and even fewer could distinguish good verse from bad. They were called "The Worms, père et fils.") These were their happy days. They lasted two full months. The Thomases wrote like demons.

Unfortunately, their bodies were hosts to the annelids. After three months they were infested. There were worms dangling and crying from their noses and ears and eyes and mouths. Whenever they moved worms dropped from them. And, when the pain of being eaten alive became unbearable and they were confined to their beds, the worms infested their bedsheets. The noise the worms made was itself agonizing, like cries of schoolchildren heard from a distance.

After six months, they were both dead. Their corpses were white as marble, but their hands and feet were ash grey. The hair on their bodies was brittle as desiccated pine needles. The nails had fallen from their fingers and toes, and their skin was light as paper. When the pathologists cut into them, millions of worms, exposed to the light, began to cry out.

The bodies of the Thomases were taken out and burned.

The worms themselves also died out. They died when exhumed. And, when the reconstruction of the cemetery was completed they were annihilated, or seemed to be, and it was not possible to conduct any further experiments.

5.

On the eleventh of January this year, all of the windows in the old firehall on Sunnyside cracked. It was a cold and unusually dry night; so dry it was thought the dryness itself had cracked the windows. There were delicate threads of glass, some as long and thin as transparent hairs, scattered over the floor inside the hall. The shards were swept up with hard-bristle brooms, and a dance scheduled for the following night went on as planned.

Martine Beauchamp and her friends attended the dance together, six fourteen-year-old girls accompanied by Madame Florence Gru, Martine's grandmother. The heat inside the firehall had been turned up to compensate for the cracked windows, so the air in the dance hall was as dry as straw in a drought. The girls took up positions against one of the walls. At the opposite end of the room, the young men stood together.

An older man, perhaps twenty years old, with light-blue eyes and extremely white skin, asked Martine to dance. He asked politely, and Martine's grandmother gave her permission.

— Mais oui, said Mme. Gru. On voit qu'il est cultivé.

And the two of them danced all night, finding that they had much to talk about.

The man's only indiscretion came when they were about to part for the evening. He put two of his fingers into Martine's mouth and pressed on her tongue. But Mme. Gru was willing to believe that this had been accidental, or else a new custom with the well-bred. (Martine was even more surprised than her grandmother, but not unpleasantly. His fingers had been dry as paper, and her tongue had stuck to them lightly.)

The following week there was another dance at the firehall. Martine and her friends went eagerly, dragging Mme. Gru with them. And this night was identical to the first. When Mr. High-smith put up his two fingers to touch her, Martine smiled and opened her mouth slightly. He said goodnight after they had danced and laughed for hours.

It was on the way home from the dance, as she and her friends talked of everything but Mr. Highsmith, about whom she was too excited to speak, that Martine realized she had forgotten her gloves. The girls and Mme. Gru had already reached the bank of the river. The river was not completely frozen. Near its centre a smooth, black strand of water flowed in the ice and snow. The moon was white in the cloudless sky, and it was as she looked down at her hands that Martine saw that she had forgotten her gloves. Asking her friends to take her grandmother home, she walked back to the firehall alone.

As she neared the building, Martine saw Mr. Highsmith leave. He walked away from her, towards Bank Street, and at the corner he turned towards the canal. Martine followed him, anxious to say goodnight again, but instead of walking along Echo Drive, Mr. Highsmith cut across the snow-covered driveway and walked to the back of the monastery.

Behind the monastery was a large stone replica of a church, the size of a small cottage. It had been built to keep the bodies of priests who died. Their remains lay on a bier for two days before burial so that the confrères of the dead could pay their final respects. Mr. Highsmith entered the building directly, and by the time Martine looked in at the window to see what he was doing, Mr. Highsmith had already stripped Father Alfred Bertrand's corpse of its shroud and he had begun to eat the priest's body.

Martine put her hand to the window to support herself, and when she did, the window creaked dryly and ice fell around her. Mr. Highsmith looked up, but by then she was already running. The snow on the monastery ground seemed deeper and colder and almost impassable.

In the days that followed, Martine avoided company. She told no one what she had seen. To her mother and her grandmother she seemed to be pining for her young man. They encouraged her to go out, and when, a month later, there was a community dance at the firehall, they insisted she attend.

— Vas y, ma chère, said her mother smiling, et sans chaperon.

— Oui, said Mme. Gru, ce monsieur Highsmith est la politesse même.

Her friends teased her and tried to encourage her, but she hid in their midst until they came to the hall.

Mr. Highsmith approached her immediately, and he was so friendly, Martine believed he had not seen her or heard her at the monastery. As they walked the dance floor, he took her missing gloves from his suit pocket.

— You must have forgotten these, he said.

— Yes, thank you, Martine answered.

— The last time we saw each other was some time ago, said Mr. Highsmith.

— Yes, said Martine.

— You followed me to the chapel.

— No.

— What was I doing there?

— I don't know.

Mr. Highsmith put up his two fingers and forced them into her mouth.

— Very well, he said. When you return home tonight you will find your grandmother dead.

And then they danced. Mr. Highsmith held her so close she could not move, and to the people around them they seemed happy. At the end of the night, when she returned home, Martine found her grandmother dead.

In Martine's bedroom there is a window that looks out on a garden, and beyond the garden, there is a curtain of pine trees. As she looked out the window several weeks later, when her grandmother had been buried for some time, she saw Mr. Highsmith come through the trees. He called out to her.

— How's your memory, my dear? Did you see me in the chapel that night?

— No, Martine answered.

— Did you see what I was doing?

— No.

— Tut tut, he said. Your mother is dead before sunrise.

She moved away from the window, and she began to cry, but in the morning her mother was dead.

Some time after her mother's death, Mr. Highsmith knocked at her front door. Martine, alone, opened the door to him, and before she could close it, he put a foot on the threshold.

— And how is your mother? he said, smiling. I was wondering, my little bitch, did you see me in the chapel that night?

— No.

— Did you see what I was doing?

— No.

— Well, said Mr. Highsmith, time is finite. If you do not tell someone, anyone, what it was you saw that night, you will die within a week. But whoever you tell will die.

And he disappeared. And from that moment, Martine began to die slowly, feeling the life pulled out of her as if it were a strand of hair pulled through her fingers. She did not know what to do, but when the pain of dying overcame her, she threw open her bedroom window and shouted out what it was she had seen. She told everything to the garden.

That's how I heard the story.

A curse on anyone who reads this.

1994

Martha and Elvira

SCENE 2

ELVIRA   *(quietly, still sitting)* Remember when we first left the south, Brother Thomas was our way out. He say . . .

MARTHA   Keep one on the North Star, and the other on your path!

ELVIRA   Say, you won't see nobody, cause there won't be no moon lighting the way.

MARTHA   And that night was black. Brother Thomas say . . .

ELVIRA   Meet down under Yansee's tree. He said, I got this here rifle, and you got one another.

MARTHA   There is no turnin back.

    (They start to march together slowly picking up speed as the song speeds up)

MARTHA   I didn't know you before that, sister.

ELVIRA   You come up with some others from one of the houses down the way. Your man, Bill, was one of Brother Thomas's right-hand men.

MARTHA   I was proud of him. My man, Billy.

ELVIRA   Brother Thomas say, "Follow that star until you reach the Canaan land."

MARTHA   *(standing up)* Say, "People, owls are quiet unless there's danger around. Then they call out. You going to do the same."

ELVIRA   *(standing)* Whoo! whoo!

MARTHA   Brother Thomas went ahead of us to guide the way. We walked along close to the bushes. Couldn't see to put one foot in front of the other. I started to get scared. And the baby started to fuss. "Billy, we got to go back. We ain't gonna make it. The baby ain't gonna make it."

ELVIRA   Billy say, "He ain't gonna make it if we stay here, we making a way for him now."

MARTHA   Billy take the baby from me and give the child oil of tincture, to make him sleep. There was a marsh we had to cross, which led to an open field.

(They sing together, walking on the spot)

Walk together, sister,
don't you get weary
Walk together, brother
don't you get weary
Walk together, sister

don't you get weary
There's a campground waitin
in the promise land.

(Martha claps her hands, they speed up their steps, still moving on the spot)

ELVIRA   Bounty hunter!

MARTHA   My baby cried out loud. There was no place to hide.

(They both crouch down)

ELVIRA   Bounty hunter come up real close behind us. One of the children, Ben, I held his hand. "Run boy! Run!"

(Elvira claps her hands)

Ben's hand slipped away. He was dead. The bounty hunter was getting closer to us.

MARTHA   The baby was crying loud now. I took the rifle from Billy.

ELVIRA   The bounty hunter started shooting. There wasn't nothing more we could do.

MARTHA   He aimed the gun at me. He would have killed me and the baby sister. I tried to stop him, but I wasn't fast enough. Bounty hunter cocked the gun. And Billy called out "No!" And he threw himself in front of me.

(Elvira claps her hands)

MARTHA   And my man was dead. My man was dead. Billy Junior fall from his daddy's arms.

ELVIRA   I picked up the baby and held him close.

MARTHA   Well, nothin seemed to matter then. I aimed my rifle straight at that bounty hunter's heart. Why all I'm seeing is my man dead. . . . That hunter see the red in my eyes. I look at him straight, and pull the trigger.

ELVIRA   You killed him, Martha.

MARTHA   *(sitting down on her chair)* I killed him dead. Never said nothin to nobody. Ceptin for you, Brother Thomas was the only one that knowed that. I killed for my Billy and for my freedom, sister. And I came too far, to turn back now.

ELVIRA   *(sitting down)* We wrapped Little Ben, and Bill, in a blanket. And then we moved on.

MARTHA   Days and nights passed, we walked and walked. We were running out of food, and the days were getting colder. But when we reached to a place called Ohio, we knew we were close. Stopped at a house on the way. Some Church people were there dressed in big hats and the women had on those big bonnets. Give us some food, I do believe it was boiled potatoes with ham, and gravy, you remember that, Vi?

ELVIRA   Unn hu. It was rice and stew.

MARTHA   Huh?

ELVIRA   Said it was rice and stew. With a mess of biscuits on the side.

MARTHA   Well, I don't remember no rice and stew. I could have sworn it was potatoes with ham, and gravy. Well, whatever it was, it sure tasted good.

ELVIRA   I got long remembrance, Martha, long remembrance. No way for me to disremember, less I die. I remember some days clear as I remember this day right here.

MARTHA   Things now days, going round so fast, and young peoples don't take no time to sit and talk things over — that's just the way it is.

ELVIRA   My mammy's name was Caroline, she come from NorCross Georgia. We moved round for a time before we settled on Lawson's plantation where we lived with my daddy and my sister Nora. My daddy's name was Egypt. That was on account of his colour. He was dark like the night. No denying he was an African man. Un uh. *(she pauses, remembering)* Oh, he used to tell me stories bout where he come from and what his mama and daddy told him about they own peoples. I knowed bout Africa since I was young girl. Times was good when I was with him and my mammy.

Then when Massa Lawson died, his brother came down from Texas to take over the plantation and he was one mean man. Was a true killer. Got in trouble the first week he was there. Had to leave straight away! So what he did was chain all the slaves round the neck and say we going back with him to Texas. And we was to walk all the way. If you try to resist, he just shoot you — just like that and leave you there to die.

Well, somewhere along the road, it got to snowing and he wouldn't let us wrap nothin round our feet. We had to sleep on the ground, right in snow.

My mammy give out on the way, round the line of Texas. Her feet were raw and bleeding and her legs swoll right out of shape.

Well, Massa just took the gun and shoot her while she lay dying. Then he kicked her two or three times and say, "Damn a nigger who can't stand nothin." "Damn a nigger who can't stand nothing!" *(pause)* Well, Daddy was never the same after. He just stopped talkin. Never said a word to me or nobody after that. I would ask him to tell me a story about Africa, but he'd just look at me and wouldn't say nothin. After a while I was sold to old man Hindley and I never seen my daddy or my sister again. *(pause)* But I'll never forget bout all those remembrances he told me. Un uh, I'll never forget that.

MARTHA *(whispering)* I know. I know.

ELVIRA I'm going to miss you, Martha.

MARTHA Well, I'm going to miss you too, but you and I both know that Hannah needs you now. Why, I'll be just fine. You the one you should be worrying bout. I'll be just fine.

(Martha pats Elvira on the hand and then gets up to leave)

MARTHA *(stopping)* All I can say is that you better make sure the white folks ain't pullin one of they tricks and tellin us we free down south, and have you runnin back down just to put you back in slavery again. Now I'm not sayin that's how it is, but it's somethin you should think about before you go. Of course I don't know what they'd want with an old Granny like you, but white folks 'ell come up with somethin!

ELVIRA   *(shaking her head and laughing)* My Lord, my Lord! *(pause)* You know when we first come up here, there was not a soul that could tell us nothin!

MARTHA   Well, there wasn't no one could get us to do something that we did not want to do.

ELVIRA   If I say, "Martha, that fire needs pokin."

MARTHA   Well, I just turn around and tell you that it ain't the first fire that died down, and it won't be the last! I'll get to it when I'm good and ready.

Then white folks used to say, "How them niggers going to do things for theyselves? Needs us to tell them what to do."

ELVIRA   We went on and did what had to be done.

MARTHA   You know there ain't nothin sweeter than fooling people who think that you is a fool.

ELVIRA   Mr. Lawson, he tried to fool us one time. He was a man that didn't low his niggers to fish. And didn't low them to hunt neither. Said it was too easy. Well, sometimes, my poppa and some mens would slip off at night and catch possum. Cook em up until they was smelling sweet like fine food stuff. Put them with cow cabbage and leeks, well, this time Massa Lawson smell the possum cookin. He wait till way in the night, and then wrap sheet over him and come a scratchin on the wall outside the cabin.

MARTHA   This was the time when Massa Lawson come lookin for possum.

ELVIRA   You has a good memory, Martha.

MARTHA   Well, I have heard this story once or twice before.

ELVIRA   Well, you know, when my poppa go to the door, he say, "Who out there?" All along he knowed it was the massa dressed up in a sheet.

MARTHA   Oh my Lord!

ELVIRA   He say *(imitating MASSA LAWSON)* "It's me. What's yee cooking in there?" And my poppa say, "I'se cookin possum." Well then he say, "Cook him and bring me the hindquarters, you and your children can eat the rest."

MARTHA   He wanted the sweet part, huh?

ELVIRA   Well, bout that time, I was fit for to be tied. I couldn't keep myself from bustin out with laughin, seein the massa all dress up and askin for possum hindquarters.

MARTHA   And then what your poppa do?

ELVIRA   He just cut up the possum and give some to the massa. Why, we had three or four of them possum left ready to cook and feedin the massa would just get him out of the way so we could enjoy ours.

MARTHA   Get to the next part now, Vira, I like this part.

ELVIRA   Well, this particular time, the massa turned to leave and, wham, tripped right on his sheet. I said, that possum flew out his hand and smack right gainst the door before it slid down to the ground.

MARTHA   Oh my Lord!

ELVIRA   Well, I couldn't move, I couldn't catch my breathin . . . said I couldn't stop my shoulders from shakin, I said laugh! Oh I was shakin up and down and up and down seeing him tryin to put that sheet back on his head, and gettin all caught up in it. Then my poppa reached over and thwacked me right behind my ear back with his fingers. Just like he was hittin a fly.

MARTHA   That cleared your head.

ELVIRA   It surely did. Poppa reached down and picked up the possum and put it back in Massa's hands. Then opened the door for him, and you know, the funny thing about it is that all the massa had to do was ask.

MARTHA   Your poppa would have shared him some of that possum, huh?

ELVIRA   I knowed he would have done that.

MARTHA   But tell me, Vi, why are white folks so fool?

ELVIRA   Want to take, take, and keep on taking, before they just ask for some and get.

MARTHA   Massa, playing he smart, and acting stupid.

ELVIRA   That was a long while ago, sister. You and me ain't nobody slaves no more. Only thing that's ruling us now is time.

MARTHA   We come a long way, sister. You helped me, and I helped you. My son is a grown man now with his own children. I only wished poppa could see what fine grandchildren that he got.

I had me eight children. Two dead, and five that were sold off to different plantations. And I never seen or heard about them again. Billy is my only child left now. All the rest gone.

ELVIRA   I was fourteen years old when the massa told me to fix that cabin for living with Jumas. I never had no learnin. I thought he meant for me to tend the cabin. That started the pestigation for me. Jumas weren't nothin but a big bully, and thought that everybody should do what he say. First night I was there, I fixed up the cabin, and then crawled in my bunk. If that old Jumas didn't come crawlin in with me. I says what you meaning by this fool? He said that this was his bunk too and he was ready to use it. I told him he was touched in the head! I put both my feet against him and shoved him out hard on the floor. That got that fool out. But he start back towards me like he ain't had enough. He looked just like a bear comin out of the bushes! So I look around, and grab me a broomstick. It was about three feet long, with those strong bristles. I said, "Nigger, come and get it," and I brought down that broom, wham, right over the head. Did that man stop in his tracks? I says he did. He just sat back and looked at me. He was lookin like a bull. So I looked back at him. We must have stayed like that for a good while. Just watchin each other's moves. After that he said, "Pretty girl, you think you smart, don't you? But you ain't smart enough. The master, he's gonna show you who's in charge." Next, old man Hindley call me up to the house and say, "Elvira, I pays big money for

you to raise children. What you think I put you with
Jumas for? Now if you don't want whuppen at the
stake, then you better do what I say." So I yields.
When my first baby was born, I named her Precious.
Cause she was the most precious thing to me. She died
three days later. Right in my arms. She just stopped
breathing. After that, every child that I had, was born
dead. Everyone but Hannah. When Hannah came
along, and live, that was the time when I decided that
this girl was special. She wasn't going to live no slave
life. And I was going to give her a home somehow.
After she was born, I just put on to everyone like she
had died, just like the others. I wrapped her up in a
blanket and said I was taking her out to the woods to
bury her. Said it wasn't meant for me to have children.
There was an old woman who lived not far from the
plantation and I had heard that she helped people who
are tryin to run. So I went to her, and I begged her to
take care of my child, until I was ready to leave and
take her with me. She took Hannah, and every day I
would go there and bring her what food I could, and
sing to her. *(she mimes rocking the baby and singing)*
"Momma's baby is sweet like honey, Momma's baby is
pretty like a flower," and then one day, I went there to
see her, and wasn't nothin there. They had found out
bout old lady Jessie and burnt down her house. And, I
didn't know if my child was alive weeks after, just
waiting, just hoping for a sign. Then, when I found
out I was going to be sold to another plantation, I went
back the night before we was to leave, and I took a
rock and carved my name on a tree should in case
Hannah ever come back. Hoping maybe she would
see that and come lookin for me. That's why I got to
go to her now. I got to tell her what little I knowed
about my momma and my poppa, and what he told me
bout his. She got to know. And I got to tell her that

somebody was carin bout her all this time. I got to let her know.

(Martha nods silently)

MARTHA   Sometimes it feels like we keep walking down a road trying to get somewhere, and just when we almost reach there, the road takes you off somewhere again, and you got to stop and see which way it is that you really want to go. Seems like I found my road, sister, and you got to find yours now. Only thing is, they going two different ways.

(Martha is weary now, and stands up slowly)

MARTHA   Well, tomorrow comes early.

ELVIRA   You go on in. I won't be long.

MARTHA   Suit yourself. *(she picks up the tea)* You never touched a drop of this, Vi. If you didn't want the tea in the first place, you should have told me, cause I wouldn't have bothered. And next time . . .

(She stops and looks at Elvira, realizing there won't be another time)

ELVIRA   *(quietly)* Goodnight, sister.

(Lights go down slightly on porch and crickets are heard again, or some sounds to indicate morning and a passage of time. Elvira should still be seen slightly, putting on her shoes)

1993

✈ ✈

LAWRENCE HILL

Some Great Thing

(EXCERPT)

As a boy, Mahatma had been told countless times about the life of Gandhi. And about famous blacks. Booker T. Washington. Marcus Garvey. Harriet Tubman. Langston Hughes. Ben had talked about them daily. But Louise, Mahatma's mother, always cut the sermons short.

"Stop filling that boy's head with nonsense," she often said.

"It's not nonsense," Ben would reply. "It is the story of his people."

"He can learn about people in school! Don't go filling his head with mumbo-jumbo."

Ben would grumble and back down. Increasingly, he would try to educate Mahatma during his wife's absence.

Mahatma remembered a certain day, when he was eleven or so. He was watching TV. His mother was ironing. Ben came into the room and tried to turn off the TV, but Louise wouldn't let him. He said there were better things to do than look at the boob tube. Why didn't they read, study about their people? Did she know that the founder of modern Russian literature was a Negro?

"I bet," Louise said.

"He was!" Ben brought a thick volume to his wife.

"Alexander who?" his wife said, reading the cover.

"Pushkin. Alexander Pushkin."

"Doesn't sound like a Negro to me," Louise said.

"He wrote poetry. He wrote prose. He wrote *The Queen of Spades*! He wrote an unfinished novel about his great-grandfather, called *The Negro of Peter the Great*."

"Didn't finish it, hunh?" Louise said. "Now *that* sounds like a Negro. So tell me, if he's Russian, how come he's black?"

"His great-grandfather was from Abyssinia," Ben said.

"From where?"

"Ancient Ethiopia."

"You're saying he had one ancestor from Africa?"

"That's right," Ben said.

"And the rest were Russians? Regular white folk?"

"Yes. But I . . ."

Louise turned back to her ironing. "Then he didn't have much coloured blood left in him, you ask me."

Ben lost his temper. Who was she to deny black heritage? One drop of coloured blood made you black, and that was that.

"Don't pay him any mind," Louise told Mahatma. "Twisting and yanking the truth out of shape, he'll fill up your head with confusion. I say, better to have your head empty and see clear."

"Don't pay *her* any mind, son," Ben countered. "If you keep your head empty, you'll see clear all right. You'll look clear at mediocrity all your life!"

Louise had wanted to name her son Paul. Paul James Grafton. Ben would have nothing to do with it. Who ever heard of a world leader named Paul? This was no ordinary baby. He was a Grafton! The baby, the story goes, started to cry. Louise rocked him protectively. That husband of hers was insane. He read too many books. Lately, he'd been reading Greek mythology. Walking all around the house spouting crazy names: Prometheus, Zacharia, Euripides, Homer. She wished he would shut up about all those books of his. He carried on as if he were a scholar, and not just a plain old railway porter.

"And how do you want to name him?" Louise asked.

"Euripides Homer Grafton."

Louise put the baby in its room, closed the door and went to the kitchen cupboard. She launched a teacup at his head. It missed and exploded against a wall. "You're not naming my baby after any Greeks," she said between clenched teeth. "And none of your Negro pride names, either." With her next missile – a teapot – she nicked one of Ben's massive ears. Years later, Ben would show the scar to Mahatma. *See that? Your mother gave it to me.* Cupping his bleeding ear, Ben consented. It was agreed that he would find the name, but that Louise retained veto rights over anything sounding Greek or Negro. There was to be no Euripides Homer Grafton. No Marcus Garvey Grafton, no Booker T. Grafton. Ben accepted his wife's conditions, because he knew that otherwise she would oppose him at every turn. She would call the boy Paul no matter what Ben called him. Ben needed her cooperation. He didn't want the boy confused about his name.

Ben found the name for his son by a devious route. Mahatma Gandhi was a great man. A man of great thoughts and great action. A credit to his race. True, he was an Indian, from India. But he had brown skin. Call him an Indian, call him what you wanted, as far as Ben Grafton was concerned, the man was coloured. Brownskinned just like Ben's son. Mahatma it would be. It was a great name. Fitting for a great person. Mahatma had a good sound to it. It was respectable. It had three syllables. Anybody who meant to pronounce that name was going to have to stop and think about it. Mahatma Grafton!

"Mahatma," Louise sniffed. "Is that a Negro name?"

"No," Ben was able to answer, "it is not."

➤➤ ◄◄

Helen Savoie had lived for ten years above a fur store east of the Red River. Initially, she had used one room to sleep and the other as a study. But after joining *The Herald*, she often slept in her study or wrote in her bedroom, noting ideas for stories late into the night.

The landlord had always assumed Helen was a secretary. She never bothered to correct him.

In her earliest days at the paper, an editor had asked her to coach one of the weaker reporters – a fellow named Chuck Maxwell – in the art of writing. Helen took the task to heart. In those days, reporters still used typewriters. Helen would bring home carbon copies of Chuck's articles. In her spare time, she would unite split infinitives, tighten leads and cross out adjectives. Helen eventually realized Chuck would never improve much. But the editing bug had infected her. From time to time, she couldn't resist red-pencilling other reporters' carbon copies and slipping the corrected work into their mailboxes at work. This unsolicited service proved unpopular in the newsroom. Helen let it drop, except for occasional comments to new reporters who appeared receptive to criticism. Although Mahatma Grafton was a capable writer, Helen detected a disturbing tendency in his work. He was too hungry for news. Too willing to write anything. In a recent article, he had happily compared police statistics on the number of rapes this year and last. Helen circled the offensive paragraph and scribbled, "What do you take these for, basketball stats?" before dropping the clipping in his mailbox.

Helen didn't hear from him. She believed that Mahatma Grafton was rudderless. Capable of producing great work, but equally likely to waste his talent on junk news. Helen pictured Mahatma lingering on the brink. He could swing one way or the other. Journalists started out honourably, but circumstances – city editors, assignment editors, tabloid competitors – plunged them into trash cans. It took less effort to grab the easy stories – dog bites boy, mayor swears at premier – than to climb out and do something.

Every day, when journalists came to work, they knew how their work had been judged: their stories ran big or small or not at all. Reporters learned how to wring the most gratification from the least work. Helen worried about Grafton. On the cop beat, he exhibited a growing tendency to grab easy news. It disturbed Helen that so many young reporters tossed aside their values to succeed. Perhaps they didn't have any values. Didn't care about anything. "I don't have an opinion, I'm a journalist," they would answer if you asked them anything about anything. Should Canada withdraw from NATO? Bar American cruise missile testing over Canadian airspace? Idiots.

Hassane Moustafa "Yoyo" Ali met Helen Savoie on the bicycle path in Lyndale Park on the east side of the Red River. Helen was out for a stroll, and Yoyo had come to see the Red River, which, he'd been informed, had been a meeting place for Cree and Assiniboine Indians before the Europeans came. "Excuse me," Yoyo said to her. He found her plumpness attractive. Yoyo worried about disturbing her. He knew that Canadians disliked talking to strangers.

"Yes?" she said, eyeing him directly.

He asked, "Is this the historic Red River, travelled once by Louis Riel, father of Manitoba?" He liked her big hips, big bones, big legs. She resembled a good strong African woman.

For her part, Helen noticed his heavy accent. She guessed that he was from Haiti. And so cute: small, like a boy, but in his late twenties, or older. Replying in English, Helen said yes, this was the Red River.

"Should I call you Madame or Mademoiselle?"

"It doesn't make any difference," she said. Oh yes, he emphasized, it made a difference. "Mademoiselle," she said. Touched by the man's struggle to carry on in English, Helen made up her mind. She began speaking to him in French. Flawless French.

"Alors, vous êtes canadienne-française," he said.

"Mais oui."

"Vraiment?" He studied her with great interest.

"Oui," she said, shyly. She admitted that she was French-Canadian. That she still carried the language with her.

Yoyo told Helen he was spending ten months in Winnipeg as a foreign correspondent while gaining experience as a contributor to the St. Boniface weekly. They spoke of St. Boniface, Canada and Cameroon as they walked through the park. A bitter autumn wind whistled across the river. She could see he was cold, and she, already wearing a heavy sweater, offered him her jacket.

He declined. "That is very kind of you. In my country, never would a white woman lend a black man her jacket."

"There are whites in Cameroon?"

"There are tourists, and there are ex-colonials, and missionaries, and those who wish to rescue us from our misery," he chuckled. "They come over, stinging from vaccinations, suffering diarrhoea from our water, melting under the heat, cursing the roads when it rains, carrying mosquito netting to protect them from malaria, never speaking our native languages, sometimes not even speaking French, yet still, somehow, they remain convinced that they must rescue us from our misery."

"And do they do it?"

"No, they leave, after a few weeks, or months, to rescue themselves from their own misery." Helen laughed again. A long, hearty, simple laugh, mirth that she had barely known in the many years she had worked at *The Herald*. Yoyo was a charming fellow. Handsome, in his way. But thin! His wrists and knuckles seemed particularly frail. Perhaps this was what she found attractive. She allowed herself to dwell for a moment on inconsequential thoughts that could never lead anywhere. Yoyo asked her name. For him, she pronounced it "Hélène." "Hélène!" Yoyo said it with urgency, as if he were warning her of a rushing bicycle.

"Oui?"

"Hélène, je t'aime."

They met the next day in the park, on the bicycle path, under a tree with a strange branch that reached straight out and then curved up, like a bent arm. Yoyo told her it resembled the arm of an African woman reaching up to adjust a water pail on her head. Yoyo kissed her cheeks. His lips were thick. Dry. As dry as a twig in the sun. Dry, perhaps, but they exerted pressure. Promising lips! He said, "Hello, my lover!"

"And what makes you think I'm your lover?"

"Come now, Mademoiselle Hélène, if we were not lovers, why would you have met me today?"

He told her she had beautiful eyes. Stunning hair, dark brown, very brown, that hung straight down, grazing her neck. "Tellement foncés, tes cheveux," he told her. As if she had *ancêtres africains*. She was going to tell him she couldn't meet him again. She was going to say she didn't want to get involved. She was going to break it off before it started, but then he told her he was returning to Cameroon in six months. Helen bit her tongue. If he were going soon, why not? He was staying in the home of an old widow; they couldn't go there. So Helen took him home.

Yoyo was a wonderful lover. Less energetic, less thrusting, than her old boyfriend. Yoyo was no bigger than Helen. In fact, laughing, she put him on the bathroom scales and found out he was two pounds lighter. He didn't perform gymnastics and he didn't display Olympian endurance. But he was caring. He made her look into his eyes when they made love; his eyes were so dark that, whenever the lights were dim, she couldn't find the line between his pupils and his irises. Sometimes he spoke in French and sometimes Bamileke, his mother tongue. He said the English language wasn't fit for bedroom conversation.

They made love again. The phone rang. It was out in the hall, on the floor. Before he had undressed her and let her strip him, Yoyo had stared at the beige receiver in the bedroom. "Canadians leave telephones in their bedrooms?" he asked.

"Yes," she said, puzzled at his confusion.

"You leave them right next to a bed?" he asked.

"Yes, why?" she asked.

"And if it rings while you sleep, won't it wake you up if it is so close to the bed?"

"Yes, of course."

"And that doesn't bother you? You would let the phone ruin your rest?" This was the first time the practice had struck Helen as absurd. But Yoyo hadn't finished. "Now, one other thing. If you and I are making love, and this phone rings, what happens then?"

"Well, normally, I would answer it."

Yoyo shook his held. Canadians really had their priorities mixed up. "I have entered you, and we are gasping together, and you are prepared to roll over and answer the phone?"

Helen grinned and said, "You never know. It could be important. Someone could be selling vacuum cleaners." They laughed and kissed, but before going further, Yoyo carried the phone into the hall.

"Do you know what I would like?" They had slept for an hour.

"Anything you want, Yoyo."

"Make me breakfast."

"What?"

"Make me breakfast."

It was 2:00 in the afternoon. "Why breakfast?"

"In my country, when a man and a woman make love, if the man does a good job, the woman makes him breakfast. A huge, whopping breakfast. She treats him like a king. It is thought that he deserves it, if he has satisfied her."

"Well, how about eggs and orange juice and toast?"

"I'll take the toast and the eggs," he said. "Many eggs and much toast. But no juice! By no means juice! Just give me tea with honey."

"You don't like orange juice?"

"I don't like what Canadians call orange juice! In those frozen cans? How can one freeze the juice of an orange? I nearly choked, the first time I tasted it. We have beautiful oranges in Cameroon and we know how to make orange juice. The richer a nation becomes, the less capable it is of producing respectable orange juice." Helen laughed hard, hearing that. It sounded particularly funny when pronounced with Yoyo's West African accent. She made him breakfast.

➤➤ ◄◄

Ben began, "In 1937, there were so few coloured people in Winnipeg that most knew each other. Many roomed off Main Street, near the Canadian Transcontinental Railway station, and everyone noticed a new man when he showed up looking for work.

"One Friday afternoon in June, Harry Carson, another railway porter, showed up at my room and asked, 'You hear about that Grenadian kid?'

"He was talking about an island boy who'd had the audacity to ask for the manager of a bank that morning, seeking employment as a clerk. Harry and I shook our heads.

"All through the next week, Harry kept bringing me news. The upstart, whose name was Melvyn Hill, tried two more banks, the City Hall, two mining companies and *The Winnipeg Herald*, spreading word of his high school diploma.

"Finally, Harry asked me, 'Who does this boy think he is, Ben?'

"I said I didn't know, but I wished him luck.

"'Ain't no luck gonna get that boy a white man's job.'

"I left town on a run down east and back. Two nights on the train plus one in Toronto, shining shoes, carrying luggage, making beds, mopping floors, dusting windows, keeping out of trouble, you know. Trouble, in those days, meant instant dismissal. There was an old porter used to say, 'Trouble's like air coming tru the winda. You can't shut the winda and you can't stop the draught; you just step aside so you don't catch cold.'

"In Toronto, I spent the night with a cousin to avoid the bunk-bed flophouse the company ran on Huron Street. When I got back I learned from the inspector that the company had just trained Melvyn Hill.

"'We'll put him in your car on the next trip to Toronto,' the inspector told me. 'Show him the ropes. Let me know how he does.'

"Melvyn Hill had piano fingers. That was the first thing I noticed: no blisters, no calluses. He was short and had little meat on him and was neither photo handsome nor fighting ugly. Small eyes that hardly blinked. Chin that stuck out. And dark skin. Not high yellow. Not brown, like mine. This baby was black.

"Though I didn't speak to Hill except when necessary, I was glad when the trip ended. He hardly spoke during the entire trip, made a fuss about cleaning toilets, refused to eat with other porters and went out alone on his night off in Toronto."

Ben had eaten his soup and he was fussing with a glass of water.

"Hill was made a full-time porter at a salary of $87 a month, plus tips. They put him on the spare board, meaning that he didn't work a regular train run, but filled in for others here and there. Weeks passed before I saw him again. But I heard Harry muttering about him from time to time. 'He acts like he knows it all. He thinks he's better than us.'

"Almost a year passed. One day while Harry and I were sitting on a window ledge upstairs in the Porters' Club, I saw a middle-aged coloured man with a serious, dignified face walking our way. Pressed grey suit. Polished shoes. With him, a woman who was also well dressed. A white woman, one hundred percent white. And that wasn't all. Two boys toddled behind them. They had straight, dark hair. The younger one's skin was very light. Almost white. The boys wore yarmulkes, which I saw as the family crossed Main at Sutherland, walking north.

"Harry and I thought they were quite a sight. Neither of us heard the footsteps on the stairs, and suddenly I found myself face to face with the coloured man in the suit. For a moment I didn't know what to say. The man stood tall and with perfect posture. His eyes were light brown and his greying hair, curled and cropped close to his head, was clipped above his large ears. He was in his mid-forties. Behind us, the room had fallen silent. The man said he was looking for me. Said he had recently been to porters' training school, and was supposed to start Monday in my car. He introduced himself as Alvin James."

Mahatma tapped his fork on the table. "Alvin James? Aren't we getting off track here, abuelo?"

"Patience. Alvin James was the first black man to graduate from the University of Manitoba with a Master's degree in sciences. Also, he had converted to Judaism because his wife was a Ukrainian Jew. That's why we called him 'the Rabbi.' It wasn't meant to be derogatory. Quite the contrary. Even though he was educated and had tried to get other jobs, all he could find was porter.

"Of course, the other porters held him in awe. Some went to him with questions. One asked him to help fill out an income tax form. Alvin James complied. Another two porters had him settle a dispute. All this time, Melvyn Hill was running to Toronto and back. So for more than a year, Melvyn, Harry, Alvin and I worked the same train down east and back.

"Melvyn pestered Alvin James all the time with questions about books and university. He even started dressing like the man, always in a jacket and tie.

"Hill was so enamoured that he told us a story about Alvin James. Apparently, the Rabbi had found twenty dollars in the bedding of a passenger and had jumped off the train at White River, Ontario, to give it back. Harry Carson said the Rabbi was a plain fool, giving up good money. But Melvyn said it showed that Alvin James had class. And that Negroes would never get ahead by dishonest means.

"A couple of weeks later, the passenger wrote a letter to the superintendent, praising James and enclosing a hundred-dollar bill. Here's the stinger. Alvin James refused that too. Though he did suggest the hundred be used to buy new mattresses for the company's flophouse on Huron Street in Toronto. The superintendent lost his temper when he heard that. Alvin didn't get the hundred, and the flophouse stayed the way it was."

Ben Grafton was starting on his meal now, an omelette with mushrooms and tomatoes. "Now we jump to 1940 when everyone was talking about enlisting. Well, just about everyone. Alvin was too old to go to war. And Harry wanted nothing to do with it. He said, 'White people wanna kill each other, they don't need my help. Anyway, I got myself a good job.'

"Melvyn applied to the Air Force, did not hear back, tried again three months later, and was told the Air Force was filled up. He applied once more and was contacted shortly thereafter for testing. Melvyn became an Air Force man. They wouldn't let him fly a plane, navigate, operate guns or aim bombs, but they let him do tarmac duty for two years. Then they taught him how to service aircraft. He stayed on ground crews in Canada until 1944 and finally made it overseas.

"I became an Army private, went overseas in '44. You know all this. When we got back in '46, we found that job doors didn't swing any wider than before the war. We got our old jobs back. Before we had a chance to see any of our old buddies, the Rabbi died. You should understand that I had just come back from a war that I was sure would kill me. Melvyn, ten years younger than me, was exhausted from the war. Neither of us could accept the news of the Rabbi's death. We'd seen all kinds survive in Europe. Why that man, of all people? He was a good man.

"Harry Carson was too upset to work the trip back to Winnipeg. In Sudbury, a doctor had to shoot tranks into his butt. He was a mess all the way home. When the train carrying the Rabbi's body got back to Winnipeg, we learned that he'd died in a fire at that flophouse. The worst part was that the company blamed him for the fire."

Ben stopped and fingered the napkin beside his plate. His omelette was only half eaten. When Mahatma coughed into his hand, Ben roused himself and went on.

"We went to a shiva, a Jewish wake that lasts seven days, in the Rabbi's home. I had my only suit pressed. We passed a hat and in two hours collected one hundred dollars. That was a lot of money in those days. Later, we heard the Canadian Transcontinental had offered the Rabbi's widow only fifty. At her house on Bannerman, we met John Novak and the Rabbi's widow, Deanna, and her two boys, now about ten and twelve years old. I was fascinated by their pigmentation. Peter, the older one, was brown-skinned, but I might not have guessed that Alvin, the ten-year-old, was born of a Negro father. Alvin Jr. seemed almost as light as his mother.

"I gave John Novak the envelope from the porters. He was impressed. He steered me toward two chairs in a corner and told me, 'The company says the porters had been drinking and partying and that Alvin had been smoking in bed.'

"He knew, like I did, that Alvin didn't smoke. He wanted to know why, if there was a party going on, only Alvin got killed. How come he was the only person in the house?

"I told him what I could. That the flophouse had two rooms upstairs, each with six bunk-beds, but that the company never filled the place. Porters resented staying in bunk-beds while white train crews slept in hotels. I hated the place and usually stayed with my cousin. Most porters avoided the place. Slept with friends, whatever.

"The Rabbi stayed there out of principle. He said nobody would end segregation if porters avoided the place. He said black people had to fill that place up and keep filling it until someone took notice. But the porters wouldn't listen. It's true that the men partied there, sometimes. About a year before, some of the boys had a real shindig there. They brought girls in and tomcatted and drank until neighbours called the police.

"After that, the doors were locked every night at 9:30. They came early in the morning to let you out. It was stupid but the company wouldn't do a thing about it. But Alvin kept staying there. He wouldn't give up. And that flophouse, that dignity cost him his life.

"He was the only man in that house. And even though firemen axed down the door, they were too late. They found him right there, dead on the floor."

Ben looked up at Mahatma. "I told all this to Novak in so many words. It was at the funeral, remember, and I didn't know that he was a lawyer, or that he would soon earn a seat on City Council and later become Winnipeg's first communist mayor. I didn't know that Novak had contacts with reporters and civil rights groups across the country. Or that he would come after all us porters to testify about that flophouse and get even with the company. All of us except Melvyn Hill, that is. He wanted to get ahead and he knew that testifying against the company could hurt his chances. He told us, 'I'm going to climb the ladder, make something of myself. You should do the same.'"

1992

GEORGE ELLIOTT CLARKE

Watercolour for Negro Expatriates in France

What are calendars to you?
And, indeed, what are atlases?
    Time is cool jazz in Bretagne,
you, hidden in berets or eccentric scarves,
somewhere over the rainbow –
where you are tin-men requiring hearts,
lion-men demanding courage,
scarecrow-men needing minds all your own
after DuBois made blackness respectable.
    Geography is brown girls in Paris
in the spring by the restless Seine
flowing like blood in chic, African colonies;
Josephine Baker on your bebop phonographs
in the lonely, brave, old rented rooms;
Gallic wines shocking you out of yourselves,
leaving you as abandoned
as obsolete locomotives whimpering Leadbelly blues
in lonesome Shantytown, U.S.A.

    What are borders/frontiers to you?
In actual seven-league sandals,

you ride Monet's shimmering waterlilies –
in your street-artist imaginations –
across the sky darkened,
here and there, by Nazi shadows,
Krupp thunderclouds,
and, in other places, by Americans
who remind you
that you are niggers,
even if you have read Victor Hugo.
      Night is winged Ethiopia in the distance,
rising on zeta beams of radio free Europe,
bringing you in for touchdown at Orleans;
or, it is strange, strychnine streetwalkers,
fleecing you for an authentic Negro poem
or rhythm and blues salutation.
This is your life –
lounging with Richard Wright in Matisse-green
parks, facing nightmares of contorted
lynchers every night. Every night.

      Scatalogical ragtime reggae haunts the caverns
of *le métro*. You pick up English-language
newspapers and *TIME* magazines,
learn that this one was arrested,
that one assassinated;
fear waking – like Gregor Samsa –
in the hands of a mob;
lust for a black Constance Chatterley,
not even knowing that
all Black people not residing in Africa
are kidnap victims.
      After all, how can you be an expatriate
of a country that was
never yours?

Pastel paintings on Paris pavement,
wall-posters Beardsley-styled:
you pause and admire them all;
and France entrances you
with its kaleidoscope cafés,
chain-smoking intelligentsia,
absinthe and pernod poets . . .
Have you ever seen postcards
of Alabama or Auschwitz,
Mussolini or Mississippi?
It is unsafe to wallow in Ulyssean dreams,
genetic theories, vignettes of Gertrude Stein,
Hemingway, other maudlin moderns,
while the godless globe
detonates its war-heart, loosing
goose-stepping geniuses
and dark, secret labs.

Perhaps I suffer aphasia.
I know not how to talk to you.
I send you greetings from *Afrique*
and spirituals of catholic *Négritude*.
Meanwhile, roses burst like red stars,
a flower explodes for a special sister.
You do not accept gravity in France
where everything floats on the premise
that the earth will rise to meet it
the next day;
where the Eiffel Tower bends over backwards
to insult the Statue of Liberty;
and a woman in the flesh of the moment
sprouts rainbow butterfly wings
and kisses a schizoid sculptor
lightly on his full, ruby lips;
and an argument is dropped over cocoa
by manic mulatto musicians

who hear whispers of Eliot –
or Ellington –
in common prayers.

     You have heard Ma Rainey, Bessie Smith.
You need no passports.
Your ticket is an all-night room
facing the ivory, voodoo moon,
full of Henri Rousseau lions and natives;
and your senses, inexplicably
homing in on gorgeous Ethiopia,
while Roman rumours of war
fly you home.

                                       1979

Salvation Army Blues

     Seeking after hard things –
muscular work or sweat-swagger action –
I rip wispy, Help Wanted ads,
dream of water-coloured sailors
pulling apart insect wings of maps,
stagger down saxophone blues avenues
where blackbirds cry for crumbs.
I yearn to be Ulyssean, to roam
foaming oceans or wrest
a wage from tough, mad adventure.
     For now, I labour language,
earn a cigarette
for a poem, a coffee
for a straight answer,

and stumble, punch-drunk,
down these drawn-and-quartered streets,
tense hands manacled
to snarling pockets.

1983

Hymn for Portia White[1]

The white, bathing moon
    ogles itself in the sea,
        all black and handsome.

1983

Look Homeward, Exile

  I can still see that soil crimsoned by butchered
Hog and imbrued with rye, lye, and homely
Spirituals everybody must know,
Still dream of folks who broke or cracked like shale:
Pushkin, who twisted his hands in boxing,
Marrocco, who ran girls like dogs and got stabbed,
Lavinia, her teeth decayed to black stumps,
Her lovemaking still in demand, spitting

---

[1] A famed Africadian contralto (1911–1968).

Black phlegm – her pension after twenty towns,
And Toof, suckled on anger that no Baptist
Church could contain, who let wrinkled Eely
Seed her moist womb when she was just thirteen.
    And the tyrant sun that reared from barbed-wire
Spewed flame that charred the idiot crops
To Depression, and hurt my granddaddy
To bottle after bottle of sweet death,
His dreams beaten to one, tremendous pulp,
Until his heart seized, choked; his love gave out.
    But Beauty survived, secreted
In freight trains snorting in their pens, in babes
Whose faces were coal-black mirrors, in strange
Strummers who plucked Ghanaian banjos, hummed
Blind blues – precise, ornate, rich needlepoint,
In sermons scorched with sulphur and brimstone,
And in my love's dark, orient skin that smelled
Like orange peels and tasted like rum, good God!
    I remember my Creator in the old ways:
I sit in taverns and stare at my fists;
I knead earth into bread, spell water into wine.
Still, nothing warms my wintry exile – neither
Prayers nor fine love, neither votes nor hard drink:
For nothing heals those saints felled in green beds,
Whose loves are smashed by just one word or glance
Or pain – a screw jammed in thick, straining wood.

1990

The River Pilgrim: A Letter

At eighteen, I thought the Sixhiboux wept.
Five years younger, you were lush, beautiful
Mystery; your limbs – scrolls of deep water.
Before your home, lost in roses, I swooned,
Drunken in the village of Whylah Falls,
And brought you apple blossoms you refused,
Wanting Hank Snow woodsmoke blues and dried smelts,
Wanting some milljerk's dumb, unlettered love.

That May, freights chimed xylophone tracks that rang
To Montréal. I scribbled postcard odes,
Painted *le fleuve Saint-Laurent comme la Seine* –
Sad watercolours for Negro exiles
In France, and dreamt Paris white with lepers,
Soft cripples who finger pawns under elms,
Drink blurry into young debauchery,
Their glasses clear with Cointreau, rain, and tears.

You hung the moon backwards, crooned crooked poems
That no voice could straighten, not even O
Who stroked guitars because he was going
To die with a bullet through his stomach.
Innocent, you curled among notes – petals
That scaled glissando from windows agape,
And remained in southwest Nova Scotia,
While I drifted, sad and tired, in the east.

I have been gone four springs. This April, pale
Apple blossoms blizzard. The garden flutes
E-flats of lilacs, G-sharps of lilies.
Too many years, too many years, are past. . . .

Past the marble and pale flowers of Paris,
Past the broken, Cubist guitars of Arles,
Shelley, I am coming down through the narrows
Of the Sixhiboux River. I will write

Beforehand. Please, please come out to meet me
                    As far as Gilbert's Cove.

                                        1990

Bees' Wings

  This washed-out morning, April rain descants,
Weeps over gravity, the broken bones
Of gravel and graveyards, and Cora puts
Away gold dandelions to sugar
And skew into gold wine, then discloses
That Pablo gutted his engine last night
Speeding to Beulah Beach under a moon
As pocked and yellowed as aged newsprint.
Now, Othello, famed guitarist, heated
By rain-clear rum, voices transparent notes
Of sad, anonymous heroes who hooked
Mackerel and slept in love-pried-open thighs
And gave out booze in vain crusades to end
Twenty centuries of Christianity.
  His voice is simple, sung air: without notes,
There's nothing. His unknown, imminent death
(The feel of iambs ending as trochees
In a slow, decasyllabic death-waltz;
His vertebrae trellised on his stripped spine
Like a xylophone or keyboard of nerves)
Will also be nothing: the sun pours gold
Upon Shelley, his sis', light as bees' wings,
Who roams a garden sprung from rotten wood
And words, picking green nouns and fresh, bright verbs,

For there's nothing I will not force language
To do to make us one — whether water
Hurts like whisky or the sun burns like oil
Or love declines to weathered names on stone.

1990

Blank Sonnet

The air smells of rhubarb, occasional
Roses, or first birth of blossoms, a fresh,
Undulant hurt, so body snaps and curls
Like flower. I step through snow as thin as script,
Watch white stars spin dizzy as drunks, and yearn
To sleep beneath a patchwork quilt of rum.
I want the slow, sure collapse of language
Washed out by alcohol. Lovely Shelley,
I have no use for measured, cadenced verse
If you won't read. Icarus-like, I'll fall
Against this page of snow, tumble blackly
Across vision to drown in the white sea
That closes every poem — the white reverse
That cancels the blackness of each image.

1990

Each Moment Is Magnificent

Othello practises *White Rum*, his scale of just music, and clears the love song of muddying his morals. He sets his glass down lovingly, a whole chorus of molecules sloshing in harmony. He vows he will not, he will not be a dead hero, no way, suffering a beautiful sleep, trimmed with ochre, hazelnut, dressed in mahogany, smelling of last-minute honey and tears, regrets rained upon him too late in the guise of wilted, frail flowers. Instead, he will sleep right now, while he still can, up to his thighs in thighs, gnaw dried, salty smelts, and water song with rum. *Sweet Sixhiboux, run softly till I end my song.*

Wearing the lineaments of ungratified desire, Selah sashays from the livingroom, watches dusk bask in the River Sixhiboux. She tells Othello to shut up because Jericho's where she's gonna go when she falls in love. Yep, when that someday man come out the blue to Whylah Falls, Beauty Town, to serenade her and close his wings around her, she'll be in Jericho at last like the fortune-teller says. She'll jump the broom and cross the Nile.

I stroll outside with strange music in my skull. Here's the Sixhiboux River, tossed tinfoil, crinkling along the ground, undistracted by all the grave lovers it attracts, all those late Romantics who spout Lake Poet Wordsworth, "The world is too much with us, late and soon," and brood upon the river's shimmering bliss before tossing themselves within, pretending to be Percy Bysshe Shelley at Lerici. I've thought of the Sixhiboux in those erotic ways, dreamt it as midnight-thick, voluptuous, folding – like a million moths, furry with a dry raininess – over one. No matter where you are in Sunflower County, you can hear it pooling, milling in a rainstorm, or thundering over a hapless town. Even now, I can hear its shining roar pouring over Shelley's house, polishing the roses that nod, drunken, or spring – petalled crude – from earth. All I hear is an old song, her voice, lilting, "Lover Man."

1990

Vision of Justice

I see the moon hunted down, spooked from hills,
Roses hammer his coffin shut, O stilled
By stuttered slander, judicial gossip,
And a killer's brawling bullet. Bludgeoned
Men, noosed by loose law, swing from pines; judges,
Chalked commandants, gabble dour commandments;
Their law books yawn like lime-white, open pits
Lettered with bones, charred gibberish, of those
Who dared to love or sing and fell to mobs.
Language has become volatile liquor,
Firewater, that lovers pour for prophets
Whom haul, from air, tongues of pentecostal fire –
Poetry come among us.

1990

Violets for Your Furs

I still dream the steamed blackness, witness, of you in rain;
I talk about that – pouring living fire on guitar strings,
And suffer Cointreau's blues aftertaste of burnt orange,
The torturous bitter flavour of the French in Africa,
The crisis of your long black hair assaulting your waist,
Your small, troubling breasts not quite spoken for,
Your spontaneous mouth unconsummated with kisses,
'Cos you cashed in your pretty *Négritude* and gone.

Ah, you were a living *S*, all Coltrane or Picasso swerves;
Your hair stranded splendid on the gold beach of your face,

So sweet, I moaned black rum, black sax, black moon,
The black trace of your eyelash like lightning,
The sonorous blackness of your skin after midnight –
The sadness of loving you glimmering in Scotch.
Now, this sheet darkens with the black snow of words;
In my sheets, a glimpse of night falls, then loneliness.

I can't sleep – haunted by sad sweetness outside the skull,
The hurtful perfume you bathed in by the yellow lamp,
Three-quarters drunk, your rouged kiss branding my neck,
The orange cry of my mouth kindling your blue night skin.
The night blossoms ugly, I down gilded damnation.
I've been lovin' you – more than words – too long to stop now.
What will happen next? I can't know, you should know:
The moon tumbles, caught in fits of grass, seizures of leaves.

1994

To Say, "I love you"

To say, "I love you,"
"je t'aime" –
your white thigh chafing my brown
in our beautiful sleep
and lovetoil,
the taking and giving,
your mouth
on mine –
the wet lustre
of our lips and sexes
becomes silver oiling,
burnishing,

dull, usual words;
French and English gleam
with fresh meaning:
leaf-sifted light
soleils, shadows,
our bared love.

1994

DAVID N. ODHIAMBO

LIP

ONE

1st movement
fall 95.

1a.

halloween. downtown dracoon. a jackhammer gets busy. crooning
times many. ushering in a scratch break – dusk. lady day tickling the
inner workings of ear. strain of rain. a truck backing up/beeping
into a loading zone.

lip stretches . . . yards. tricking himself to sit. peeling out of a
duvet stuck to sweat on ebony skin. a mottled scar from shoulder
to elbow above hands opening rusted ramshackle latches at
windows. opening the door. water put to boil in an aluminum pan.
as he gives in to an urge to piss. thinking on a shave. startling the
face, in the mouth of a doorway, with warm drips/rain instead.

he fights an urge to distract the mind – calls to make; calls to
take. as he has himself a du maurier. something to give up for
months now. so as to avoid yellowing teeth.

the jackhammer. laid back now. another groove he's begun, yet
again, to give over to. another remix, yet again, of the sound
outside his window with an internal clamour of gothic blue . . . a

sign/another exploration begins . . . yet again . . . tentative . . . yearning to move away from . . . structure/obligation (this back to work/back to work) that has beached itself where prodigal notes/tones stray all up inside the marrow of his bone.

he stands, yet again/as he does once more, in this doorway. trying, once again – not for the last time – to outwit this foe (he knows this much at least). to outwit this death – his sometime friend. as secrets he's forgotten to remember, once again, snarl and prance/prance and snarl inside the coffin beat/beat/beating beneath a pierced nipple in his chest. this snarl and prance/prance and snarl locking into configurations known, for now, only as a drag/downward into nicotine; tricks turned by smacked up whores from the district; liquor sweetened trolling the day before the mourning after. as he thinks, crawl back under covers. wanting to sleep off a fatigue which never lifts. away from this city his body has begun, yet again, to drag itself through.

he flicks the butt – not for the last time – out onto damp grass. lights up a stick of incense – jasmine. crafted state side. slipping on a c.d./j.b.'s – sex machine. phunking his bad ass to awake. as he high steps into sweats. staring at a drip of shuffle steps leaking through his ceiling. leaking into walls.

i told you tomorrow. TOMORROW. is tomorrow today?

she needs a father.

what she needs is to go to jail. that's what she needs.

for chrissakes, pritchard.

for chrissakes, pritchard . . . if you want to go to this party. fine. but i'm not taking ula.

he rubs eyes. yawns. eyes attaching to a mustard mug on the windowsill.

we were going to do this as a family.

a FAMILY! a table leaps/tumbles and glass – splintered deci-belzzz – chatters against floor. i said tomorrow.

why . . . why must you break things?

he pours the bristle and steam of water into the mug.

i said tomorrow.

sprinkling it with clove and slabs of ginger.

now i'm going to have to clean up again.

TOMORROW.

the j.b.'s testily holding off. slick. tight. before crackling sideways . . . the bridge.

. . . why don't you just . . . just kill me. KILL ME. here. here's the
knife. just do it. RIGHT NOW.

honey dribbles from an abandoned teaspoon as lip scrambles
through piles of ageing sheet music. knocking ink flecked bars and
measures to the hardwood floor. fingers reaching/tapping out
digits on a telephone . . .

ta. i'm calling to repor' a 'omestic 'ispute.

a what?

a 'omestic 'ispute. 'omestic 'ispute.

what seems to be happening, sir?

'ere's bin smashin. un a woman jos said . . . she jos said . . . ere's
the knoife. kiw me. KIW ME roight now.

do you know the address?

uhhhhhhh . . . i . . . dunknow ma'e. ummm. moine is 1000
houghton. it's . . . uh . . . east of moine.

can you go out and take a quick look?

culd i wha?

can you take a look at what the address is, sir?

phhuuuck . . . he drops the phone. and thuds out into blue of
new moon breaking through shifty leaks of charcoal cloud. frisky
wind whispering all up inside pant legs.

. . . 1004 houghton.

and what's your name?

me naime?

yes. your name, sir.

lip. lip osland.

liplip osland.

no(w) . . . LIP OSLAND.

and you're a . . . neighbour.

crikey . . . yeh oi'm a goddamn neyeburr. 'ook she said, kiw me
roight now.

don't panic, mr. osland. an officer will be there shortly.

b.

a clock ticks. tick. seconds passing into minutes. tock. that lick and shriek up on the hour. tick. wind scratching the nail of branches up against a silky sulk/wettened drip – snaky wracks . . . trumpet. tock.

. . . a flutter of footsteps at the door. tick. a bag clatters to cement. tock.

TRICK OR TREAT.

tick. he crawls under a piano bench. tock. waiting. tick. until . . . feet scamper back into rain/buckets full for days. tock. out past cars/trucks galloping through traffic lights winking red. tick. blinking green. tock. among leaves bruised to discolour by autumn. tick. aged by wind. tock. tanned by grey tabled to mauve for day after night after fucking day.

. . . the phone . . .

juwain. oi ma'e . . . no' baad. yewe . . . shi's appenin nex' door. pritchard un simone a' it agin . . . alf un 'our. the cops aven't shown op . . . no. nuffin . . . she said kiw me. KIW ME roight now. un the bleedin opera'or a' the steyetion ad me ronnin aroun' fo' mus a bin . . . ole on a sec, he listens . . . noises at the gate. i's the cops . . . yeh . . . yeh. no(w). listen 'aveta, ron. and hangs up. to skulk outside. behind a bush. sky wailing water to socks at feet. tock. watching two officers knock at a door. tick. pritchard opening up/soused n' stumbling out in a sailor costume.

c.

good evening, officers.

good evening, mr. charles. i'm constable gray. a balding fellow flushed overripe beet stands beside the rookie that is his partner. and this is inspector roger.

good evening, mr. charles.

good evening, inspector.

sorry to bother you. but –

there's been a ca —

BUT there's been a call.

everything is fine, officer. just a little disagreement with the missis.

the neighbours —

PARDON ME for asking. but some of the guys down at the station are big fans. do you . . . do you think we could get an autograph?

certainly.

he's handed a parking ticket. on which he distractedly scrawls a signature.

the wife will be tickled pink by this . . . thank you.

inspector gray steps back. slips. fumbling pen and paper to muck. both pritchard and inspector roger reaching out to help him stay on feet.

tickled pink.

he picks up after himself. hastily doubling back. clambering into the passenger seat of a cop car. inspector roger sliding in beside him. starting the engine. backing up . . . into a fire hydrant. coffee spilling onto clothes. before they scoot off through puddles. out into night. pritchard scurrying back inside.

d.

lip slinks/slunks back to his tea. and takes it to the piano — opening the lid. standing up twice to go elsewhere. sitting back down again before, fingers tackle ivory. improvising on a scale. something easy — g major. away from lull/sleep. towards obsessings over tempo/tone. shuttling in and out of phrasing . . . pacing.

too damn slow.

his fingers — tremble. crumpling into one octave. colliding up against another. eyes up and down. his mind . . . finding — notes curved/cupped — the taste of rouge. then . . . nothing/back to his reflection in the window. knuckles stuck at — day set/a disruption of horizontal dark smeared west. unable to script familiar faces scuttling off to cappuccino bar flights too long n' brief. into un-filtered tobacco retreats, unfiltered monoxide scented beats. trips . . . lips. lists of the murdered till centre page — frederick sin-clair/frederick sinclair — empty and alone.

he balls a hand up into a fist. empty. reaches for a smoke. alone. three puffs out and back to idling time away. empty. a percussive thing out of key. alone. clock ticking ass backwards. tick. nine minutes to the hour. tock. nineteen minutes to the hour. tick. fifteen stars and a firefly between. tock. drenched by the cymbal clap/thunder brokered rain. tick. into a swig of herbal brew. tock. stuttered to absent moon a scar cutting the windowpane. tick.

he gathers himself. tock. stands — arid/dry — closing the lid. tick. before huddling out back. tock. plucking melancholia leaf by petal. tick. dragging heavy on a camel light. tock. tick. tock . . .

2a.

an airplane taxis into port. in from lofton city. way the hell 'cross the country. hi hat treble to stand still. rilca unclapping a seat belt. a dark glassed bad assed baby. trunk jewellery at neck n' upper arm. piercing in tongue. dark eyes. dark tights. off to baggage check — mellow.

she hops a cab. dark glasses behind dark eyes. squinting — yet again — at sheets of rain. like when she'd left — at a smudged bungle of hotels. wondering, as they lurch through traffic, where the fuck am i now. after frederick sinclair. which had been inconceivable to most. but had happened. where the fuck was she now. after having gone to the places she'd been. sketching straklanders who'd sur-vived that other time — inconceivable to most, but it had happened. straklanders who'd endured with their song sprung from among the graves behind the cane fields and coffee plantations of the panoans. the panoans — merchants who'd deposited the salucians like sediment up on a foreign shore. the salucians — indentured labour who'd watched as the straklanders had been driven or fled or suicided in droves from the land, which up until that other time, had been their own.

she'd sketched. collecting charcoal portrayals of crooked hands and shattered feet and backs scarred the cut and feel of corrugated iron. unable – unwilling perhaps – to look too close. uncertain what, if she watched too long, this would reveal about them to her/about her to them. and, what toxins the ensuing torment, inevitable as the rising sun, would work in her.

i'm dressed up as thales. the cabby suspends bait – worms of chatter – into dizzy – live – trickling in through the radio. caffeine jump started eyes staring at her from the rear view mirror. unwittingly drawing her back into dracoon. this city which, up until that fated trip, had been her refuge. had been a taste and odour so familiar she no longer noticed the purple mountain dominating its perimeter.

thales?

uhuh. the philosopher. the first to talk of unity in multiplicity. he predicted a solar eclipse . . . 585 b.c. said . . . all is water.

the speedometer drifts – 60/70/80 klicks an hour – past homes/replicas of each other endlessly for blocks. past trees the shape of sketches rolled up in the tubes at her feet. just like that. all is water and there was an . . . eclipse?

no. he also said all is water.

RED LIGHT.

he slams both feet to brakes. the car swerving/tires flirting with an embankment. skidding to a halting in the intersection. the guy was a giant. he hits reverse. a genius. his ideas . . . do you know much about quantum physics?

green light.

his ideas . . . fucking genius . . . imply what we've come to know after splitting the atom.

left . . . LEFT.

that matter is comprised of one entity – ENERGY.

it's the house with the blue staircase at the top of the street.

thales was a milesian. they decelerate. brake. rain beating numbly against the windshield. $22.80 up on the metre. the school responsible for this whole notion of corporeal monism.

she roots through a purse for rumpled bills. could i get a receipt?

one substance. he gropes through the glove compartment. finding pen and paper. one substance. for thales . . . water. for anaximander/an ineffable boundless and limitless entity. she takes his offering of slurry scribble. and opens her door. for anaximenes/air. with a sense that mechanical process led to the creation of objects. a tentative step. and she's saturated. tights clasping skin the fizz n' kick of cola. listen . . . i don't often meet people i can talk to about these things . . . and was . . . would you like to go for a coffee sometime?

my husband . . .

he smiles. baring purple gums. then splashes away. towards the next fish in the drink/catch in the ocean. as she lugs her sketches up stairs. stripping into jammies. quick brush of teeth. moon sliding. clouds shifting. night skipping. into a craving for a smoke.

b.

pritchard and odelle in a boozy tumble in among jackets. she, a chiffon blouse. lace of bra peeping through. neck long and brown the aroma of coffee. her riding crop/beige jodhpurs tossed aside with boots.

they're seeing one another again. fucking around like before. though she'd said . . . never again. and he . . . but my family . . . yet again.

a bail of clothing collapses in heaps of laughter. the midnight train barking away somewhere – how beautiful it all was. a stubbled cheek grazing a chap in the bill of painted lip. as they straighten up. reluctantly. his hands steeped mahogany the sonority of tuba, buttoning up her shirt – reluctantly. him noticing, for the first time, what her powder had failed to conceal – creases above a rash beneath the eye. her cuticles finding – one last time – the razor bumps beneath his chin/the bulge at his belly. as he – reluctantly – steals into sailor gear. reluctantly. before a . . . quick . . . clandestine slip back to a room full of costumes chasing a diminishing supply of dry wine.

. . . imitations of picasso hang from walls. vladimir horowitz breaking down a mozart sonata on the hi fi. fingers making music of math – a harmony of fractions as odelle plucks carpet from hair. pritchard straightens his cap. nobody noticing their back to business as usual. this their secret. that they wish to return to more than often.

his throat. gulp. that she watches. eyes touching up/lingering for appoggiatura's. till evening ends. everyone ushered out of doors. to happening late night joints. to homes.

c.

simone drowsily lifts cream limbs out of stockings. hanging a stewardess's uniform up in a closet. pritchard, sluggishly unbuttoning cufflinks. sitting on the edge of their bed folding trousers.

the pattersons'. what . . . cal couldn't wait to tell everyone about their goddamn pool . . . infernal bores. i don't know why you insist on going to these things. the room has begun to spin. how he managed to drive home he does not know. she applies aloe vera to wrinkles in skin. the details of their hazy evening somehow eluding her. and that spoilt brat of theirs. private school . . . private school! whatever happened to the public education system. not good en . . . serves the prat right. who wouldn't beat on the little shit.

pritchard!

come on, simone. you know i'm right.

she dabs powder under arms. popping sleeping pills. as he flosses in the bathroom mirror – a vigil in which he will, once again, examine the lay of a receding hairline. brushing teeth before clambering into a double bed – their harried nest. him groggily setting the alarm. turning out an antique lamp on an antique table.

her listlessly placing slices of cucumber on her eyes. before . . . the distant tinkle/tankle of traffic/sirens – this bloody neighbourhood; how many times had they had this conversation. the goddamned sound of it scalding another night that will not sleep.

pritchard.

—

pritchard.
mmm . . .
can't we . . .
i don't want to talk about that right now.
but . . .
come on, shuga. it's late.

—

—

pritchard.

—

pritchard.
WHAT?
do you still find me . . . attractive?
he struggles up onto elbows. leans in to slop a kiss to her cheek. before turning away. leaving her to drift uneasily off to seconal kissed/liquor stained slumber in another one of those damn dracoonian nights that will not sleep.

d.

1 a.m.
simone . . . simone.

—

he shakes her. i can't get any bloody sleep.
she turns away.
i've got to get out. go for a drive.

—

simone!

—

e.

rilca slides into sweats. obsessing over her morning shift. another eight to eight. another early morning that this sleepless night will not let her forget . . . uneasy. far from settled – which may take . . . god knows how long. maybe . . . who knows this time. and heads outside to wander a bathe of praple glaze/lamplit sidewalk. drowning in the hood of a parka. chill n' rain looping a noose around stems on leaves – green to beige. tightening around a widower. bum hip. umbrella. stumbling sideways down stairs. pumpkins toppled by wind to lawns. black and orange streamers dazed and dangling from bush.

she turns a corner. startles/twisting ligaments at joints in an effort to avoid stepping on ula – tattered tobacco stained pullover/whisky shot eyes – hunched n' grimacing beside the 7 eleven. a puppy (slouched eyes) her friend.

sorry. didn't see you . . . you okay?

spare some change?

i'm really sorry?

change?

you sure you're all right.

ula peeps up from beneath a tangle of bleached hair. you going to give me change or what. then moans. eyes startling wide open as she tightly clutches at her sides. the puppy leaping up to lick her face.

i'll . . . i'll have to get some first.

she hurries in. shaking beads of water from sleeves. blowing in hands as she moves up to the register. a brown face beneath a red uniform waiting for her there.

could i get a pack of extra lights?

will that be all?

she grabs a handful of licorice. uh huh.

that'll be $6.03 . . . ten. do you have three cents?

nah.

okay. that'll be . . . two, one annnnd ninety-seven cents.

she hurries back outside. here.

got any cigarettes?

i can't give you cigarettes.

you smoke.

and you don't seem to be doing so well.

whatever.

listen, if you're looking for a place to sta –

not interested.

not my place. i mean, a shelter.

not interested.

here's a number anyway. she pushes a card into grubby palms. the puppy now resting its golden head in ula's lap. and pulls away. reluctantly. into . . . another autumn, fall, indian summer – starting to lose count of how many – that she bundles up in preparation for. reluctantly. the air – rumours of strife 'cross mountains/'cross the sea.

she's fractions of seconds slow. yet again. detached from the busted sidewalk; fallen leaves. still ruminating on the girl hunched n' grimacing beside the 7 eleven. eyes darting/clinging to images at restaurant windows; petty technocrats – cleanly pressed. knocking back a coffee – slave labour/death squads. as they . . . fractions of seconds slow . . . submerge/merge at breathless. hidden behind conversation . . . rallies/marches – take back the night; end the arms race – they don't go to any more. not like they used to. when younger. with a sense of purpose.

fractions of seconds slow an ageing dog stoops/strains/shits on the walk. owner marching on. crows sharpening bills on telephone wire. descending to pick at garbage. the odd pedestrian happening by. fractions of seconds slow. struggling ahead of bills; to do's to do; people to socialize with. fractions of seconds slow on streets refusing comment on; strangulation – #318; shooting – #412; suicide – #723. rain continuing to steady piss from sky.

suddenly – woozy/overwhelmed – she stops. fractions of seconds slow. her head a swill of images – hands wrenched apart. gripping at fingertips. receding into . . . headlights; the burn of screeching rubber; a horn; water splashing up; pricking eyes.

WATCH WHERE THE FUCK YOU'RE GOING.

sorry.

i just had my goddamn bumper fixed.

—

goddamn whore. go peddle your ass in someone else's neighbourhood.

before the car motors away leaving rilca to stare at the hurried
retreat of pritchard's tail lights.

1997

→→ ←←

SUZETTE MAYR

Moon Honey

(EXCERPT)

Bedelia in her nightgown gives a sudden squawk that Fran only half hears and believes comes from outside the window. That afternoon during nap time, the last day Fran sees her mother alive, Bedelia's rash bursts open and pin-feathers, then adult feathers, sprout through her pores. She stretches her wings and opens her sharp mouth wide, clicks it closed one two three times. This is how meta-morphoses work; angry old women transform into magpies, white girls turn brown, lose their lovers, but discover themselves in the television set. Metamorphosis always signals a happy alternative.

Bedelia shits on the pillow, flies from the room. A farmer shoots at her but misses. Of course he misses. She's already dead.

What now? thinks Bedelia. What now? In her small skull she is no longer mother of Fran, or the daughter of Fran's grandparents, but a hungry and cold brand new magpie, requiring nourishment and warmth. Her beak and wings slice through the air. She leans her bird-body west in the direction of British Columbia. West is where all heroes go when they retire. West to where she'll rest on the beach among rotting gull bodies and used hypodermics washed up on the sand. Maybe she'll look up her great-grandmother turned into a fountain, or her best friend Vesta who passed to the other side years ago. West is where heroes go.

Or this is what Fran would like to believe. This is what her mother *says*, promises her, that Bedelia will live forever in one form or another. Fran never believes that Bedelia died. Bedelia can't die, she'd never allow it. Bedelia has too many angry bones in her body to die peacefully like other people, lie in the ground and just *stay* there.

Fran is her accident, Bedelia always says, you're my accident and thank God you were a girl. Boy accidents are too hard to control, Bedelia says, don't marry off so easily.

Bedelia planned on being a nun, she tells Fran, before she had her accident, even makes it as far as the convent gates before her father grips her by the upper arm and swings her in the direction of their Protestant home where the potatoes wait to be peeled and the table to be set.

You can be a teacher or a nurse or a wife if it's a career you want, says her father, but no goddamn nun.

So Bedelia teaches. Looks out the window at the Catholic church across the street when she teaches, then turns her back to the window to stare at the children in their desks. She is afraid of them, of their hairy skulls too big for their bodies, back-talking mouths. The principal tours Bedelia's class every so often; her work is impeccable, but she feels like an easy target, prey, a Canada goose during hunting season, X-marks-the-spot tattooed on her forehead, her back, her mouth. At times she feels she would be more fulfilled as a lizard. She would rather hide under a rock, her tongue flicking in and out, than teach.

She envies her mother's cat lying around all day, doing nothing but eating and chasing birds in the garden.

Sometimes Bedelia prays that she will be struck with laryngitis, mononucleosis, but illness will never eliminate the job, she'll still have to come back when she gets better. She wishes she were an animal in the zoo. Perhaps she already is an animal in a zoo, a passer-by just has to look in the classroom window and there she is, trapped in front of the children, her arms flailing wildly, her lips flapping pointlessly, her body turning circles and circles and circles from the board to the children to the board to the children like an armadillo trapped in a sandy-bottomed aquarium, while the children doodle and whisper among themselves, stare out the window and count down the minutes until freedom. Bedelia counts, too. Bedelia prancing up and down like a monkey in a floral-print dress trying to keep her audience, her keepers, engaged.

Bedelia stands in front of the class, day after day, the chalk gritty between her fingers. She hands out papers, takes back papers which after months of her useless prancing are nothing more than blank sheets.

One morning she turns to write on the board and has no words. Her arm, the chalk in her hand, reach out.

The chalk drives itself, leaves its trail over the board space, arches and swirls, crosses and bumps. Her arm follows the chalk, also swirls and crosses, bumps and screeches. She swirls and crosses, bumps and screeches, swirls and crosses, bumps and screeches; her arm stretches long and thin and blue, her face transparent and dissolving, and her body swells, bursts into water vapours, she evaporates before her students. They don't notice, they look forward to getting to leave early, or will they have to suffer a substitute?

She whirls in many pieces through the air, whirls and slides out the window, smoke, she will whirl and drift until nightfall, until her pieces reassemble and she condenses into a dew drop, coats the tip of a long blade of grass.

Back at home, she wraps up her dripping hair in a towel, throws her wet clothes into a pile and puts on her nightgown. Daddy, she announces, I've had enough.

One by one she carries her books to the burning fireplace, one by one cleans her bookshelves, one by one discards her career as a teacher. She will not, she has decided, be a teacher, a nurse, a wife, or a nun. She will do nothing. Absolutely nothing, a career choice that finally makes sense to her. Her family has money, why didn't she think of doing nothing before?

Bedelia resists until she is fifty-five, everyone's busy-at-doing-nothing spinster aunt and maybe even funny with her housekeeper the family thinks, until the arrival of Fran. The summer she turns fifty-five, Bedelia drinks too much punch at an engagement party for her niece and loses her virginity in the back garden, behind the garden shed, with the charming young priest visiting from Thunder Bay.

Now that she has reached her fifty-fifth birthday Bedelia believes she is safe from being impregnated, as does the young priest. Having sex with the priest, she feels, is the next best thing to becoming the nun she wanted to be. Besides, she loves the sound of an Ontario accent.

The priest loves women over fifty, likes his women mature and capable and not pregnable. He especially loves Bedelia's hair, her long smooth hands, her size eleven and a half triple A feet. He has been having doubts about staying in the priesthood lately anyway, but he doesn't want to upset his mother.

Soon after the priest's visit, Bedelia throws up regularly, every day. Breaks wind and belches, craves pickles dipped in brown sugar. The beginning of the end, she thinks, dares not think, she keeps cinching in the waists of her dresses and skirts more and more tightly, until the housekeeper opens her big mouth, says to Bedelia, You're pregnant, stop pretending you aren't.

The horror of the word.

Bedelia doesn't contact the priest, never speaks to him again – she felt embarrassed enough the morning after when she woke up with a headache and no hymen. Besides, if she were to tell him, he would just want to hang around, force her into making decisions she might not want to make. That would be out of the question.

He's done enough poking around, Bedelia tells her housekeeper, and the housekeeper pats her hand reassuringly.

Bedelia tries hot baths, scalds her thighs, the skin on her arms and belly. She vomits and curses after drinking glass after glass of gin especially purchased by the housekeeper. Bedelia contemplates throwing herself down the stairs but is afraid of the pain, afraid of breaking one of her fifty-five-year-old bones. Having a baby is probably less dangerous than cracking her skull on the hard steps. She feels she is too old for such gymnastics anyway. In the fifth month she hits her stomach once, twice, as hard as she can, but only winds herself and starts to cry. She can't dislodge this thing, this accident in her womb, can't simply stick her finger down her throat and vomit it out. Time to give up. She looks out the window at the grey clouds which roll like the tiny fluid animal in her stomach, watches rain pour abruptly and sharply from the sky.

Bedelia walks out the back door and into the blades of rain, rests her back against the wall of her house, in the garden. Lets the rain fall all over her, seep into her clothes, her ears, dribble through her hair. She sinks to the ground, huddles in the slick dirt.

Face pattered and spattered with rain, rain pounds into her eyes, drizzles into her mouth. She sighs, spreads her legs out in a V, lets her arms dangle in the muck. Single brown ants move slowly up her legs and arms; her hair rebels against the combs holding it in place and puffs out in the dampness and the rain. Her slender hands – her best feature, the priest said over a thin china cup of tea – trail in the mud, grow thin and green, and shine in the wetness. Her belly explodes, a bushy clump of leaves and stems.

Buds round as marbles appear, baby fists, at the tips of Bedelia's fingers, at the ends of stalks sprouted from her centre. Pop open into blossoms sweet and full, pink and white bundles amid the green, Bedelia's fingers and stalks bob and wave, full and fine as magic wands.

The housekeeper runs from the farthest part of the garden where she was frantically taking in the washing. Her feet pound across the grass, the ground rumbles with her steps, her breath steams out panicked and heavily. She pulls Bedelia from the ground and slaps the leaves where Bedelia's face used to be.

This just won't do, pants the housekeeper. This won't do at all, stand up and be a man, take responsibility for your actions, face the music. You've made your bed now lie in it lie in it lie in it! The housekeeper shakes Bedelia, shakes until the leaves fall away and reveal the tired and frightened woman inside the shrub.

The Blessed Virgin Mary did it, says the housekeeper, I suppose you can too. You have money and you have me. Running away is the coward's way. We'll raise her together. Your baby will be our pride and she will be our joy.

Bedelia looks sadly at the brown, wet face of her housekeeper, Bedelia's hair wet and still puffy as peonies, but she nods and lets herself be led to the house, into a nice warm bath, and then into a nice warm bed. She sleeps and sleeps, her hands on her stomach. Her mind makes itself up, thread winding around a spool.

Bedelia arrives at the family Easter brunch seven and a half months pregnant in an oversized dress, her stomach round as a tortoise's shell. A modern medical miracle.

Vesta is eating with us, announces Bedelia, and after an awkward pause, another place is set. The housekeeper sits down graciously, spreads her skirt thoughtfully over her knees. Vesta is not stupid, she knows she is unwelcome, but to hell with them all, this baby in Bedelia's stomach is hers too, which makes Vesta a member of the family. She picks up her fork and begins to eat. Eat and eat and eat. Eating for two.

Bedelia homes in on the nearest baby. Pats the baby's knees, strokes the baby's cheeks, pries open the baby's mouth and peers at the gums, down the throat, at the small wriggling fish of a tongue.

Do you want to hold her? asks the baby's mother, a woman thirty years younger than Bedelia. The mother drapes a dish towel over Bedelia's shoulder, settles her baby into Bedelia's arms.

They grow so quickly, says the mother.

Do they, says Bedelia as she arranges the baby carefully over the round shelf of her stomach. Bedelia and Vesta cluck over the baby admiringly, but know secretly that *their* baby will of course be superior. Vesta pops a sliver of fried ham into her mouth, chews, then offers the chewed ham to the baby. The baby's mouth opens, an electric garage door, and the baby swallows the ham. Vesta and Bedelia beam at the family seated around the table.

Bedelia holds the baby cautiously all through that Easter brunch, aware of the cloud of urine and baby powder surrounding them both, and she sneezes. Her relatives watch her, watch her stomach, her fingers stroking the baby's stomach inquisitively. None of the relatives would dare say anything. Bedelia, the unofficial, do-nothing queen wasp of the family nest, does what she wants, when she wants, and how she wants.

Outside the family, however, Bedelia is forced to poke her umbrella at little boys who waddle behind her in the street.

Her friends no longer come to call.

Too busy, they say.

But Bedelia doesn't let other people's petty politics bother her, she and Vesta are too busy planning for the baby, choosing wallpaper for the nursery, getting the crib ready.

Fran is born with teeth and thick black hair. The baby clutches avidly at Bedelia's breasts for milk, Bedelia who only nine months before suddenly realized she had breasts when the priest from Thunder Bay pointed them out to her with moist fingertips.

Fran grows up an accident, spills things, trips over clothing throughout her life until her knees and elbows are knotted with scars.

Your father was a holy man, says Bedelia. That's all you have to know.

Vesta rolls her eyes. Hole in the head more like it, she grumbles. Arranges chocolate-chip cookies on a plate and pours out three glasses of lemonade.

You girls come have a snack, she calls, and waits for Bedelia and Fran to come sit with her at the small table on the back porch.

Vesta holds out her arms and Fran runs and jumps into Vesta's lap. No other girl Fran knows has two such loving mothers.

1995

Glossary

abuelo – old man
ackees – a fruit, often eaten with saltfish (cod)
Africadian – a black Nova Scotian
avoirdupois – system of weights; bodily weight
Ba'ma – Bahama grass: a low, creeping grass
badda – bother
beeny – tiny, very little
boasy – boastful
box hot-hot – to slap someone hard
brassing – a dressing down
bull-buck-and-duppy conqueror – "the baddest" (slang)
bully beef – cornbeef
cerasee – a bitter bush used in folk medicine
chaklata – chocolate
coumbite – a term describing a communal system of work
   exchange, expecially prevalent in rural areas in Haiti; it also
   connotes solidarity among workers
conchs – shellfish
cut eye – to cast a quick, mean look
cyann – can't

dandy-shandy – a ball game with three or more players, in which one, at the shout "dandy-shandy," runs out of the line of a thrown ball

dokunu – pudding wrapped in banana leaf or leaves and boiled or roasted

dotish – (derived from "doltish") senile; mentally slow

dray – a flat, open-sided, mule-drawn cart

dutty – dirty

facety – describes someone with a lot of gumption

goat water – a stew made from goat meat, vegetables, and dumplings

grater cakes – cakes made of grated coconut and unrefined "wet" or "new" sugar

guava cheese – a conserve of guavas, strained and boiled down with sugar to a solid consistency

gwaan – go on, behave

hard-back – a mature person

heng-pon-me – straw knapsack

johnny shirt – hospital smock

ku – look at

maljeu – sorcery or witchcraft

meke-meke – (onomatopoeic): sticky or oozing

mussi – must be

petchary bird – a belligerent bird

pickney/pickni – a child or children

pingwing – a dry-land cousin to the mangrove; its sword-shaped leaves are used for basket-weaving

sampata – sandals

smadi – somebody, people

tata – term of respect for a father or an elderly person

trupence – three pennies or a three-penny piece

About the Contributors

ANDRÉ ALEXIS is a Toronto writer whose collection of short stories, *Despair, and Other Stories of Ottawa*, was published in 1994. His play, *Lambton and Kent*, was produced in Toronto in 1995. He is on the editorial board of *This Magazine*, has been writer-in-residence at the Canadian Stage, and writes book reviews for the *Globe and Mail* and the *Toronto Star*. He is working on his first novel, a slow torture from which he may never really recover.

DIANA BRAITHWAITE is a third-generation Canadian of African descent. She studied at the University of California at San Jose in the mid-1970s and has pursued a career in dramatic arts. Her moving one-act play, *Martha and Elvira*, took First Prize at the Afro-American Women in the Arts Festival in Chicago, Illinois, in 1992.

Vero Boncompagni

DIONNE BRAND was born in Trinidad and has lived in Canada since 1970. Renowned as a poet, her book *No Language Is Neutral* was shortlisted for the Governor General's Award in 1990. She was writer-in-residence at the University of Toronto in 1991, and has taught creative writing at York University and the University of Guelph. In 1996, she published her first novel, *In Another Place, Not Here*. She lives north of Toronto.

AUSTIN CLARKE was born in Barbados in 1934 and emigrated to Canada to attend the University of Toronto in 1955. Since 1964, he has published seven novels and five short-story collections in the United States, England, and Canada. *The Origin of Waves*, Clarke's first novel in ten years, was published in 1997. He will publish his *Illustrated Black History of Canada* in 1998.

Julie Morin

GEORGE ELLIOTT CLARKE was born in Windsor, Nova Scotia, in 1960. He has published three books of poetry, including the acclaimed *Whylah Falls* (1990), which has been adapted for radio and the stage. Clarke lectures in poco theory and Canadian and African-American *littérature* at Duke University in Durham, North Carolina.

FRED COGSWELL was born in 1917 in East Centreville, New Brunswick. A graduate of the University of New Brunswick and Edinburgh University, he was the editor of *The Fiddlehead* (1952–1966) and the founding publisher of Fiddlehead Poetry Books (1955–1982). The author of twenty-two books and chapbooks of poetry as well as seven books of poetry in translation, his latest book, *The Trouble with Light*, was published in 1996.

Don Hall

ARCHIBALD J. CRAIL was born in Paarl, South Africa, and now lives in Regina, Saskatchewan. Nominated for the Governor General's Award for short fiction in 1992, Crail has written numerous pieces of short fiction and feature articles for the CBC, a feature-length script, *Birdsong*, for the NFB, and a number of stage plays, one of which, *Exile*, was produced in both Canada and South Africa.

JO-ANNE ELDER has translated poetry for *ellipse* and books in the areas of Acadian culture and visual arts. With Fred Cogswell, she edited and translated *Unfinished Dreams: Contemporary Poetry of Acadie* (1990). She holds a PhD from the Université de Sherbrooke and is co-editing an anthology on women's spirituality, *Voices and Echoes*.

Daniel St. Louis

GÉRARD ÉTIENNE was born in Cap-Haïtien, Haiti, but left in 1964 to escape the dictatorship of Papa Doc Duvalier. Educated at the Université de Montréal and the Université de Strasbourg, France, his *œuvre* includes twenty works of *belles lettres* and sixty critical studies in literary criticism, linguistics, and semiology. He has received several prizes and honours for his writing. He is a professor of linguistics and journalism at the Université de Moncton.

CECIL FOSTER, born in Barbados, has reported for the *Globe and Mail*, the *Financial Post* as a senior editor, and the *Toronto Star*, where he is now a columnist. His articles have also appeared in several Canadian magazines. His most recent book is *A Place Called Heaven: The Meaning of Being Black in Canada*. His two novels, *No Man in the House* and *Sleep On, Beloved*, received critical acclaim in Canada and the United States.

CLAIRE HARRIS came to Calgary from Trinidad in 1966. She won the Commonwealth Regional Award (Americas Area) for *Fables from the Women's Quarters* (1984), The Writers Guild of Alberta Poetry prize, and the Alberta Culture Poetry Prize for *Travelling to Find a Remedy* (1986). *Drawing Down a Daughter* was short-listed for the Governor General's Award in 1993. *Dipped in Shadow* was published in 1996.

LAWRENCE HILL is the author of the novel *Some Great Thing*. He has also written *Women of Vision: The Story of the Canadian Negro Women's Association* and the children's history text *Trial and Triumphs: The Story of African-Canadians*. In 1996, he completed a new novel, *Any Known Blood*. Hill teaches creative writing at Ryerson Polytechnic University in Toronto and lives in Oakville with his wife and three children.

John Reeves

DAVID HOMEL was born and raised in Chicago. After study and travel in Europe and America, he settled in Montreal. He is the author of three award-winning novels: *Electrical Storms*, *Rat Palms*, and *Sonya & Jack*. As a translator, he has put all of Dany Laferrière's writing into English, and he won the 1995 Governor-General's Award for his translation of Laferrière's *Why Must a Black Writer Write About Sex?*

Martine Doyon

DANY LAFERRIÈRE was born in Port-au-Prince, Haiti, where he practised journalism under Duvalier. He went into exile in Canada in 1976. His first novel, *How to Make Love to a Negro*, was made into a feature film. He has published seven books, which have been translated into several languages. He is married and the father of three daughters (like King Lear). Laferrière divides his time between Miami and Montreal.

SUZETTE MAYR is of German and Caribbean descent. Her poetry and fiction have appeared in a number of literary journals across Canada. She has published one poetry chapbook, *Zebra Talk*, and her first novel, *Moon Honey*, was published in 1995. She lives and works in Calgary, Alberta.

PAMELA MORDECAI was born in Jamaica, educated there and in Massachusetts. She has written five books of poetry and has edited/co-edited four landmark collections of Caribbean writing, received the Institute of Jamaica's Centenary Medal, and won Jamaica's inaugural Vic Reid Award for Children's Literature. She lives in Toronto.

M. NOURBESE PHILIP is an award-winning poet and writer who lives in Toronto. Her poetry, prose, essays, reviews, and articles have been widely published in Canada, the U.K., and the U.S.A. She has published four books of poetry and a novel, *Harriet's Daughter*. In 1990, she was made a Guggenheim Fellow in poetry and, in 1995, was awarded the Arts Foundation of Toronto award in writing and publishing.

Joanna Eldredge Morrissey

DAVID N. ODHIAMBO was born in Kenya and studied at McGill University in Montreal. He currently lives and writes in Vancouver. His works include a play, *afrocentric*, and a novel, *diss/ed banded nation*. His poetry, articles, and fiction have appeared in several magazines. Odhiambo is currently working on a second novel.

Stephanie Martin

ALTHEA PRINCE was born and grew up in Antigua. After moving to Canada in 1965, she earned a doctorate in sociology. Prince writes adult fiction, poetry, essays, and articles in the disciplines of sociology and children's books. Her books include *Ladies of the Night*, *How the East Pond Got Its Flowers*, and *How the Star Fish Got to the Sea*. She is working on a new novel and a collection of short stories.

Bently Quast

OLIVE SENIOR, born in Jamaica, has worked in journalism both in Canada and Jamaica. Her first work of fiction, *Summer Lightning*, won the 1987 Commonwealth Writers Prize, and was followed by two acclaimed short-story collections, *Arrival of the Snake-Woman* and *Discerner of Hearts*. She is also the author of two poetry collections, *Talking of Trees* and *Gardening in the Tropics*, and several non-fiction books. Senior lives in Toronto.

Sarkis of Toronto

MAKEDA SILVERA is an African-Caribbean lesbian feminist writer. She has edited numerous anthologies and has appeared in too many to count. She has been in the forefront of publishing and developing writings by women of colour for over twelve years in Canada. Her two collections of short stories are *Remembering G* and *Her Head a Village*. She is at work on something new.

H. NIGEL THOMAS, a native of St. Vincent and the Grenadines, is an associate professor in the département des littératures at Université Laval. His poems, short stories, and literary criticism have been widely published. He is also the author of *From Folklore to Fiction: A Study of Folk Heroes and Rituals in the Black American Novel*; a novel, *Spirits in the Dark*; and a collection of short stories, *How Loud Can the Village Cock Crow?*

KEITH LOUIS WALKER is a professor of French and francophone literature at Dartmouth College in Hanover, New Hampshire. He is the author of *La Cohésion poétique de l'œuvre césairienne* and the forthcoming *Counter Modernism and Francophone Literary Culture: The Game of Slipknot*. He is co-editor of *Postcolonial Subjects: Francophone Women Writers*.

FREDERICK WARD, author-playwright-screen-writer-composer, has written three novels, two plays, a small collection of prose-poetry, and has had his work extensively anthologized. In 1992, he was awarded Doctor of Laws, *honoris causa*, and he now teaches at Dawson College in its Professional Theatre Department. Ward makes his home in Westmount, Quebec.

PAUL TIYAMBE ZELEZA, the director of the Center for African Studies at the University of Illinois at Urbana-Champaign, was born in Zimbabwe and educated in Malawi, England, and Canada. A professor of history, he has published two volumes of short stories. *The Sunday Nation* in Nairobi declared that his first novel, *Smouldering Charcoal*, should be "compulsory reading for every citizen of Africa."

Acknowledgements

To begin where I must, I am deeply grateful to Ellen Seligman, the editorial director of fiction at McClelland & Stewart, who generated the idea for this anthology in a conversation we had during the Harbourfront launch for *Writing Away: The PEN Canada Travel Anthology*, in May 1994. Ideally patient, her precise editing and guidance have magnified the virtues of the collection. Consummately professional, she made the process of anthology compilation almost pleasurable. (I will be forever appreciative of her indulgence of my passion for Fournier typeface.)

Heather Sangster, the copy editor, is a fabulous artisan of words. Cheerfully, she queried the instances of original orthography and eccentric typography, correcting only the errors.

Ayanna Black, who has edited two anthologies of African-Canadian literature, was an inspiration. Her choices have elicited my own.

Makeda Silvera of Sister Vision Press was unfailingly kind. Suzanne Alexander of Goose Lane Editions was equally charitable.

Natania Feuerwerker ensured that I received Keith Walker's translation of Gérard Étienne's fiction. She tolerated, *très poliment*, my unchurched French.

The generosity of Duke University permitted me to post letters, make long-distance phone calls, and dispatch faxes. And I thank the staff of the Department of English – Catherine Allen, Susie Parsons, Roz Wolbarsht, Carol Renegar, Megan Winget, and Ann Duffy – as well as Janice Engelhardt of the Canadian Studies Center and Edwina Daye-Newman and Pat Scott of the African and African-American Studies Program – for fielding the faxes, phone calls, and travel compensation requests.

My departmental colleagues, Karla Holloway and Cathy Davidson, were powerful mentors. In addition, I salute the work of Smaro Kamboureli of the University of Victoria, whose recent anthology, *Making a Difference: Canadian Multicultural Literature* (1996), provided an exquisite model for this endeavour.

I must also express my appreciation for the gracious assistance of Canadian Studies Center Director John H. Thompson, Arnold (Ted) Davidson, and Jean Jonassaint, all fellow Canadians. I must also acknowledge Nahum D. Chandler, a colleague and a true brother.

And there are three beloveds: Julie Morin, *une belle Québécoise*, whose love I treasure; my aunt, Joan Mendes, whose signifying voice I cherish; and my mother, Geraldine Elizabeth Clarke, for the obvious reasons. And I acknowledge sweetness.

ANDRÉ ALEXIS. "Despair: Five Stories of Ottawa" from *Despair, and Other Stories of Ottawa* by André Alexis (Toronto: Coach House Press, 1994). Reprinted by permission of the author.

DIANA BRAITHWAITE. Scene Two from *Martha and Elvira: A One-Act Play* by Diana Braithwaite (Toronto: Sister Vision Press, 1993). Reprinted by permission of the author and Sister Vision Press.

DIONNE BRAND. "Winter Epigrams – 4" from *Winter Epigrams and Epigrams to Ernesto Cardenal in Defence of Claudia* by Dionne Brand (Toronto: Williams-Wallace Publishers Inc., 1983), "I am

not that strong woman" from *Chronicles of the Hostile Sun* by
Dionne Brand (Toronto: Williams-Wallace Publishers Inc., 1984),
"Hard Against the Soul – X" from *No Language Is Neutral* by
Dionne Brand (Toronto: Coach House Press, 1990), and "Just
Rain, Bacolet" from *Bread Out of Stone* by Dionne Brand
(Toronto: Coach House Press, 1994). Reprinted by permission of
the author.

AUSTIN CLARKE. "When He Was Free and Young and He Used
to Wear Silks" by Austin Clarke from the book of the same name,
copyright 1971 by Austin Clarke. Published in Canada by House
of Anansi Press Ltd. Used by permission of the author via The
Bukowski Agency, Toronto.

GEORGE ELLIOTT CLARKE. "Watercolour for Negro Expatriates
in France," "Salvation Army Blues," "Hymn for Portia White,"
"Violets for Your Furs," and "To Say, 'I love you'" from *Lush
Dreams, Blue Exile: Fugitive Poems, 1978-1993* by George Elliott
Clarke (Lawrencetown Beach, NS: Pottersfield Press, 1994) and
"Look Homeward, Exile," "The River Pilgrim: A Letter," "Bees'
Wings," "Blank Sonnet," "Each Moment Is Magnificent," and
"Vision of Justice" from *Whylah Falls* by George Elliott Clarke
(Vancouver: Polestar Book Publishers, 1990). Reprinted by permis-
sion of the author and Polestar Book Publishers.

ARCHIBALD J. CRAIL. "The New Order" from *The Bonus Deal*
by Archibald J. Crail (Regina: Coteau, 1992). Reprinted by permission of the author.

GÉRARD ÉTIENNE. "Ah My Love Flutters . . ." is a translation of
"Ah voltige mon amour. . ." from *La Raison et mon amour* (Les Édi-
tions Port-au-princiennes, 1961); "It Is Snowing Outside" is a
translation of *"Il neige dehors"* from *La Poésie acadienne, 1948-1988*
(Les Écrits des Forges & Le Castor Astral, 1988), both poems ©
Gérard Étienne. The English translations of these poems are
reprinted from *Unfinished Dreams: Contemporary Poetry of Acadie*

M. NOURBESE PHILIP. "And Over Every Land and Sea" and "Meditations on the Declension of Beauty by the Girl with the Flying Cheek-bones" from *She Tries Her Tongue, The Silence Softly Breaks* by M. Nourbese Philip (Charlottetown: Ragweed, 1989). "Commitment to Hardness," by M. Nourbese Philip, is from *Érotique Noire/Black Erotica*, edited by Miriam Decosta-Willis, Reginald Martin, and Roseann P. Bell (New York: Anchor Books, 1992). Reprinted by permission of the author.

DAVID N. ODHIAMBO. "LIP." © David N. Odhiambo, 1997. Printed by permission of the author.

ALTHEA PRINCE. "Ladies of the Night" from *Ladies of the Night and Other Stories* by Althea Prince (Toronto: Sister Vision Press, 1993). Reprinted with the permission of the author.

OLIVE SENIOR. "All Clear, 1928" from *Gardening in the Tropics: Poems* by Olive Senior (Toronto: McClelland & Stewart Inc., 1994) and "Swimming in the Ba'ma Grass" from *Discerner of Hearts* by Olive Senior (Toronto: McClelland & Stewart Inc., 1995). Used by permission of McClelland & Stewart Inc., Toronto.

MAKEDA SILVERA. "No Beating Like Dis One" from *Remembering G and Other Stories* by Makeda Silvera (Toronto: Sister Vision Press, 1991) and "Old Habits Die Hard" from *Her Head a Village and Other Stories* by Makeda Silvera (Vancouver: Press Gang Publishers, 1994). Reprinted by permission of the author.

H. NIGEL THOMAS. Chapter 3 from *Spirits in the Dark* by H. Nigel Thomas (Concord, ON: House of Anansi, 1993). © The House of Anansi Press, in association with Stoddart Publishing Co. Limited. Published in the United Kingdom by William Heinemann Publishers. Reprinted with the permission of Stoddart Publishing Co. Limited, Don Mills.

FREDERICK WARD. "Purella Munificance" from *Riverlisp: Black Memories* by Frederick Ward (Montreal: Tundra Books, 1974) and "Who," "Mary" (from "Who All Was There"), "Blind Man's Blues," "Dialogue #1: Mama," "Dialogue #3: Old Man (to the Squatter)," and "The Death of Lady Susuma" from *The Curing Berry* by Frederick Ward (Toronto: Williams-Wallace, 1983). Reprinted by permission of the author.

PAUL TIYAMBE ZELEZA. "The Rocking Chair" from *The Joys of Exile: Stories* by Paul Tiyambe Zeleza (Toronto: House of Anansi, 1994). Reprinted by permission of the author.

Every effort has been made to determine copyright holders. If an omission exists, the publisher will make suitable acknowledgement in future editions.